The Eagle
and
The Raven

by

Maggie Shaw

The Eagle
and
The Raven

by

Maggie Shaw

eregendal.com

Also by the Author
The Vision and Beyond (2018)
Diviner's Nemesis I – Avenger (2019)
Diviner's Nemesis II – Retribution (2020)
The Eagle and The Butterfly (2020)
The Last Thursday Ritual in Little Piddlington (2021)

First published in the United Kingdom in 2021 by
eregendal.com, Rosehill Road, Crewe, Cheshire, CW2 8AR.
Printed in the United Kingdom by Lulu.com.

ISBN 978-1-8381313-6-4 (paperback)

Contents

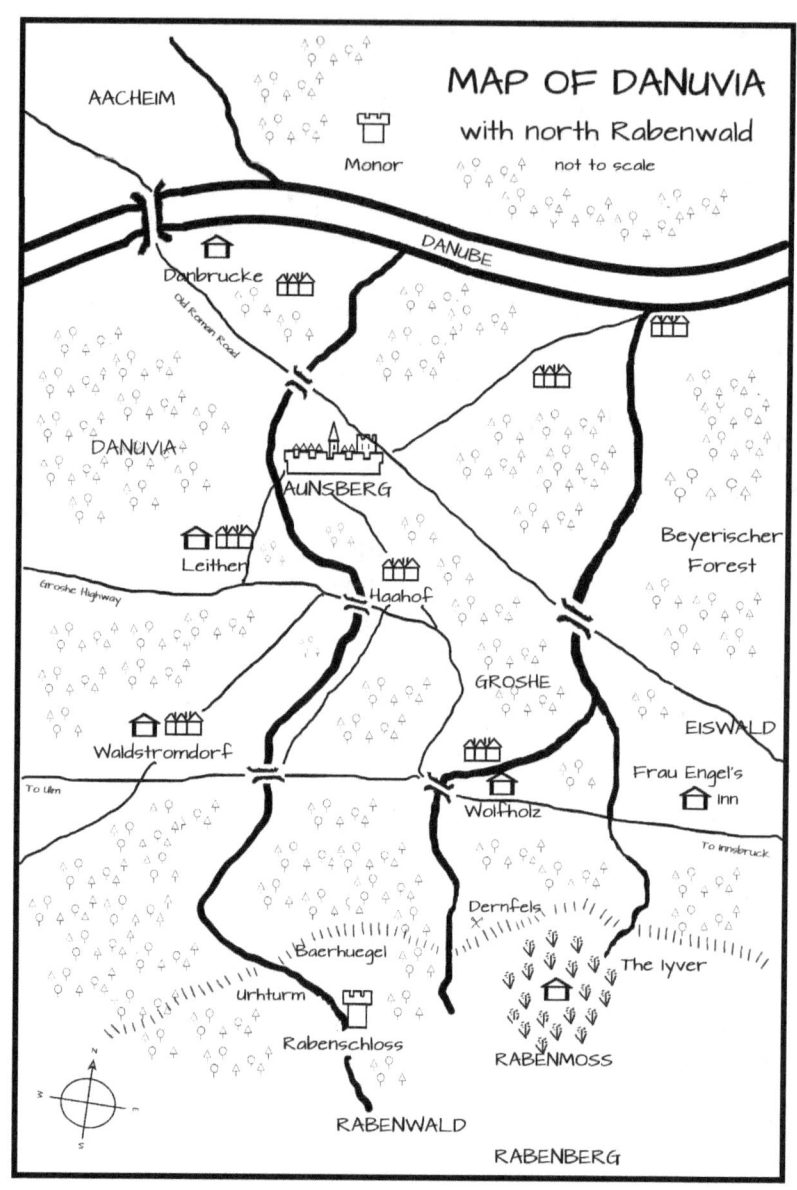

Map of Danuvia

Introduction
and Acknowledgements

The Eagle and The Raven is a sequel to *The Eagle and The Butterfly,* published in 2020. The butterfly eagle person Eregéndal has returned to the dreamworlds and now works as the human guide and messenger Knight Gendal in 14th century Holy Roman Empire. Gendal's travels draw the guide into a civil war between an independent mountain clan and the Duke of Danuvia, who had been given the land of Rabenwald by the King of Rome in return for the Duke's political support during his election to be Imperator. Gendal is supported by friend and disgraced Prince Rehlein Hirschmann, who finds himself saddled with the responsibility of leading the mountain clan when their chief, Count Bertram, is imprisoned.

This novel is less mystical than its prequel and develops into a powerful adventure story. The theme is a working out of the commission given to Gendal at the end of the previous book, to 'go out into all the world in the name of God: seek justice for the poor, defend the oppressed, and set the captive free.' The world in which Gendal moves is feudal, brutal and treacherous, making that commission a challenge to obey.

With sword fights, battles, duplicity, tenderness and cruelty, and a memorable cast of flawed yet often heroic characters, this exciting fast-paced story will keep you guessing to the end with its many unexpected twists and turns.

As always, I would like to thank those who helped with the book in any way, including Roy Butler and Helen Lamb for their guidance in the development of the manuscript, F Durrant & Co. Ltd of Worcester, for letting me handle a longsword similar to those mentioned in this book, and Canva for the original cover photographs. Any faults in the work are my own alone.

Map of Aunsberg

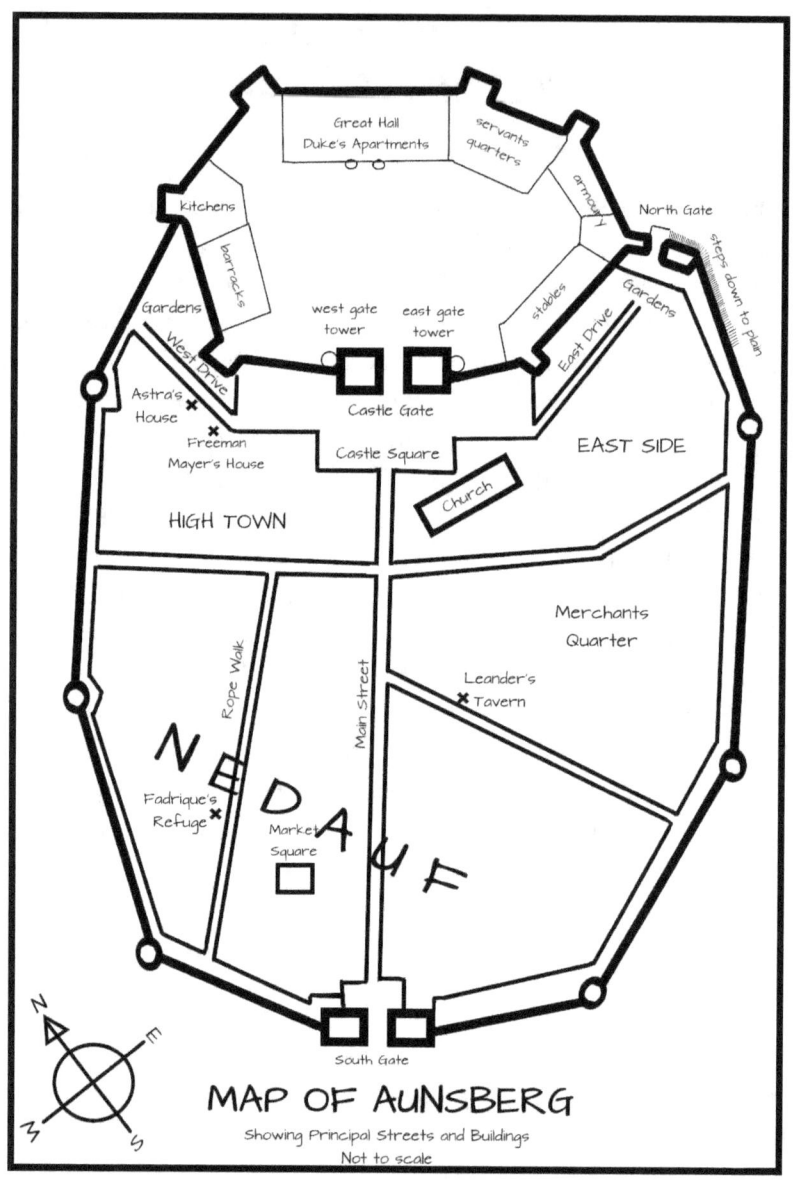

MAP OF AUNSBERG

Showing Principal Streets and Buildings

Not to scale

Chapter 1
The Messenger

A fist pounded urgently on the tavern door. We travellers looked up from our bread and stew to watch the ostler check the bolts on the door were fast. It was evening, and this remote roadside inn at the base of the long moorland ridge of Rabenwald was not the place to welcome strangers after curfew.

'Who is it?' the ostler demanded.

'It's Thiemo. Help me, please!'

'Let him in, Herman,' said the widowed innkeeper, Frau Engel. She was a plump, homely woman dressed in a practical beige linen tunic. She looked more than capable of taking care of herself in her sometimes tough line of work.

Her son, the lean ostler, drew back the bolts and cautiously opened the door. He checked to make sure the caller was who he claimed and pulled the thin young man inside. Thiemo dragged himself to the bar. His ragged clothes were muddy and he looked bruised and bloodied from a fight.

'What's happened to you, Thiemo?' Frau Engel asked.

She put a motherly arm around his shoulders and offered him some food. He shook her off.

'Not now, Frau Engel. Is there a messenger here?' he demanded.

The five travellers shook their heads, not wanting to get involved. I saw the pain on the young man's sallow, bearded face and sensed he sought to send a message rather than learn one.

'I am Guide Gendal. An it be important, I will take a message for you, lad.'

THE EAGLE AND THE RAVEN

'Heavens be praised – at last a rider willing. For my master's sake, leave your meal, and ride to the Iyver tavern on Rabenmoss. There seek out Count Bertram.'

'Hold, young sir. Oft have I ridden Rabenwald, but never has the Iyver welcomed me. It is a local spot.'

'Aye, but the name of Count Bertram and the message will gain you entry. For Raban is dead.'

A knife clattered. Frau Engel blushed.

'Heaven save them and him,' she whispered.

'How did it happen, Thiemo?' the ostler demanded, his mouth agape in dismay.

'Not now! Precious time is being wasted!'

'Aye, but my horse could use a little rest after our hard day,' I said, my mouth full. Whatever his urgency, I needed more than a mouthful of sopped bread to face Rabenwald's night. 'If I am to ride with such heavy news, I should know more. Count Bertram is sure to question me.'

Thiemo nodded and sat at our table. My tall, blond companion Rehlein Hirschmann moved his plate to give him room. The ostler gave the young man a tankard of ale.

Thiemo eyed my black brigandine with some interest. He recognised the studded velvet jacket lined with overlapping metal plates, as the coat of someone who was used to handling trouble on the road. He noticed too the seals on my rings: the splayed eagle of a free imperial knight, and my own splayed eagle overlaid with a butterfly. They seemed to give him confidence in me as he embarked on his tale.

'Last week, Duke Nicolaus' men arrested Raban and took him to Aunsberg. They tortured him to learn about the rebels. He said nothing and would have died by their hands. A soldier who was a secret sympathiser helped him escape. As they came south across Danuvia for Rabenwald, the Duke's men overtook them. They killed the traitor and mortally wounded Raban. He fell at my door and died in my arms. With his last breath, he charged me to send word to Count Bertram, and gave me his ring. I ran to find a messenger. Thank you, stranger, for stepping forward.'

'Yes, and stepping right back again,' said Rehlein. My well-dressed friend was broad-shouldered with flabby muscles. Life had been kind to him, but that had been some time before he had joined me on the road. He warned, 'Cara Gendal, I have no mind to go gallivanting on fell tops at the witching hour after a day's ride.'

'What, do you fear I will take your soul?' I scoffed. 'Forsake not your soft warm bed, friend – a messenger carrying this message is better off alone. Meet me at the Rabenwald Iyver tomorrow sunset, should Count Bertram let us stay there the night.'

'He will, I promise you,' said Thiemo: 'All Rabenwald will respect you for your service.'

'Are you also one of them, then?'

Thiemo leapt back, ale spilling, fearing me to be Duke Nicolaus's spy.

'Calm yourself, friend Thiemo,' I said: 'I am neutral in this region's politics. As a true messenger, I will say naught about the sender elsewhere. My reason for asking is this. Though I know I do not support the cause, should the Duke's men arrest me, they might not believe me. If your mission is innocent, forget my question and forgive me. If it is not, tell me, lest I forfeit my life and the message doesn't get through.'

Thiemo nodded, settling again. He took Raban's ring out of his pocket and looked fondly at it before handing it to me. It bore the Raven seal of the Count of Rabenwald.

'Raban was my greatest teacher and my truest friend, though I was but one of many to him. Our pennons will skim the ground for him.'

He paused, but then broke down and wept, not selfishly but like a lover separated forever. His tears moved me.

'Ostler, saddle my horse. I ride.'

Herman hurried to obey. I checked details of Rabenwald's dangers with one of the other travellers, who had come off the hill that day. The man was short and portly with a greasy red face and dark beard. He wore expensive clothes for the class of inn where he had chosen to stay.

'Be warned,' he said in an accent that was not local: 'It is a foolhardy mission. No self-respecting messenger would take it.'

'Aye?' said I: 'Well, I have little respect, good sir, but I do have pride.'

I donned my cloak and strode out into the night-darkened stable yard. Rehlein followed and embraced me.

'Welcome back, friend,' he said as I opened the saddlebags on my black horse, Finstar. Rehlein recognised the ethical mountain I had crossed when I had weighed the political dangers and still said I would go.

I packed my brigandine and put on my padded leather gambeson coat instead. Though it would afford less protection in a straight fight, it was much quieter than the rattling plates of the brigandine. To ride out again after the curfew hour required more stealth than strength.

'Nay: there is no change,' I said: 'This is still Eregendal, adventuring.'

'Not to ride out tonight. Till tomorrow, at the Iyver.'

We clasped hands. I threw the reins over the pommel of the

saddle, checked my longswords in their saddle scabbards, and mounted my horse.

'Do you want a lantern?' asked the ostler.

'Nay: the rising moon is still near full. But you should take care. The travellers who rode off the hill today may well be the Duke's men. One tried to warn me off.'

'Thank you, friend, but they can do little here. This is Eiswald, not Danuvia.'

'Perhaps. But what are ducal marches when Nicolaus is cousin to the King of Rome?'

I saluted and rode off into the night.

Chapter 2
The Message is Delivered

Rabenberg is an awkward mountain to travel even during the day. It grows out of the Eiswald plain as a wooded foothill spur of the Bavarian alps. I was glad of the moon's early light to guide me through my memories of its paths. I rode its base westerly for three miles to pass the long side of treacherous ghylls, and at length climbed the safest ascent from the Eiswald plain, a worn sandstone-tipped granite spur stretching out from the forest into the fields. Its aggressive square-edged boulder cliffs slowed my ascent. Several times I had to lead my horse, hoping I would not lose the little-worn path in the moon's cold light. At length I reached the brow of the spur and remounted to ride to the top of the fell's last rounded bluff. When I rounded the bluff, I could see far: east across Eiswald to the distant Beyerischer forest, north towards Aunsberg, and south across the wetlands of Rabenmoss. I should have seen the lights of the Iyver to the south, but the bog was in darkness. I assumed the inn keeper slept.

The Iyver stood in the heart of Rabenmoss, on a small central island in a peat bog held in the bowl of mountain rock. Three main routes crossed the bog to the island, marked by whitewashed boulders. The easiest route of the three started from a sandstone outcrop which marked the entrance to the morass.

I doubled back along the lip of the mountain bowl for about four miles east to the sandstone outcrop. When I got there, I looked for the first white guide stone showing the way into the bog. It had vanished.

I did not know whether to set foot across the morass. What was more important: my safety, or the urgent nature of the message I carried?

Small lights gleamed in the near distance against the darkness to the north. As only Danuvia lay north, the lights could only be the lanterns of Duke Nicolaus's men. It was after curfew time. If they found me abroad, they would give me no quarter.

I dismounted and led my horse into the bog, glad that I had refused the ostler's lantern. Though the moon was setting, making it much harder fo see my way in the darkness, I could easily conceal my cloaked body and my black horse among the clumps of sedge.

Rabenmoss shuddered with an odour of earthy decay each time I placed a foot off the path onto the quaking peat. I recalled past ordeals crossing bogs and marshes, and used a technique I had learned from them, tapping the tarry surface with the toe of my riding boot until I found firmer ground. After a few steps, I stumbled over a reed clump and landed with my arms around a white boulder. What joy it was to find the guide stones had not gone, but were just hidden!

I led my horse on across the bog in greater confidence.

Lights gathered by the sandstone outcrop marker at the edge of the mire. They were now only about three hundred paces away. The still night air carried the sounds of men's voices speaking in an Italian dialect. My heart fell.

The only Italians that far north had to be Condottiero mercenaries, contracted to Duke Nicolaus to protect Danuvia. I had let myself become trapped in the Rabenmoss by professional solders; and already there was no going back.

'These bastard bog dwellers,' swore one of the Italians. In the still air, he sounded closer than I had thought. His voice had a distinctive roughness, which alerted me to be very wary of him.

I turned my head towards his voice, and my food slipped from the path. I fell into an earthy, wet hollow. The hungry peat engulfed my body up to my hips.

I grasped the roots and stems in the earthy wall above me as I tried to pull myself out. The stalks snapped and broke in my hands. The heavier soil and stones were soon engulfed by the hungry mud. As I sank with them, I felt my panic rise. To calm it, I recalled the time hell had discarded me in a similar highland bog, and prayed.

The setting moon shed a cloud. Its faint beams lit the scabbard of my heavier longsword hanging above my head.

'Finstar,' I whispered: 'Lie down.'

It was a command I had given him before, but then I had been standing at his shoulders and holding his reins, ready to guide him to the ground.

He bent his head towards me. His reins dropped a little. I called to him again, reaching out my right hand. He seemed to grasp my predicament and knelt down on his forelegs. The scabbard hung over the edge of the hole.

THE EAGLE AND THE RAVEN

I reached up and grabbed the scabbard with both hands. When my grip was secure, I urged Finstar to stand again. He rolled a little as he took my weight with the additional pull of the greedy bog. One foreleg unbent and then the other. The uneven tug of war between the horse and the hungry peat bog stretched my shoulder muscles as I tried to hold on. My grip held, my horse pulled, and together we forced the mire to relinquish its hold on me. The mud fell away from my legs with irritated reluctance. Once free, I dragged myself out of the hollow and hugged Finstar's neck in silent gratitude. Then I gave thanks to God in wordless prayer.

The mercenaries fell silent. They had heard the quagmire battle across the moss, and peered into the darkness, looking for the source of the noises. I stood still, tense with fear, my arm around my horse's withers to quieten him. The peaty smell of the bog clung to my body. The night chill crept through my wet clothes.

'It must have been a bog man,' a soldier said in Italian. He told the others some Will o' Wisp tales with a bloodthirsty zest which unsettled the more superstitious ones. Once their thoughts were engrossed with myth, I thanked God again and led my horse on across the bog.

After some time working my way across the mire, I calculated that I should have covered the distance to the Iyver, but my feet had not yet found the firmer ground of the island. I had not got lost along the peat-turfing side tracks. Bewildered, I stood in the darkness, looking for the outline of a building that obscured the starry sky.

Across the bog, the soldiers had ventured onto the path I had taken. When one missed his footing, all leapt back from the mire, unsettled after the bogman tales. With no master to witness their daring, they were not hasty to risk their lives for possibly little gain. They agreed to wait at the sandstone outcrop for dawn's light to show them the way. A stirring of the air warned me they would not have to wait long.

My horse pulled me forward along the path. We felt firm ground beneath our legs at last: the island I had been seeking. The tension fled from my body after the danger of the crossing. A sapping tiredness replaced it.

After a brief rest, I walked around the edge of the island looking for the Iyver. I found it when a large silhouette blocked out the sky's low light. I tried the doors of the inn. They were locked and barred.

I did not want to wake the soldiers as well as those within by knocking on the door. Instead, I picked up a pebble and threw it through the view hole in the window shutter.

Arms took me from behind. A hand filled my mouth to silence me. Another gripped my waist to lift me off the ground. The people bundled me into the Iyver stables and threw me into a straw-strewn corner. Someone led in my horse and shut the door. Then the night shade was taken off a coaching lantern near my face. I shied back from the dazzling light.

'Who are you? What do you want?'

The man was massive: six foot six, broad; pure muscle. I saw beyond his peasant clothes and his unkept black curls and beard; forced to respect. Six other people gathered round him. They had all been sleeping fully clad with their weapons beside them, ready for a fight.

'Who I am matters little. I…'

He struck my face, throwing me hard against the corner.

'Facts, not puling, stranger!'

'Give the traveller a chance to speak,' said a woman with a hard beauty. She was dressed like a man in riding breeches, and her long black hair was tied back with a fine scarf.

'If I must, Cara Rea,' he replied.

Her name brought to mind my early days as a messenger and guide. I had escorted the young Cara Rea shortly after she had earned the right to use the Celtic title Anam Cara, soul friend and advisor. Our journey had taken us through the dangers of Flanders around the time of the Battle of Courtrai. I stood up and gave her a courteous bow.

'Cara Rea,' I greeted: 'Do you not remember me?'

'No,' she rebuffed. 'Who are you?'

Her question surprised me. I had not expected her to forget me after such a perilous journey, despite the intervening years.

'Gendal the Guide. I took you through the fields of Flanders.'

She drew a deep breath, as if realising her mistake.

'And what are you doing here?' demanded the big man.

'Thiemo sent me to play messenger, to Count Bertram.'

I hoped that if the massive man was the Count, he would not bridle at my not realising it. To my surprise, he paled. His voice dropped low.

'I am Bertram. What is your message?'

'Raban is dead.'

Count Bertram shook. Cara Rea paled. She asked me for details. I handed Bertram Raban's ring and repeated Thiemo's tale. As they listened, one of their companions shook his head in doubt. He was a brave, stocky man, with bushy red hair whose name I learned later was Gawin.

'Lies! Duke Nicolaus tries to demoralise us! Throw this bog reject back into the bog he escaped from.'

Cara Rea shook her head. 'Guide Gendal does not look the sort to lie.'

Her womanly command of the water consciousness, magnified

by her arts, coaxed her listeners to believe her silvery tongue.

'Many years have passed since I escorted you, Cara Rea. But still I cannot lie.'

The doubter scoffed. I raised my hand to silence him.

'Whether Thiemo's message is true, I cannot say but ask Thiemo. And for now it makes no odds. Mercenaries wait on dawn's light at the guide rock, ready to cross the bog for the Iyver. Luck alone saved me from them by making me refuse an ostler's lantern.'

'How did you cross Rabenmoss then?' asked one.

'By patience, prayer and moonlight. Thiemo's tears spurred me on.'

'Prayer?' Cara Rea mocked gently. 'Gendal, you will soon lose your head with prayers alone for armour.'

'Perhaps; but if prayer is not wrought into your armour, you lack the strongest steel of all.'

'Enough!' roared Count Bertram. 'What of Raban?'

'Aye,' said the doubter, 'and what of us?'

Chapter 3
The Revelation at Rabenschloss

Count Bertram's party left the Iyver as the curlews roused in the first chill light that silhouetted the horizon. We were delayed by the ostler Hans, a study, dark-haired villein with peat-stained hands.

'I'm not leaving the Iyver,' he insisted: 'This farmstead has never been without tenant, and I don't intend it to now.'

'And I will stay here too, with my husband,' his wife Anna said. She too was sturdy and dark-haired, but more homely and with a simple understanding of life.

'But what if the soldiers find their way here?' Bertram warned.

'Then take our daughter Ilse with you. Anna and I will stay.'

'The moss has always kept us safe before.'

'If you are both staying, then I would like to, too,' I said. 'I've arranged to meet my travelling companion Rehlein here tonight. I'd love to wash away the bog and sleep the day here until he arrives.'

'No, Gendal,' Cara Rea ordered: 'Even one stranger found here at present could endanger Rabenwald's cause.' Her fear had good grounds with the Iyver being watched by the mercenaries.

She gave me a reviving potion to keep me alert for the additional journey. As Count Bertram prepared to depart, I made arrangements with the ostler.

'I'll come back around sunset. If you see my friend, please give him your help. He's tall and blond and well-appointed; nothing like those Italian mercenaries.'

'I'll look out for him and guide him across the moss. And I'll leave a light on in the Iyver as a beacon for you,' Hans promised.

Seven of us led our horses out into the bog, leaving just two behind. We had no time to cross the mire and clear the summit brow by dawn. Cara Rea was prepared for this. When the sun's first silver rays gleamed above Rabenwald's wall, she produced a green stoppered bottle.

'This shall give them nightmares for a week!' she laughed.

She smashed the bottle on a guide stone in the mire behind us. The water exploded with a blinding white light and thick smoke which I recognised as a form of Greek Fire. My horse Finstar started, almost taking me into the bog. I struggled to control him.

'Quick! We must make our escape,' Cara Rea ordered through the billowing smoke.

'Your power is terrible, Cara Rea,' said Count Bertram.

'How do we find our way through this fog with the boulders hidden?' I asked.

Count Bertram laughed.

'Rabenwald is my birth right. On this mountain my mother bore me, and when she died, she joined my family buried in this mire. Here was I raised and taught of Rabenwald, how she blesses those who love her and curses those who curse her.'

He sighed and shook his head. 'And here stands the ruins of my castle, which Duke Nicolaus destroyed. How can a man who hates Rabenwald hope to tame her? She and her children will always despise him. We must regain our freedom from his cruel sway.'

The Count led us all across the mire, each of us taking our horse's head and holding the tail of the horse in front. He took us in swift safety to the far bank, while the gentle early morning breeze kept the smog around us, hiding us from the mercenaries.

We remounted on the edge of the bog and rode over the brow of the hill. Though the unnatural cloud had almost gone, the mercenaries did not notice our departure. They had ventured into the bog and found their feet more important to watch than the horizon.

We stopped to rest once out of their sight. I scanned the northerly view over Rabenwald's wooded side to the fertile Danuvian plain and the distant granite tor of Aunsberg, where the Duke's forefathers had founded his citadel. No smoke smudged the air above the forest below us to betray a nearby settlement or castle.

'Where is this Rabenschloss I know naught of?' I asked.

'Strangers have no cause to know,' said Count Bertram. 'Three years back, a traitor gave it to Nicolaus. Though the ravens picked clean his bones, our revenge could not regain us our land. We must fight and build, as our motto requires of us; we can do no more.'

THE EAGLE AND THE RAVEN

Tears filled his eyes. I turned away from watching such grief in so awesome a man, to look at Cara Rea who had remounted.

'We must take the news back to the castle,' she said, and gave her horse its head.

We galloped after her down sleep wooded gullies, along narrow paths across jagged scars. When the party straggled, she called out to hasten each slacker but Count Bertram. All felt tired, but my horse and I were exhausted. We stumbled along the forest paths as our party continually descended towards the plain. To keep us going, Cara Rea promised our goal around the next corner, but so many more promise corners came after the first, that I came to disbelieve her every word. Only when her own horse quickened its pace did I know we were soon to arrive. Around the next bend we trotted, and finally reached our destination.

Rabenschloss stood before us in all her damaged glory. She was a towering castle built on a promontory which had been cut away by the winding river beneath, a distant tributary of the Danube. Her damaged walls were nigh on hidden by the ancient oak, pine and beech trees growing all around.

'No stranger ever ventures here alone! *Rabenwald folk are a clannish lot!*' mocked Cara Rea. 'Come, we need our rest.'

She led us along the neck of land and over the fallen drawbridge. Nicolaus had ordered its chains to be cut to stop it being raised against him again. We entered through the open gateway, which could not be closed because the Duke's men had thrown its gates and portcullis down into the river below. Around us in the cobbled courtyard, gathered a crowd of welcoming people with fear in their eyes. Count Bertram let them cheer his return for a few moments before raising his arms to quieten them. His grief was plain.

'People. Raban is dead.'

A hard silence stilled the crowd. The men's faces looked drawn and bitter. The women did not hide their tears. A chilling wail rose up like the wind, to fade and redouble with a people's grief.

Count Bertram dismounted and handed his horse's reins to his waiting page, his young cousin Barthram. The young lad looked as Bertram might have done when twelve, with his long black curly hair and flashing eyes.

'Stable our horses, and bring food to the Great Hall for the rest. If any want a bed, see to it,' the Count said and turned away.

'Bertram, you must also eat,' said Cara Rea.

She caught hold of his sleeve. He shook her off.

'Aunt, you may have the strength to hide your tears, but I have not,' he said: 'I must go mourn my father.'

Then I understood why my news had so dismayed such a hero. I had been the first to address Bertram by his inherited title. It was Count Raban who was dead.

Chapter 4
The Vision in The Will

Bertram's page Barthram roused me an hour before sunset. I woke on a bracken-covered cot in a small cell in the castle walls, and struggled to remember where I was. Page Barthram served me a meal of bread and cheese washed down with a malty local beer. Once I had eaten, he led me out to my horse in the castle courtyard. I checked Finstar over. He had been groomed and well-cared for while I had slept. Although he had been saddled again with the saddle scabbards and their swords in place, the saddlebags were missing.

THE EAGLE AND THE RAVEN

'Where are my bags?' I asked Barthram as I mounted.

'Cara Rea told me to leave them off.'

She must have been close enough to overhear what we said as she appeared from nowhere to join us.

'Is your signet ring real, Gendal?' she asked me, her manner abrupt: 'Are you now a knight?'

'Aye, I have earned imperial immediacy,' I replied.

'Then, eagle, fly swiftly now and bring your friend back with you. Count Bertram has read his father's will, and you and he are mentioned.'

'What? We have never met Count Raban.'

'Quite. So fetch Rehlein Hirschmann here before midnight. We cannot delay the public reading of the will much longer.'

She beckoned over my escort for the journey and slapped my horse's rump. Finstar galloped across the castle drawbridge and along a track through the dense forest.

My escort soon caught up with us. Black-haired Gotfrid was a brave young warrior with an excellent seat on his bay horse and a longsword almost as impressive as my own. I assumed Count Bertram had sent him to travel with me because he feared more trouble from the mercenaries when we reached Rabenmoss.

As we climbed through the woods, retracing our steps from the morning, I became more grateful for Gotfrid's company. Though my geographical memory was usually excellent, my exhaustion had dulled it when I had ridden the path before. I would have quickly lost the path without him. We wove through a landscape of steep ghyll sides and fast beck torrents, with a dense canopy of evergreen branches above our heads to shade our path in twilight.

We reached Rabenmoss after sunset. The sky was still edged with light in the west and north, silhouetting the mountain bowl's rugged rim against its fiery orange. The three-quarter moon had just risen over the horizon. A light twinkled far across the bog, but none shone from the Iyver, though Hans had promised me one would.

Unease quickened my heart. I rode quickly round the bog's edge towards the light with Gotfrid beside me. He feared the light was a trap laid by the mercenaries. I reassured him I would be able to convince any mercenaries that we were lost travellers seeking a friend and a bed for the night on a strange fell.

The twilight had hardly dimmed when we reached the light. It proved to be a lantern balanced on the sandstone outcrop. Below the outcrop sheltered my friend Rehlein Hirschmann, huddled in his riding cloak. I dismounted and embraced him.

'Friend, it is good to see you safe. But did no-one come to guide you across the mire?'

'No,' said he gruffly, put out with waiting. 'Did you deliver your message?'

'Aye, and for it we must ride much further this night. First, to the Iyver. The ostler promised me he would meet you. Follow me.'

'What, across that quagmire?'

'But aye. Gotfrid will guide us. Lead your horse. We must go on foot.'

Rehlein followed begrudgingly, complaining of tiredness and hunger.

'Why must we ride even further tonight when the Iyver is prepared for us?'

'Aye, but how will it be prepared?'

I told Rehlein all that had happened since I had left him at the inn the night before, while Gotfrid led us both safely across the bog. By the time I had told all my story, we had reached the Iyver island.

'I still think we should back out while we can, Cara Gendal,'

Rehlein said. 'Your lust for adventure will only get your head forcibly removed from your neck. Let me do it now! It would be pleasanter for us both. I should have heeded last full moon's warning of your lunacy... What in heaven's name?'

'Hark! Do you still invoke heaven, friend?'

My light jest fell heavily as he and Gotfrid raised their lanterns. Scattered on our path were the remains of the ostler, Hans. His limbs had been struck off one by one and his hair set alight before he had been decapitated.

'And his wife was here too?' Gotfrid asked, his voice low with fear.

He hurried to the ransacked Iyver with Rehlein beside him. I followed more slowly, knowing what to expect. I was more surprised that the building had not been torched and still stood.

They found the ostler's wife in her sleeping quarters. Anna had been cruelly abused. As Gotfrid picked her up in his arms, she used her last breath to ask our names. Gotfrid cradled her dead body, weeping.

Rehlein turned his face towards me. The anger in his fiery expression made me step back.

'God curse those bastards who committed this atrocity!' he swore, his voice bitter; 'And God curse me if I do not avenge her death and her husband's!'

'Rehlein, hold,' I cautioned, laying a gentle hand on his shoulder. He shook me off.

'Why did you not tell me we face devils in human guise, Gendal? I would have followed you at once.'

'Let us bury their bodies and be gone,' Gotfrid said.

'Let the dead bury themselves. We don't have the time,' I replied.

'What if their daughter returns to see this?' he warned.

I nodded in understanding. 'You are right, of course. What would you have us do?'

'We can give them to the mire, where they can join their ancestors.'

Gotfrid carried the dead woman to the bog. Rehlein followed with the body of the ostler, and I cleaned up after them. The bog took Hans' and Anna's bodies with hardly a murmur. As the mud resettled and looked unmoved once more, we whispered a brief prayer to God to receive their souls. Few traces of the carnage remained when we left the Iyver to head for the castle.

The moon had risen high enough by then for Rehlein and Gotfrid to douse their lights. We walked across the mire in silence, condemning that part of humankind which could perpetrate such foul crimes in the name of politics. Once out of the bog, we rode over the summit brow to the steep wooded slopes. Gotfrid led us back down through the trees to the Castle.

We arrived shortly before midnight. Cara Rea was waiting for us in the gateway as our horses crossed the drawbridge. She saw Gotfrid's face in the torchlight and knew better than to ask him what had happened. She turned to me.

'How went it, eagle?'

'Rough, madam, so let me keep it till your people meet. It is no tale to delight in telling.'

'The people are already waiting in the Great Hall.'

We dismounted in the courtyard. Page Barthram and two other lads led our horses away to stable them. Cara Rea's manner softened when she looked at Rehlein. The blond knight had made a clear impression on her.

'So this is your friend?' she said to me, showing her surprise.

THE EAGLE AND THE RAVEN

'Aye, this is Rehlein Hirschmann.'

She held out her hand for him to take. He lifted it slightly and nodded over it in wary courtesy.

'You at least are come in safety, Sir Rehlein,' she said. her eyes noticing the image of the hart on the signet ring on his middle finger.

We entered the Great Hall directly from the courtyard. This ground-floor chamber was the largest room in the castle and had been built against its south-east wall. Some eighty people had already gathered there. At a refectory table opposite the fireplace in the outer wall, sat red-eyed Count Bertram, a sealed document and a rolled standard lying in front of him. He smiled us a welcome, but his face fell at our expressions.

'What news?' whispered Ilse, Hans' and Anna's daughter from the Iyver.

'Bad news,' I said.

I went to sit next to her in the crowd. Cara Rea pulled me back to sit on the top table between her and Count Bertram. They also gave Rehlein a place at the table, placing him on Bertram's left.

'Aye, bad news it is of the Iyver,' Rehlein said: 'The tenant and his wife are dead. I have pledged myself to avenge their fate, though I need no vow to compel my destruction of the vermin responsible.'

'Dead?' cried the daughter. 'Oh, God, what world is this?'

'Sadly, death was their blessed release,' I said. 'They now sleep in the bosom of the mire, having kept their Iyver safe. What of the matter at hand? It is the midnight hour.'

Bertram shook his head.

'Let it rest. Too much blood has been shed through my family's desire to keep Rabenwald. When your lords have failed in their feudal duty, how can I ask you to stand by me still?'

The Children of The Raven protested their loyalty. Far from

destroying their spirit, our bad news had intensified their determination to rebel. Cara Rea struggled to quieten them enough to hear her speak.

'My nephew is very troubled by his father, my brother's death. Your loyalty gives him the strength to stand tall despite his grief; nor shall we stop fighting till our dear land is free. Nicolaus shall not quell Rabenwald till her last child dies!'

A cheer filled the hall. She let it quieten naturally before raising her arm for silence.

'Now let us hear my dear brother Raban's will, that Rabenwald might know what her father in his wisdom had planned for us. Bertram?'

The young Count picked up the will but could not find a voice to read it. My heart reached out to this brave new leader who was not ashamed of his humanity. He sensed my sympathy and offered me the will to read in his stead. I looked for Cara Rea's permission. She waved impatiently and forced the paper on me.

To the Children of Rabenwald, let it be known that this is my last will, written on the eve of my journey to Aunsberg and the Court of Duke Nicolaus. Dear Children, I hope that I may destroy these words on my return, for now I can bequeath my sons and daughters naught but strife and rebellion. Support my blood heir Bertram in his task to reclaim his birth right, for his devotion in duty and love is worthy of your devotion. And support my beloved sister Cara Rea as she works beside him, though it may seem otherwise.

For this night I awoke from a dream, where I looked down upon myself in chains shadowed by the Wolf, and though one praiseworthy broke my chains, he could not carry me out of its shadow. An eagle came with the message of my death; and behind the eagle came another, an antelope, to whom ye lent the mantle of the Count of

THE EAGLE AND THE RAVEN

Rabenwald that Duke Nicolaus might be deceived.

The omens are against us, but still we can win if we have faith. Our enemies fear the Children of The Raven, so make heirs, my children, that they shall have another generation of us to fear, whatever our fate. If I die, do not mourn me, but celebrate the marriage of my son Bertram to the maiden Ened, who were betrothed as infants. Then take to heart my family's motto: fight and build, that your children might receive their rightful inheritance.

I sat down and handed the will back to Bertram. After a moment of silent reflection, some of the women present wept; while some of the men cheered: all felt moved. Rehlein looked perplexed.

'What of this dream?'

'Aye, what indeed,' said Count Bertram as the crowd fell silent. 'Would my father have me run away? But if he were against it, he would not have bequeathed us his dream.'

'My brother wanted you to temper your courage with prudence,' said Cara Rea. 'What of his premonition? For Guide Gendal the Eagle brought us Thiemo's message of Raban's death at the Duke's behest. And behind the eagle came Rehlein or "little deer" Hirschmann wearing an antelope engraved on his signet ring.'

'That is the seal of my family, the Hart of Harzland,' said Rehlein with indignant pride.

I looked at Rehlein in surprise. Over the many miles we had ridden together in our younger days and since we happened upon each other in the past month, he had never revealed his true identity to me. Now I knew of his ancestry, I understood why he had given in to doubt and abandoned his youthful search for truth years before. Who would not hanker for the best feather beds of the richest demesne in the north after a year of suffering the hardships of the road?

'Near enough an antelope except on a plate,' said Cara Rea.

Bertram rebuked her with a look. A change came over him as we watched. He shed the look of the grieving son. His back became straighter and his face more decisive as he accepted the mantle of his leadership role. He stood up to address the clan.

'Tonight, Children, we must sleep, as we have much work ahead of us. Tomorrow sunrise, the horn master will sound the alphorn to call all the Children of the Raven home from their work on the mountain. I will meet with my generals, Aldwin and Walther, in the Lesser Hall, to plan our response to these provocations by Duke Nicolaus. Cara Rea, you will go to fetch my betrothed Ened and bring her back by noon, for our wedding tomorrow afternoon.'

Cara Rea scowled. I sensed she had wanted to attend his meeting with the Generals.

Bertram picked up the rolled cloth which had lain before him on the table and unrolled it with a flourish. The gathering cheered as he revealed the gules scarlet and sable black standard of Rabenwald: the Raven against a field of blood.

'It is time for the Raven of Rabenberg to fly once more!'

Chapter 5
The Meeting

'Glad I am that my family has no such customs,' said Rehlein, as sleep evaded him that night.

We were sharing the same servant's room I had slept in earlier, in the separate kitchen block across the courtyard from the Great Hall. The bracken-covered canvas beds were basic, but I had experienced far worse in my travels, and Rehlein had too.

'Though my family would have had me marry for peace, Gendal, they knew better than to betroth me before the age of understanding. That is why I am still single now.'

I fell asleep, lulled by his endless prattle. When I woke next dawn, he was still rambling on.

'With this diversion, I'll wager we'll not see the north this winter. The quest appeals at least. Far better to discard life valiantly than to raise one's hand against one's self.'

'Have you chattered this night away, Rehlein?'

'Cara Gendal, I thought you listened. You answered several times.'

'Aye, in my sleep. Has anything happened?'

'No. The mountain rested all night in preparation to fight and build today, as required by the family motto.'

Rehlein's demeanour had improved a lot since we met by my locket's prompting at The Bush Inn in Strasbourg about a month before. At first, I had not recognised the wealthy drunkard with the stern expression, until he had spoken. When I had greeted him, he demanded, 'Who are you to hail a stranger?'

'Do you not remember me, Rehlein Hirschmann? Has Gendal changed as much as you?' I answered him.

He scowled at the memory. 'Eregendal, the travelling companion of my youth! From that time long past when we had hope and optimism! Does life still hold three stars for you? For I have lost a star, and must find it to make a new compact with this life. Existence is so tedious, and yet I am so loath to leave. Waiter, another drink! And one for all this fine company too!'

Though I supped a beer with him, I promised him nothing, and dragged him away from the drinking hole before he could waste any more money on his fair-weather friends. Whatever I had said to him next morning must have given him some small glimmer of hope though, for he abandoned his drinking companions and joined me on the road that day. We had ridden together since.

The powerful tones of an alphorn brought me back to the present. The hornmaster was blowing the summons some distance away from Rabenschloss, calling across the mountains for the Children of the Raven to come home to the castle.

Our chamber door crashed open. Cara Rea swept in. Her presence filled our little stone-walled cell.

'Leave your beds, travellers! Your presence is required in the Lesser Hall.'

Her resentment at our being included in Bertram's planning meeting while she was not, touched her face and manner with an ugliness I took as a warning.

I rose and threw my brigandine coat over my singlet while she watched and waited. Rehlein held back beneath his blanket.

'Pray, leave this room, Madam. I will not rise before a lady.'

'Why, have you aught that's different to any other man?' she retorted, mocking his false modesty.

Her scorn raised his indignation.

'Do not try to rule a Hirschmann, lady,' he growled: 'I bow to my liege lord alone; and will therefore be treated courteously, or I shall surely leave you and yours to redeem my vow alone.'

'Do you seek an excuse to get away?'

'Pray, leave each other's throat,' I bade them. 'Cara Rea, permit us to complete our ablutions in private. We shall make our way to the Lesser Hall as soon as we are able.'

She snorted and left our cell. When we emerged some minutes later and crossed the courtyard to the Lesser Hall, we saw her canter off through the castle gateway to fetch Ened, Bertram's bride.

The courtyard was busy with people preparing for the wedding, which was to be held that afternoon. People were coming and going from the forest, bringing game for the feast and firewood for the spits and ovens to cook it. Young women made decorations and posies, while young men carried benches and tables across the courtyard and into the Great Hall. We dodged the bustle and entered the doorway to the Lesser Hall beside it.

Bertram welcomed us as we came in. The new leader radiated an energy I had seen before in people who contemplated battle and welcomed it. Some men find their greatest sense of being alive on the battlefield rather than in the bridal chamber.

'Ah, you have come at last, Sir Rehlein, Knight Gendal. Help yourselves to bread and cheese. Let me introduce my Generals, Aldwin and Walther.'

We nodded to the two generals as Bertram named them. Aldwin was a tall, lean, powerful man in his forties, with unkempt chestnut hair and beard, and a hawklike look to his face. Walther had a similar build to Aldwin, but his face looked older and more fleshy, and his long black ringlets of hair hung in greasy ropes on his shoulders. They wore the practical undyed linen shirts, short wool tabards and long breeches that were traditional working clothes in the region.

'I have asked Sir Rehlein and Knight Gendal to join us in our planning, because of their training and experience,' Bertram said: 'Sir Rehlein, I believe you have undergone far more extensive training in leadership in Harzland than I have here in Rabenwald.'

Rehlein nodded, but he had a strange expression on his face, as if that training had been squandered in some way.

'And Knight Gendal: the Imperator's ring you wear marks you as a free Imperial Knight, under the direct authority of our Holy

Roman Emperor.'

I nodded. 'I gained my Imperial Immediacy as a ministerialis, upon King Henry's accession to the Imperator's throne, for my services as a guide and messenger during his election.'

'You are a long way from Luxemburg,' said Aldwin.

'For the help I gave, King Henry granted me leave to roam.'

'So you'll be handy with a sword,' said Walther, knowing how dangerous the road could be when politics were in flux.

I gave a reluctant smile. Though I was a skilled longsword fighter and my brigandine protected me well, I abhorred violence and preferred to end conflict by more peaceful means. In the violent world of the 1300s, I usually kept such views to myself.

'It is unusual to have two generals in charge of such a small nation force as you could muster,' said Rehlein. 'Is there a reason for this?'

'I saw service in the County of Wurttemberg, but I have retired now,' said Walther. 'Aldwin is our senior general. I advise and support, from the benefit of my experience.'

I tired of their polite game of setting precedence and cut myself a hunk of bread and cheese. The bread had been baked fresh that morning and had the aroma and body of a product baked by a master baker. The alpine cheese had a firm texture and a faintly herbal flavour. I washed the simple meal down with fresh water which had been drawn from the castle well. I turned my attention back to Count Bertram when he started to outline his proposed plans.

'I have thought long and hard about what my father chose to tell us in his will, and how we can avenge his death, and the deaths of our brother and sister Hans and Anna at the Iyver.'

'We do not have a defensible castle here,' said Walther.

'No, we don't, and I have taken that into consideration. All our people are gathering here today for my wedding to Ened. We will all stay here overnight. Tomorrow, my bride and I will go to Eiswald, to find my father Raban's body and bring back what we can of it for a decent burial here. We should be gone no more than four days.'

'Surely one of us can go. Don't put yourself and Ened at risk,' said Walther.

'No, I owe it to my father. And that way, I can carry out the instructions he gave in his will. For if you are willing, Sir Rehlein, I want you to deputise for me while I am away. Oversee the rebuilding of the castle, to make it fit for battle once again. Organise the Children of the Raven to prepare for war: have them make pikes and arrows and protective clothing. Duke Nicolaus will suspect nothing while Ened and I honeymoon away from Rabenberg.'

'This is early September,' said Aldwin: 'The season for battle will soon be over: the beginning of October is the latest we can reasonably ask our forces to go out and fight.'

'Yes: the weather will turn against us after then,' Walther agreed.

'We will return before the end of the week. Once I am back, I will send out messengers to call people to unite against the Duke. I believe there are many in the Duchy of Danuvia who would rise up against him to break the yoke of his punitive taxation, and the cruel enforcement of his laws by the mercenary forces he employs.'

'First, let me take a letter to the King of Rome, stating your case against Duke Nicolaus,' I offered, seeking a way to avoid his headlong rush to war.

'No, it is too late for that. It was Louis who granted his cousin Nicolaus the rights to Rabenwald without our agreement, in return for his vote to elect him as the new Imperator.'

I nodded to accept his judgement there. 'Then I shall draw a map of Danuvia to help us decide where to send our spies.'

Rehlein had sat in silence through our discussion, leaning back in a carver chair with his elbows on its arms and his fingers pressed together over his mouth as he considered Bertram's plan. He came to a decision and sat more upright.

'I am ready to act as your regent while you are away, Bertram, if your people agree to me doing so. But what if you are delayed?'

'I'm sure we won't be. But if by chance we are, continue to lead in our best interests, supported by Aldwin and Walther, with the help of your friend Knight Gendal and my sister Cara Rea.'

Rehlein turned his piercing blue eyes towards Aldwin and Walther.

'Generals, are you prepared to accept my authority in Count Bertram's absence?'

They looked at each other and held their gaze for several seconds before both turned back.

'When Count Bertram gives us the order to do so, we will,' said Aldwin.

I breathed in deeply. This was going to be a challenging regency, if it went ahead.

Chapter 6
The Wedding

The castle thronged with people arriving for the wedding. As it was a beautiful warm sunny day, Cara Rea elected to hold the ceremony in the courtyard. She set up a temporary altar in front of the windows of the Lesser Hall. Benches were provided for those who were too frail to stand, with an aisle between them for the wedding procession.

The altar was decorated with seasonal flowers and herbs to ward off evil. On the centre of the altar stood a statue of the ancient goddess of flowing waters, Danu. Her wide eyes gazed from a motherly, compassionate face. In her right hand, she held a rod of command. In her left hand, she bore an urn from which poured the endless waters of life to feed her creatures of the rivers and oceans and to bring plenty to all. Part Celt, part Scythian, her uneasy alliance of two dead cultures had levelled her early with so many fallen gods. That her worship should still exist in Rabenwald spoke eloquently of the county's continued insularity.

Around the goddess stood objects symbolising the elements: a lantern to reflect the fire of the north, a fan to reflect the air of the south, a piece of granite from the mountain to reflect the earth of the west, and a bowl of water from the castle well to represent the water from the east.

The pagan elements in the wedding surprised me when I first saw them. As I thought about them while we waited for the bride and groom, they helped me understand the deep-seated roots of the conflict between Rabenwald and Danuvia. In our era when Christianity is being imposed by coercion on Jews in the cities and in battle on the Saracens in the Crusades, this pocket of folk religion hidden in the heart of the Holy Roman Empire, would be considered a poisonous cancer which must be destroyed.

Count Bertram came out from the Lesser Hall, dressed in a white surcoat with the device of the Raven in a red shield on his chest. Ened came from the Great Hall, dressed in a green gown, with a bouquet of herbs and flowers in her hands. Both wore crowns of ivy. The green ivy leaves looked luminous against their curling black hair. Ened's build was that of a capable mountain woman, with strong shoulders and hands that knew hard work. She also had an ethereal beauty, like that of the moon when she faces the sun, her benefactor in the sky. I could not have imagined a more suitable consort for the practical young Count.

Cara Rea met them at the altar and conducted the ceremony. For the occasion she wore the colours of Danu: a blue surcoat over her black dress, belted with a silver chain. She invited Bertram and Ened to kneel on a hassock before the altar and blessed them and all who were there. She instructed the bride and groom to stand and asked first Ened and then Bertram whether they consented to the marriage. They both voiced their consent firmly so that all could hear. The congregation applauded their decision with joy.

The oldest person present, an ancient bent woman known by all the clan as Mother Agatha, came forward from the crowd. She sat on a stool in front of the couple at the altar and asked them to hold hands. They clasped each other's right hand and offered the fist they had made up to her. She bound their wrists loosely with a long cord of different coloured threads woven together. Her gnarled fingers knotted each loop of the cord, binding their youthful, work-hardened hands a total of four times.

'Now you are tied to each other with a tie that only you can break,' she said over their clasped hands: 'You have taken the time since your first binding in betrothal, to learn what you need to know, to grow in wisdom and love. May Danu grant you a love that lasts and a marriage that is strong, in this life and beyond.'

The couple relaxed their fists and slid their hands out of the cord. Ened placed the cord in a small pocket in her green gown and gave Bertram an intensely loving smile.

Cara Rea dipped a small earthenware cup that had never been

used into the water in the bowl on the altar. She offered the cup to the couple. Enid drank from it first and handed it to Bertram. After he had drunk from it, he smashed the cup on the cobbles.

Finally, they recited their vows, each naming the other, repeating the words given to them by Cara Rea:

'Before Danu and the deep waters, the high mountains, the stars in the sky, the fire in the hearth and the air that I breathe, I give you my heart, and I accept your heart, to love and honour you in all I do, through all that may come, in our lives together. In all our lives, may we be reborn to meet again, and love again, as we love now.'

Bertram kissed Ened with such a passion that the entire crowd cheered, some lewdly. The married couple led the procession into the Great Hall for the wedding feast.

The tables were laden with food from the forests, the pastures and the mountain. Roast venison, boar, duck, heron and crane were served, with peas, beans, squashes and fine golden white bread, washed down with the malty local ale. There were also baskets of fruit on every table: apples, wild pears, blackberries, plums, medlars and nuts. The meal finished with a delicious steamed honey pudding, a speciality of Rabenwald. The abundance reflected in the meal came as a surprise to me: I had mistakenly imagined the region had been too severely taxed to afford such a feast, especially after the Great Famine that had ended only two years before, in 1317.

So many people had attended from across Rabenberg that they outnumbered the table places in the Great Hall. The youngsters carried in the benches from the courtyard to make sure everyone at least had a seat. Cara Rea had placed me on the end of the top table, beside General Walther. He was on great form, eating and drinking as if there were no tomorrow. When he finally had to pause for a rest, he turned to me with a knowing look.

'So where did you slip off to, after our meeting finished this morning?' He tapped his nose with a greasy forefinger, and drank another deep draught from his cup.

'I went to exercise my horse, Finstar. We explored the paths round the castle. This forest is quite a warren.'

'I thought you would be working still.'

'I have drawn a map to prove it. I will show it to you tomorrow, for your comments. You will know the forest far better than I do.'

'You have a wise head on you for such a youngster. I told Aldwin that. Sir Rehlein may be our regent for a day, but you will be the wits behind the throne.'

The time for speeches came. Johannes, Ened's father, spoke well and thanked all who had helped to create such a magnificent event in so a short time. He offered his condolences to Count Bertram on the death of his father, Raban. He praised Bertram's prowess as a hunter and a leader, and wished him every blessing for the future.

Count Bertram then stood to reply. He opened with the classic, 'My wife and I,' which drew forth a chorus of cheers, applause and a drumming of feet. Next, he thanked Johannes and all who had helped and supported them both. Then he praised Ened for her many virtues and raised his goblet to toast her. All drank to her good health and wished them a long and happy marriage.

Bertram's face became grave.

'Children of the Raven, I now have difficult things to say to you. You will have heard of the cruel deaths of my father, Count Raban, and Hans and Anna at the Iyver. This is the repayment we have received for trying to negotiate with Duke Nicolaus of Danuvia.'

The Duke's name brought forth a chorus of boos from some of the more drunken guests.

THE EAGLE AND THE RAVEN

'Our home was gifted to him without our agreement - to a leader we do not respect and who has no respect for us. We must now decide whether we accept the Duke's authority, or fight to regain our independence.'

The chorus among the guests cried, 'Fight, fight, fight!'

'But the Duke is a powerful man. He has a large army. Many of us could die.'

'Fight! Fight! Fight!' shouted the crowd, their voices louder.

'This will mean a lot of labour and a lot of sacrifice.'

'Fight! Fight! Fight!' shouted the crowd, now women as well as men: almost every adult present. Only Rehlein and I did not join in. We knew the reality of what they were baying for.

I marvelled at the way Count Bertram had manipulated the crowd to choose what he wanted. He let them bay on for some time until the chanting lessened a little. Then he raised his arms again. They fell silent.

'Thank you for pledging your support. This is what we must do. First, we will need to prepare for battle. During the next week, those who are able will work under General Aldwin, to repair our castle and make it our true fortress once again. The rest of you will work under General Walther: making weapons, organising provisions, and all those other tasks needed for us to prepare for war.'

The crowd now stayed silent, as the reality of what they had called for dawned on them too.

'Tomorrow, Countess Ened and I go to retrieve the body of my father, Count Raban, and bring him back to Rabenwald for a proper burial, according to our custom. During the short time we are away, Sir Rehlein has done us the great honour of agreeing to act as my regent, to support our preparations for battle. Sir Rehlein?'

My friend stood up to speak. I knew from his expression that he was bemused by the turn of events, though his years of training ensured he kept it hidden from the crowd. The atmosphere turned from belligerence to suspicion of the blond-haired stranger being foisted upon them as their new leader.

'Children of the Raven,' said Rehlein, 'Though I have not known you long, be assured I have your best interests at heart. Your brave warrior, Gotfrid and I were the ones who found the bodies of Hans and Anna at the Iyver. I vowed vengeance against the cruel vermin who could perpetrate such atrocities. So your fight is my fight, a fight we all need to win!'

His delivery was astounding. His words moved the crowd from suspicion, through compassion, to righteous anger and total support. The people cheered and drank to the fight ahead.

The speeches over, Count Bertram and Countess Ened left the gathering to much applause and shouted innuendo. The tables and benches were cleared away for dancing, and more barrels of beer were set up and broached.

Rehlein joined me in a quieter corner of the hall from which I was observing the celebrations.

'Can you believe them, Gendal?' he asked. 'How can they drink and dance like this when they could be dead tomorrow?'

'Perhaps it is because they could be dead tomorrow, that they drink and dance today.'

Cara Rea saw us on the edge of the crowd and wove her way through to join us. Page Barthram was at her side. Rehlein glared at her as she approached us.

'Sir Rehlein, Knight Gendal: it is time we left the celebrations,' she ordered. 'Sir Rehlein, Page Barthram will take you to the new apartment that has been prepared for you. Knight Gendal, you will come with me.'

Chapter 7
Cara Rea's Departure

Cara Rea led me along the castle courtyard, talking as we went.

'Bertram's feint of going to find his father's grave is a clever one. Duke Nicolaus will not suspect us of preparing for battle while our Count is away with his bride searching the Danuvian marches. I too have other work to do.' She laughed.

We entered the Lesser Hall and crossed to a wall tapestry which showed a hunting scene.

'The enemy knows only that a new Count has inherited Rabenwald and its unseen Adviser plays priest after the Pope's displeasure. I shall go to Aunsberg and enter Duke Nicolaus's service. There I shall use my position to weaken his forces, that our side may gain the advantage and win the victory. Once I am gone, you shall hear little of me. Before I go, I must tell you the traditions of Rabenwald, so that they do not get lost to future generations.'

She raised the corner of the tapestry and revealed a small door. The door opened onto a cramped staircase cut down a natural fault in the living rock. The stairs took us sixty feet below the castle to a cavernous chamber hollowed out by the river, Cara Rea's secret den. Human handiwork had blocked the river's entrance into the cave, reducing the flow to a small stream. This ran through the chamber along one wall and escaped below a large balanced slab of rock. A niche carved in the rock between the stream and the staircase held the statue of the river goddess Danu who had graced the wedding altar.

Smoking torches lit a low couch, a long workbench, and shelves of glass storage bottles containing plants, powders and liquids, all carefully labelled. In the shadows of the room, gleamed eyes red as the embers of the dying fire in the hearth. I peered at the gleaming eyes, heard the rustle of God's creatures fretting to be freed from their living tombs, and knew that Rea was a witch, not a Cara. She stood tall, proud beside her library of grimoires, an ambitious woman with a ruthless heart.

'Gendal, take off your knight's disguise and go,' she ordered.

'Do you say I am an impostor?' I replied, wondering if she accused me of her own crime.

She studied me in silence.

'Whoever heard of a messenger graduating to a free knight?'

'The same who sees a witch at bay. So do not stand to hide your necromantic books. They have not unmasked you. You are not Cara of the element water, Rea, despite the emblem on your signet ring and the statue of Danu beside you. The way my element air fans your temper to blaze, I would adjudge you to be of fire.'

'So you have read a little to make your act more convincing.'

'What do you fear, Rea? And why do you quit your homeland? You have no faith in your accusations, for you know the butterfly symbol on my eagle signet ring is of the philosopher, not the militarist. Do not despise my reborn status. Even death has its victory, and not even Caras can escape it.'

'Nor would we try. No, Gendal: I would have you save yourself. You have a noble bearing, but there is no honour or glory here.'

'Nor do I seek it, for I have no noble blood. My life is in our Lord's hands. I do not yearn to keep it but would not throw it away. Here have I found a cause to satisfy the commission given me by my Lord: to seek justice for the poor, to defend the oppressed and set the captive free.'

'I cannot believe the Imperator would have sent you on such a quest. He would be censuring his own kin: the Imperator and Duke Nicolaus are cousins.'

'Though I bow to no man but the Imperator, in truth I live under the orders of a higher Lord than he.'

'If you are claiming God's protection, think again. Duke Nicolaus fights The Raven as a holy cause. It is him you should fear, not me.'

I looked down at her tense hands gripping the edge of the table.

'Why do you say I fear, Rea? When it is your knuckles which whiten on the bench?'

She moved her hands from the table in controlled anger, and crossed the chamber to the stone statue of Danu. The goddess gazed at us with wide eyes set in her compassionate, motherly face.

'The old gods still rule, Gendal, and though they may be forgotten by men, they never die.'

Cara Rea moved a catch in the side of the niche and pressed the stone wall to its left. A portion of the wall opened to reveal a small chamber with no other exit. On a table in the centre of the room stood an old earthen bottle.

'Here is kept the luck of Rabenberg, Gendal. No, it is not the bottle or the myrrh which it contains. It is the table itself which this secret chamber hides. The table was a present from Danu to Iyverid, the first Count of Rabenwald who lived in the centre of the bog. Iyverid had been helpful to Danu in the war of the gods, and for his help she gave Rabenwald to his descendants. As Iyverid settled at the Iyver, Danu came to him in the guise of a toad and asked him what he most needed in his new land. Iyverid did not recognise the Goddess and answered flippantly: "Why, a table, of course. Life could not be complete without one." Enraged, Danu gave him this table, cursed so that when it leaves Rabenwald, Iyverid's children will die.'

Cara Rea laughed and touched the table's top.

'The family grew large and became good Christians. They no longer believed in Danu. One man tried to chop up the table to challenge the curse. The axe rebounded from the unmarked wood and split the hewer in twain. From that day, Rabenwald quietly renounced its new faith. But since then, its large family has dwindled to the two hundred people who supped at the wedding breakfast this morning.'

She contemplated the statue for a moment before turning back to me.

'I tell you all this, trusting in your past integrity, that you may understand the loyalty of the Children of the Raven to their Count. For their blood and his blood are the same. Their war is a truly religious war, whereas though Nicolaus claims this fight is a Christian crusade, he wars only for more land.'

She swung the stone door and closed it again.

'Tell no-one about this chamber. Gendal. Though it takes four strong men to lift the luck, secrecy is its greatest defence and protection. And remember never to enter the chamber alone without warning someone who knows about the catch. It is a secret hole, and for the unwary, there is no escape from inside.'

'Who else knows about the catch?'

'None but thee and me.'

She had politely told me to keep out. I bowed to her and turned away.

'What friends can Rabenwald count upon?'

'None. This lonely island of the past has only herself to save her.

THE EAGLE AND THE RAVEN

Few love the Raven.'

Cara Rea crossed the chamber and sat on her couch. She opened the door of the small cupboard beside it and took out a handful of small trinkets and keepsakes. These she packed in a saddlebag with some of her books and other possessions.

'I must go, Gendal. Here is my last secret for you.'

She went to the massive stone above the stream's channel out of the chamber. With an ease that surprised me, she moved the stone's balanced mass to reveal the larger tunnel once worn through the rock by the river when it had first eroded the cave. She showed me her trick of moving the stone, and gave me time to practise moving it, while she sorted and burned the last of her papers. When she had finished her packing, she picked up her saddlebag and opened the balanced stone once more to let us out.

She led me along the tunnel to where the stream emerged on a gravel bank at the base of the Castle's promontory. A saddled bay horse stood tethered in the bushes that screened the tunnel's opening. She strapped her bag onto the saddle and then turned to me.

'Farewells are best without ceremony. Good luck, Gendal.'

'Aye, sister; and the same to you.'

Cara Rea mounted and rode off across the river into the forest. Her steed's every step increased my sense of foreboding. I hurried back into the cavern chamber and stood by the caged creatures for company.

The creatures fretted against their bars and cried for release with a plaintiveness I could not refuse. I set each bird, each animal, each insect and each worm free in the forest, watching them with pity as they took their first steps back into the wild in the forgotten light of evening. Then I shut myself in the cavern chamber and sat by Cara Rea's dying fire to reflect awhile.

Chapter 8
Rehlein Takes Command

The next morning, I met up with Rehlein in the Great Hall. The castle kitchens had set up a canteen for the workers to help themselves to breakfast, with oatcakes and cheese, water, milk, porridge and fruit. Though servants were ready to wait on us, we served ourselves and sat at a table some distance from the rest. Many of the men had sore heads after excessive drinking the night before, but all seemed ready to apply themselves to their motto, to fight and build.

'Where have you been, Gendal? I couldn't find you last night,' Rehlein grumbled in a low voice to avoid us being overheard.

'Discovering Cara secrets to help you and yours. And you?'

'The first night here, we slept in serfs' cells. Last night, they treated me like a prince and promoted me to a bed in the apartments above this hall. Count Bertram gave me his aunt's bedroom, with all its menagerie of stuffed creatures. He said Cara Rea now has another place to sleep. He and the Countess have already left to find Raban's remains.'

'How curious. Cara Rea gave me her secret chamber to sleep in. And then she too left, bound for Aunsberg.'

'So the Count and his aunt have dropped all this on our shoulders, and run.'

Rehlein thought about our situation as he ate some oatcake and cheese. He had that wary look on his face that always warned me he was feeling used.

'Tell me, Gendal. How did we meet up again?' he asked.

I took out the locket I kept as a reminder of the magical locket held by the keeper of Fate, the wizard Arzandel, beyond the Tarn of Mirrors.

'I had left Mannheim, looking for a new adventure. My locket sent me to the Bush at Strasbourg, where I found you drinking yourself to death.'

'I don't remember that bit.'

'I'm not surprised. I don't suppose you'd remember all the so-called friends you had there, either. They were none too happy when I dragged you away. Are you ready to talk about it yet?'

'About what?'

'Whatever it is that made you try to drink yourself to death?'

'Not yet.'

He ate more oatcake and cheese as he thought further.

'Gendal, are they taking us for fools here?'

'Perhaps. But does that matter? I have found that new adventure. And you have stopped trying to drink yourself to death.'

We finished our breakfast and parted company to go about our different tasks.

I went out to explore the terrain, before coming back to draw maps and take what advice I could find to correct them. Rehlein worked with the generals, Aldwin and Walther, to rebuild the castle and prepare for battle.

Over the four days Bertram had asked Rehlein to deputise for him, I saw astonishing progress in the repairs to the castle walls, and the armoury filled with arrows and pikes. At the communal meals in the Great Hall, I saw a change in the workers' attitudes to Rehlein. Not only did they respect him as a knight and Bertram's deputy: they came to admire him in his own right as an able leader with sound judgement, a strong sense of fairness and a common touch which enabled him to understand their situation.

Five days passed. Still Bertram and Ened had not returned to the castle. That evening, Rehlein and the Generals held a crisis meeting to review the situation. Rehlein insisted I attend too.

We met in the Lesser Hall. The chamber acted as a scriptorium during the day. My maps lay scattered across the tables there, as the scribes and illustrators had left them when they finished their copying for the night.

'Today, we should have sent out our spies to incite rebellion in Danuvia,' said Aldwin.

'Count Bertram told us not to send them out until his return,' said Walther.

'What if Count Bertram does not return?' I asked.

The two generals looked at me with expressions which said, of course the Count would return.

'The additional time is helping us make good progress in repairing the castle,' said Rehlein.

'Yes,' said Aldwin: 'Most of the walls are now complete, and tomorrow we will raise the portcullis from the riverbed. The blacksmith has finished repairing the drawbridge chains. We plan to fit those tomorrow too.'

'Our arsenal is filling well also,' said Walther.

'Then this extra time has not been wasted,' said Rehlein.

'Yes, but what if Count Bertram does not return?' I insisted. 'Do we go ahead with the Count's plan, under Sir Rehlein's leadership? Or do we give up and all go back to where we were before.'

'It would be wrong for us to call a halt to our preparations. But Count Bertram did not give me authority to lead your people into war, only to rebuild.'

'I don't think this is an issue,' said Walther. 'The Count has probably just been delayed.'

'Yes: he could come back up the hill at any time,' agreed Aldwin. 'We could send someone to follow his path and find him. Then they could come back with his next instructions.'

'I will go,' I said. 'Let Gotfrid ride with me, to show me Bertram's most likely path. His presence will reassure people like Thiemo that my enquiries are not suspect.'

'That is a good plan,' said Rehlein. 'Generals, are you in agreement that Gendal and Gotfrid should go on this mission?'

They nodded.

'Thank you, sirs,' I said. 'I shall aim to be back here by this time two days hence.'

Aldwin sent for Gotfrid. We arranged to ride out the following day, as soon after sunrise as we could safely pick our way.

Gotfrid was delighted that I had asked him to join me on our expedition.

'I'm not a one for four walls,' he said with a smile.

We were riding down the mountain at the time, heading towards the Eiswald inn where I had first met Thiemo and agreed to take the message of Raban's death. Gotfrid took me a different route to the one I knew and brought us down to the inn by late morning.

The plump inn keeper, Frau Engel, recognised me from the week before and welcomed us both with a good meal of dumpling soup and local bread, while her son the ostler Herman stabled our horses. When Herman came back, they joined us at table.

'Have you had any other visitors from Rabenwald since I was last here.' I asked them as we ate.

They shook their heads.

'The only visitors we have seen, apart from the usual travellers, are those Italian soldiers,' Frau Engel said.

Herman spat on the ground to show his contempt for them.

Gotfrid and I looked at each other in dismay.

'Perhaps Thiemo has seen them,' I suggested. 'Where can we find him?'

'Thiemo has been hiding, from those Italian soldiers,' said Herman. 'If you wait here, I'll see if I can find him for you.'

Gotfrid's apprehensive eyes watched him go. Frau Engel saw his expression and tried to reassure him.

'This is not Danuvia. Those of us on the border of Eiswald have no love for the Duke of Aunsberg's men. They encroach on the Duke of Munich's lands, and try to treat us like their serfs too.'

Herman was gone for some two hours. We had long finished our lunch before he returned.

'Thiemo said I can take you to him. You need to come with me on foot.'

Gotfrid and I looked at each other, uncertain about the instruction. I strapped my shorter longsword to my belt in case of danger, and saw how Gotfrid's hand was covering the pommel of the dagger on his waist. He seemed as suspicious of this development as I did.

Herman took us along a track through the woods to a farming hamlet hidden on the edge of the trees. There in a hay barn, full to the brim before the end of summer, hid Thiemo. When he saw who we were, he slid down from the top of the stacked hay to land in front of us.

Young Thiemo looked even thinner than before, but his clothes were freshly laundered and the holes were mended, as if someone were taking care of him. The marks that suggested a fight had gone, and the blood- and sweat-matted hair and beard were now a clean mousy blond.

'Messenger Gendal, reporting back, to confirm I delivered your message,' I said.

'And I am the proof,' Gotfrid said.

Thiemo hugged me and then hugged Gotfrid.

'Are you going back to Rabenschloss? Can you take me with you?' he asked.

'We return tomorrow,' I said. 'First, we have other business to complete. Has Count Bertram come this way in the past week?'

'I don't know. I have been hiding.'

We looked across at Herman. He shook his head.

'We've not seen anyone like him pass by the inn. There was a skirmish in the woods about six days ago, some distance from here. Not far from where Count Raban fell.'

'Can you take us there?' I asked.

'Only to the border. I can give you directions for the rest of the journey.'

I nodded and turned to Thiemo.

'Return to the inn this time tomorrow, and we will take you back to Rabenwald with us. We will complete our business and return to the inn before we go back into the hills.'

Thiemo nodded and wriggled back up the stacked hay to his hide among the rafters.

Herman led us back to the inn. We rode out with him to the border between Eiswald and Danuvia, which was marked by a tributary river. He gave us further instructions and left us on the bridge between the two dukedoms.

The land looked little different on either side of the river border. Harvested wheat fields stretched away from us as we rode along the road into Danuvia. After a few miles, we came to a deserted hamlet.

The fields were cared for, but no-one was about. We rode on down the road to another deserted hamlet. Again, all was in good order, but no-one could be seen.

We rode on into early evening through a deserted landscape. At sunset, we found a house with a bush hanging outside and stopped to ask for lodging for the night. The host was an old woman who looked incapable of fending for herself. Her lodgings were as basic as most bush inns tend to be. We saw to our horses and helped her with the fire and the simple evening meal of bread and boiled eggs.

Once our creature comforts had been taken care of, we sat and talked with the old woman for a while.

'Where has everyone gone?' asked Gotfrid.

'The Duke's men came through here, a week ago,' she said. 'They left their mark. They spared me because I was no use to them.'

Gotfrid and I looked at each other, both knowing she must be talking of the skirmish that Herman had mentioned.

'What happened to your neighbours?' he asked her.

'The soldiers were cross because they didn't find what they wanted. They beat up some of the men, and they forced themselves on some of the girls, and they took some people away. When we hear the sound of horses now, those they left here hide away, in case they come back for more.'

The atrocities she then proceeded to describe, sickened us.

'Tell me, where did the Duke's men come from?' I asked after she had finished her tale.

She looked at me, puzzled by my question.

'What language did they speak among themselves – could you understand them?'

She shook her head. 'No, they babbled. We didn't know what they were saying.'

'They will be some of the Condottiero's mercenaries,' I told Gotfrid: 'Probably the same ones we evaded at the Iyver, the men who went on to murder Hans and Anna.'

'Could they have taken Ened and the Count?' he replied.

The old woman did not know enough to answer that question. The information she had given us, warned me of a unit of predatory mercenary soldiers who had gone wildly out of control.

We slept the night at the bush inn and crossed the border back into Eiswald the next morning. Thiemo was waiting for us at Frau Engel's inn when we arrived. After resting our horses, we rode back into Rabenwald. We each took turns in letting Thiemo ride on the back of our saddles, to avoid tiring our horses too much while ensuring he did not delay us.

When we reached Rabenschloss after sundown, the drawbridge had been raised, stopping us from entering. While heartened to see how successfully the repairs had been progressing over the two days we were away, we felt less than charitable about having to wait for entry after two days spent mainly in the saddle.

I called out, hoping a sentry had been placed on look-out. After a brief pause, we heard a babble of voices and the rattling of chains as the drawbridge dropped for us. In the gateway behind stood the portcullis, also repaired and back in place. When the guards saw our faces in the torchlight, they waved in welcome and raised the portcullis to admit us.

We handed our horses over to the care of Page Barthram and hurried across the courtyard to the Lesser Hall. There, Rehlein was waiting for us with Generals Aldwin and Walther.

'Sirs, you have done excellent work with the repairs,' I said as I entered.

'You're back!' Rehlein exclaimed with such joy that he hugged me, taking me by surprise.

'What news of Count Bertram?' asked Aldwin.

'We were not able to pick up his trail in so short a time,' Gotfrid replied. 'We have brought Thiemo back with us.'

'Thiemo is the young man who sent me here to tell you of Count Raban's death,' I explained. 'He has been in hiding ever since. He asked to come back with us. You may be able to get more details about Count Bertram and Ened from him.'

Rehlein and the generals questioned us at length about our trip and then let us go to find some supper while they interviewed Thiemo. They recalled me to the Lesser Hall shortly before midnight.

'Thank you for bringing Thiemo back with you. Unfortunately, he was unable to tell us much more than you did,' Rehlein said.

'We suspect the commotion he and Herman told you about, was probably caused by the mercenaries coming across Count Bertram,' said Walther.

'My concern now is that had Count Bertram returned on the day he said he would, we would already be acting on stage two of his plan,' said Rehlein. 'Our men would be travelling across Danuvia at this moment, spreading the word about the Raven's uprising. Instead, we are waiting for the Count to come back. But what if he doesn't?'

'He will come back. He will not abandon us,' said Aldwin.

'What if he can't come back?' I asked.

The men's expressions told me they had all been thinking the same, but did not want to voice the possibility.

'Do we go ahead, anyway?' I added, to reinforce the point.

'We do have Count Bertram's plan,' said Walther.

'But will the Children of the Raven be prepared to follow me into battle?' asked Rehlein.

'We are not that far through the Count's plan yet,' said Aldwin. 'We could send out our agents as he planned, giving him the time to return to us before we reach the final stage of taking up our arms.'

'If you are willing to take on that additional role, Rehlein,' I cautioned.

I looked at my blond friend's handsome face and powerful physical presence. When I had met him a few short weeks before at the Bush at Strasbourg, he had looked a cowed and defeated man, as though life had dealt him some great calamity from which he was struggling to recover. Now, his posture was upright, his eyes bright, his wits sharp. He had found a cause in life again. I had no doubt what his answer would be.

'Yes, I will continue,' he agreed: 'for as long as Rabenwald wants me to be Regent, I shall lead.'

Chapter 9
Betrayal in Aunsberg

Thirty children of Rabenwald left with me to travel into Danuvia, just thirty-two hours later. Some of us travelled on horseback, others walked. We scattered on the edge of the Danuvian plain as each of us headed separately for our designated settlements.

I rode for the capital Aunsberg. Rehlein had allocated that most dangerous of postings to me because he knew I had friends and contacts in almost every town and city in the Empire, and trusted my ability to turn challenging situations to my favour. While my horse had enjoyed a much needed rest the day before, I had helped Rehlein and the Generals plan the campaign and allocate the different towns to the people who had volunteered to take part in the dangerous task.

The stubble was being ploughed into the late summer fields, ready for the winter. The closer to the capital I came, the thinner stood what little forest the woodcutters had left, with broad glades connecting the villages of timber-framed houses. I made good time and reached Aunsberg before the late afternoon sun had touched the horizon.

Aunsberg had been founded on a granite tor which rose defiantly from the Danuvian plain. The castle stood on the highest part of the tor. Stone and timber-framed buildings crowded together down the southwest hillside leading from the summit, with the poorest quarter, Nedauf crumbling at the bottom, near a tributary of the Danube. Tall walls surrounded the city, not for defence but for civic control. Night was curfew time for most residents of Danuvia, except the chosen few, and when the gates shut at sunset, no-one could enter or leave until they opened again the following dawn.

Although I had travelled up from the south, I entered the city by the north gate, riding Finstar up the shallow steps cut into the granite tor. To my surprise, the gate was shut. A guard demanded my business.

'I am Guide Gendal, come to rest from my travels a few days in your pleasant city,' I said, and flashed my company seal.

'Who will vouch for Gendal?'

I considered those I knew who lived there. Acquaintances rarely vouch for each other when city entry is at stake.

'Leander the Taverner,' I said, certain that he would appreciate my custom.

The gatekeeper sent a messenger to Leander as I had no letter to prove my claim. While I waited without, he admitted other travellers to the city. I felt relieved that we had not sent anyone else to Aunsberg.

Leander himself walked to the gate to greet me, probably to make sure that I was not a total brigand despite my brigandine coat. He was a short, fat man with an oily-looking skin, greying hair, and a taverner's apron over his singlet and breeches. He eyed me up first, calculating my net worth from the possessions he could see.

'Guide Gendal, what a pleasure to see you again! Yes, I can see how tired you are after your latest assignment. You are welcome to stay with me for as long as you like while you pay your way.'

The guard let me through the gate into the city. I dismounted and walked beside Leander to the tavern, leading my horse through the cobbled streets. The tavern was in the lower part of town, not quite in the poor Nedauf quarter.

The streets were quietening down after a busy day. The tavern did not have much custom. As there was no ostler, I took care of Finstar myself before going inside to eat the evening meal, a dumpling stew.

After my meal, I invited Leander to share a bottle of wine with me. At first our conversation centred on the mundane: the weather, how far I had travelled, how the prices in the market had gone up. Then he leaned across the table to whisper hoarsely at me.

'Who are you? You don't look like the Gendal I knew, Eregendal.'

'Then why did you let me enter the citadel?'

'Someone asks for me, I know I will get his custom. Money is scarce these days, what with the taxes and all. I need any extra trade I can get. So who are you? You can already get me hanged. You are a free knight, at least. I can tell from your ring.'

'Then you know that I am Knight Gendal with your quick eye.

But I was once Guide Eregendal who brought you at your request from Thuringia to this prosperous land, before Nicolaus learnt the vice of greed.'

'Hah! You would cross your sword with our illustrious Duke.'

'As much as any Guide of our Worshipful Company.'

'Aha! A Guide of the Company would not take it upon himself to influence the politics of Lords, beyond helping travellers reach their destinations. Can Knight and Guide live happily in the same person?'

'As easily as Danuvia and Rabenwald in Nicolaus's rule.'

Leander laughed.

'So you are with the rebels. You have come to the right place here, traveller. Rebels are ten-a-penny here when they are drunk, though you'll find no sober ones. Sober ones fear friend, foe and stranger alike as the Duke's spies.'

'Have many been arrested here recently?'

'All the time. They pay a penny a head. People even bring them in from the fields.'

'What happens to them?'

'Tortured for information; and the Italian mercenaries are such bastard sons they torture folk to death whether they tell or not. The soldiers confiscate their possessions and throw the families out on the streets. The women rebels have it worse, the way they ill-use them. Only children can risk talking against Nicolaus now, and even then some meet with a sorry fate.'

'So there is no hope of meeting anyone willing to throw his lot in with Rabenwald?'

'Come on! Those brigands were finished, when their leader Raban was butchered a fortnight ago.'

'Raban had a son, and was brother to a Cara.'

'No! Oh, my, my! What if I were to put it about in the other bar that I thought a certain visitor was, er, connected with Rabenwald? It would be enough to interest the rebels, without the Duke's men getting to hear of it.'

'What if the Duke's men did hear?'

'One need not leave a house by its door.'

'Unless one takes to horse inside. Go fetch more wine. I fancy a game of pegs, as we used to play on the road.'

'Certainly, friend. Right away.'

Leander was gone a long time. He finally returned, clutching the pegboard and looking a little breathless.

'What kept you?' I asked.

'I was just starting a rumour for you,' he replied as if it were nothing. 'Here is the pegboard. I cannot mind you besting me once at pegs while we were on the road.'

'I was always intent on other things. I need all my wits to play a champion like you.'

Leander had always won because he cheated. I took heed of the warning from our past.

He set out the triangular board with its fifteen pegs and started to play. He played recklessly and lost every game, which soon bored me. At least he had lost his cheating habits, I thought; or had Aunsberg brayed them out of him? As I set up the board for another game, a knock came at the tavern door. It was the harsh knock of officialdom.

'Make way for the Duke's men!' shouted a soldier. Two mercenaries marched through the tavern to our table. They were short, wiry men with tanned Mediterranean complexions. They wore tabards displaying the eight-pointed star of the mercenaries over their chain mail and were armed with daggers and longswords.

'Knight Gendal?' demanded one. He spoke with a heavy Italian accent.

'Men do call me that,' I admitted.

'We have a warrant for your arrest, Knight Gendal, for inciting rebellion against the Duke in his Dukedom.'

I responded in Italian, his home tongue. His manner improved towards me.

'I think there must be some mistake, sirs. I do not come from Danuvia. I am a Guide of the Worshipful Company of Messengers and Guides, stopping by here to rest before I return to my homeland city. Here, see my papers, and my Company seal.'

I pulled out my Company seal on its blue ribbon from under my brigandine. The mercenaries almost tore it from my neck to look. They inspected my papers and found them in order. After looking at each other, they both turned on Leander, speaking in his tongue.

'Yes, there has been a mistake,' said one. 'Leander, you named yourself as witness.'

'But yes. This infidel prated at length about Rabenwald and its people; asked me to tell everyone who would throw their lot in with them. I told you instead.'

Perplexed, the mercenaries turned back to me for my version of the story. I replied in Italian again.

'I fear that we have both drunk a little overmuch. Leander too prated at length, putting words into my mouth as we played at pegs and he kept losing. I doubt the strength of his loyalty to Duke Nicolaus; I would sooner trust his loyalty to the penny reward on a rebel head. A man in his straits would betray his mother to the devil for that sum.'

The mercenaries turned back to Leander, who stared open-mouthed at them. One of the soldiers tore up the warrant and stuffed it in Leander's mouth.

'Pick your rebels with more care tomorrow, gutter rat!'

The soldiers marched out into the street. I stood up to follow them, but Leander caught my arm. He spat out the warrant.

'Would you have had me hanged, friend, me with a wife and three children to support?'

'In your greed for pennies, sirrah, you had little more planned for me.'

I threw the wine price on the table and marched out of the tavern. As I saddled my horse again, I reflected on how my recent acquaintance here had got me into town, but also into trouble. I rode down the hill towards the poorer Nedauf quarter, hoping the next person I called upon would prove more circumspect.

Chapter 10
In Search of Allies

The neglected Nedauf quarter of the city lay mainly in ruins. Though even man's greatest works fall into disrepair over time, there is nothing more humbling than the ugly ruins of poverty in a minor capital. A country house falls gracefully beneath nature's beautiful cloak; but a city slum disintegrates beneath a throttling mound of refuse. Its empty facades betrayed a society which happily let rats infest the rotten interiors while evicted tenants died on the streets outside. A fallen city cries tears of stone, not only for the builders' lifetimes of wasted labour, but for man's mighty expectations, which time ever and again prove unfounded.

With the hour already past curfew, I was aware of suspicious eyes watching me from each inhabited hovel among the ruins. I found the address of another former acquaintance, halfway down the main south thoroughfare of Rope Walk. The address was a stone tenement building, in far better condition than the half-timber hovels around it. I knocked on the door several times. No-one answered.

As I did not want to be caught breaking the city curfew before completing my task in Aunsberg, I led my horse back up Rope Walk to a deserted ruin of a building I had noticed on the way down. The walls were tall enough for me to hide Finstar as well as myself, and the partial roof gave some semblance of protection against the persistent drizzle that had settled in for the night. We rested in what had once been a kitchen, though the grate had been torn out of the brick hearth and a good part of two wattle and daub walls were missing. I drew my riding cloak around me and tried to sleep. Sometime later, I started awake again, roused by a footstep nearby.

A shadowy figure had entered through the ramshackle gateway. He wore a monk's black habit but moved furtively, like a thief. When Finstar snorted and tapped a hoof in warning, he jumped.

'Who's there?' he asked softly. Though he spoke the local dialect, his accent sounded Iberian.

'Gendal the Messenger,' I whispered. 'I had to leave Leander's in a hurry.'

The man chuckled and came closer. I could barely see him in the shadows, but sensed he no longer feared me.

'Biggest crook in town, Leander. You did well to escape his trap. I am Friar Fadrique. You are welcome to stay in my lovely residence.'

'Thank you, Friar. I appreciate your hospitality. But why aren't you living in your friary?'

'A little difference of opinion. I cannot conceive our blessed

Lord of love agreeing to the Inquisition.'

'A man after my own heart. I studied theology at Toulouse for a term, until I realised the university was set up to denounce Catharism. My teachers did not want to win arguments with words alone: they supported their logic with inquisitions and crusades.'

'That is the way of the world these days. What brings you to Aunsberg?'

'A commission. I seek the Widow Astra. The last address I had for her was near here on Rope Walk.'

'The Widow Astra, you say!' The friar's tone alerted me to his love of telling a good tale. 'Well, there's a story for you. It's some years since she lived here in Nedauf, so they tell me. She lives at the top of the hill now, in one of the best houses in town.'

'How did she manage that?'

'She worked her way up the ranks, from what I hear. An affair here, a dalliance there. Some even say she entertains the Duke at times, when he's not pursuing some other less fortunate female.'

'She always was a resourceful lady.'

The friar's tale surprised me. The woman I recalled as Astra had been devoted to her husband. I had escorted him home to her after he had been wounded in a border skirmish. He had died soon after. Then creditors had stepped in, stripping her estate and destroying her status. I had escorted her to Danuvia to let her escape the derision she would have faced had she continued to live in the region her husband had called home.

'Resourceful?' Fadrique chuckled. 'That is one way you could put it.'

We talked on into the night. Despite his love of a good story, I warmed to the disgraced friar and enjoyed his company. He told me how Nedauf had fallen into ruins, wrecked by the mercenaries on the orders of the Duke after Nicolaus feared rebels based there were plotting to remove him. Fadrique then described the politics in Duke Nicolaus's court with great relish as he hinted at some of the particularly unsavoury details. I listened more carefully than my manner suggested, thinking that some of the information might later prove useful to our cause.

Our conversation was interrupted by a patrol of Italian mercenaries who were checking the area for curfew breakers. Fadrique cautioned me to be quiet and did not speak again that night. Some time after the patrol had moved on down the street, I heard his snoring. I settled down to sleep too.

Soon after first light, Fadrique woke me with a basin of fresh water which he had drawn from the horse trough in a nearby square. With daylight, I could see my host properly at last. He had a distinctive lined face with a bulbous nose which suggested a life of hardship and fighting.

We washed and drank and gave my horse the rest of the water. The monk was taken aback to see my brigandine coat and swords.

'I thought you said you were a man of peace.'

'I have seen enough of war to always seek peace first.'

He nodded, accepting that. His expression took on a glint of mischief.

'Is that why you seek the Widow Astra?'

I laughed. 'Airy though your guest house is, I am rather partial to accommodation that boasts a complete roof and four solid walls.'

He laughed with me. 'Then ride up the hill to the Castle quarter. You will find the Widow Astra's house on the West Drive.'

I thanked him and gave him a penny in room rent, which made him laugh all the more. We parted on good terms. I hoped I would see him again.

THE EAGLE AND THE RAVEN

The city was waking, and in a nearby square I could hear the sounds of a market being set up for the morning. The market enabled me to buy what I needed for both myself and my horse. I waited there until the socially appropriate time for unexpected visiting and then followed Friar Fadrique's directions. They took me to a beautiful stone-built house in the richest quarter of Aunsberg.

A uniformed servant answered my knock on the sturdy front door. She politely invited me to wait on Madam in a room on the ground floor and sent a page to take Finstar to the stable. The room she showed me to was bright and airy, with large leaded glass windows, cream walls, and wooden seats with cushioned chairs. A fire lay ready in the hearth below an elaborately carved mantlepiece, but had not been lit as the day was pleasantly warm. Had it not been for Fadrique's tales, I would have thought I had come to the wrong house.

The door swung open to admit Madam. Although her outer trappings had changed, the coquettish smile on Astra's plump face had not. She was beautifully dressed in sky blue silk, brocade and white lace, her hair hidden beneath an elaborate matching headdress.

'Astra! But I can hardly recognise you! Where are the widow's dowdy weeds now?'

'Gendal! You are also well changed. How good it is to see you! Think on! I am a courtier now. The Duke finds favour in my company.'

Her refined accent was also mocking. Though I had known her husband better, I knew her well enough to recognise that. She realised I saw through her act. Her painted face relaxed and her tone became less arch.

'How did you enter this fair city?'

'Leander the Taverner vouched for me, and then betrayed me

wrongly as rebel to the Duke.'

'Yes, Leander is a renowned blackguard. You were fortunate indeed to escape with your life.'

'Even mercenaries respect my status enough not to kill me off needlessly,' I said, and flashed the Imperator's ring. 'So, what news do you have for me?'

Astra equalled Fadrique for gossip, but she was much closer to the court than he. She waded through half an hour of trivia before moving on to a subject I found of interest. It concerned a recent arrival at court.

'Nicolaus is quite irritable at present, what with the troubles his latest annex has given him. He had thought the Rabenwald brigands would be silenced after Raban died. But no! The man who betrayed him had not told us the whole truth. The new advisor to the court says that in her glass she saw a son and another advisor. It was someone quite like you. But you are no advisor.'

'Naught but a Guide too tired to accept another commission yet.'

'Yes? Then I insist my Gendal stay here till you find your strength again. Your features are so drawn, my dear one. I could almost believe you had not rested once since we last met.'

'Astra! How can I show my gratitude? You were ever the generous hostess.'

Astra had turned into a formidable gossip, thanks to her position now at court. She had not yet attempted to discover my recent past, but I knew her cunning interrogation would not be long in coming.

'You are too kind, dear Gendal. Tonight I attend a court ball given in honour of the new advisor. Would you like to attend also? But perhaps you do not carry your finery when riding country wastes.'

'Aye, I have my court surcoat with me. There are times when finery is as necessary as practical wear. Who is this new advisor? What happened to the old?'

'Nicolaus banished his last advisor for warning him against taking on Rabenwald. The new advisor is a beautiful woman, but as hard as stone. She arrived a few days ago from the north, saying she had a vision to impart to Nicolaus. She then tried to leave; but our Duke pressed her to stay. He feels naked without such arts to save him and his troops. Our dear Christian Duke is so noble and so brave! So you rode out taking your court robes. Have you a royal quest?'

'Nay, I was but moving house. As usual, fate distracted me with another commission when I least needed it. Hence my present yearning for rest. Who will attend this ball in honour of the new advisor?'

'Only the Duke's court. But Nicolaus would not refuse you if I told him of your exploits. What important commission could take you from domestic necessities?'

'A matter of loyalty. One cannot refuse a friend. Aye, I have a mind to attend this ball with you. It will make a refreshing change.'

'A little diversion? Perhaps a flutter of the heart? But no, you were never one to dally frivolously with affection.'

'Aye. Some people, like you, play such games with more skill than a champion at chequers. But I find affairs of the heart a useless distraction. So slight a hunger can easily be ignored.'

'Perhaps now, Gendal. But one day you'll find your butterfly wings clipped and the prison of matrimony taming your restlessness.'

Astra smiled archly at me. I bowed to her and pleaded travel-weariness to rest before the ball.

Servants had installed my saddlebags in an impressive chamber made more homely by a small fire in the hearth to air the room. The beautifully carved bed was also comfortable, and I had hardly glanced at the canopy's religious carving above my head before sleep crept over me. Several hours later, a knock at the door woke me.

'Madam requests you prepare for dinner,' called the servant through the door. 'Would you like help to get ready for the ball?'

The offer of assistance told me Astra planned for us to leave for the ball straight after dinner.

'Thank Madam for sending you to wake me. I need no help to dress,' I called back through the door.

Not wishing to give a hint of my rebel sympathies at court, I paid careful attention to my appearance. My complexion was already ruddy from weeks of riding through the day, and my lean cheeks had filled a little with the good food and regular meals I had enjoyed at Rabenschloss. In the plain fashion of my calling, I tied back my long dark brown hair from my face. I wore a long white belted surcoat with my device on my chest: the tawny brown butterfly over the dark brown spread eagle in a vert field. Once more in the mirror stood the dashing young Gendal, all too ready to play foolish games of heroism again.

The dinner gong struck. I swept downstairs. Astra met me in the hall and affectionately took my hand.

'At last, the Gendal I remember. But why do you freelancers dress with so little style? You could be man or woman in that sack.'

'Your radiant beauty more than compensates for my dullness, dear Astra.'

She looked magnificent. Her small-waisted scarlet gown billowed out from hips to floor in folds of finest satin, and dainty red slippers clad her tiny feet. She had changed her headdress for another tiered higher with ruby-red ribbon woven into the design. Rubies and diamonds gleamed on her neck, her wrists and her fingers. Only her maquillage was out of form as pastiness of face was fashionable at that time. Paints could not hide her sparkling charm, her bright hazel eyes, her roman nose, the perfect oval of her face. I bowed to her beauty and escorted her to dinner.

The best china, glass and silver; the most refreshing wines, the tastiest dishes were placed before us. Had I not seen the discreet opulence of her home, I would have thought she had arranged the meal specially for me. Astra's constant bright chatter enchanted me at first, then amused, but finally somewhat bored me. Astra could be very boring at times. Past experience had taught me that was when she was at her most dangerous.

'Of course, that was not my reason for going, as yours is not tonight. But with such a catch before me, would I have admitted it?' she said gaily. 'Then I did not have you here, dear Gendal. How many kings did you save that earlier journey?'

'None, my dear vain Astra. Only three princes.'

'Who were each to inherit a kingdom. What kingdom employs you now?'

'None at present; but though you are able to, find me no more work yet. My youthful looks will wipe off all too easily tonight.'

'You are tired now, I know, my dear. But you were never one for resting. In two days, you will yearn for the road again. And though I held you with chains, I could not keep you back. So let me find you some commission anon.'

'Aye, then. Look. But force no man to favour me. Exhaustion has given me the ire to pick and choose, and I need no work to see me home.'

'Home? But you were moving when you were called away.'

'Home is my valley, green and mellow, where rugged snow-capped fells fall out of the sky into the smooth clear lake, and everyone embraces me as I walk down the lonning from Sluthe Wood. *Welcome home,* they say: *Be sure you stay this time.* And this time, the mill cottage is empty, or the shepherd's hut, or above a shop in the marketplace. And there is young Zana playing in the sunshine. She asks to ride my horse and leads me far across the fell.'

I sighed at the memory of that dream of heaven which had haunted me through my life since and given me my great commission.

'Everyone should have a home like that, Astra, though they may never return there again in life. Without homeland love, we are incomplete, our lives have no foundation.'

'And we flutter from promising flower to promising flower like some summer-spawned butterfly, Eregendal.'

Astra's pointed use of my younger name told me she did not believe one jot of my dreams.

'You are waxing lyrical in your old age. When you escorted my dear late husband, I mind well you saying, "Home is wherever I lay my head the night." And also, "What should I do with four walls for thieves to break through? The world is my home. No less a place will do me".'

'Experience can change a body, Astra. This tired body has seen too much not to change.'

'What has happened to make you talk so, dearest?'

'A dream called life, a world of empty faith and countless wasted lives. When will man's greed end?'

Astra blushed and pushed away her unfinished pudding.

'When man's hunger is everlastingly satisfied,' she replied. 'See, I have finished. Let us away to the ball.'

Chapter 11
A Shock at The Ball

Astra glided gracefully up the steps from her yellow and black carriage to the impressive portico of Nicolaus's residence inside Aunsberg castle. I ambled behind her like some awkward bear. Straightway, she swept me through the foyer into a large hall, brightly lit by candle-flame dancing in suspended bronze candelabra. The floor was crowded with milling ladies and gentlemen in extravagantly embroidered court dress. In the Musicians Gallery, a septet played modern and traditional music while many of the guests danced. Upon the dais, surrounded by large sprays of white flowers not naturally found in autumn, sat Duke Nicolaus, his spouse Isadora, Cara Rea and Countess Ened, Bertram's wife.

'Lady Astra and Knight Gendal,' announced the crier.

Cara Rea looked sharply at me. Our eyes met across the room and she blushed. My eyes turned to Ened, and my heart sank. The Countess looked deeply unhappy. A creature of the hills, she wore a blue court gown as if it were a punishment. I wondered what had happened for her to have turned up there.

Courtesy demanded we should meet the hosts and the guest of honour. Astra led me across to the dais and gave Nicolaus a deep curtsey. The Duke had long greying brown hair and a long cruel face, and he carried himself with arrogant insouciance. He wore an elaborately embroidered and decorated maroon doublet which overstated his status. He eyed me suspiciously, noticing the ministerialis mark on the Imperator's ring.

'A tradesman?' he demanded.

'A hero,' Astra replied: 'It was Gendal who saved three princes in Sicily.' She regaled him with an incident from my early past which bore no resemblance to what had actually happened. It was none the better for her embellishments, but Nicolaus appeared impressed, though Rea was not amused.

'And are you resting here, Knight Gendal?' the Duke asked.

'Aye, Duke Nicolaus.'

My reply did not please Astra, who wanted me to address her lord devotionally as if I too were his chattel. She could not understand my pride in having no lord before God but the Imperator.

'We shall have need of an honest ministerialis,' said Nicolaus.

'Then I hope you shall find one, Duke Nicolaus.'

Cara Rea shook her head in warning. Astra noticed the slight movement.

'Would you refuse me, messenger?' Nicolaus demanded.

'Ministerialis I am, Duke Nicolaus, with the Imperator's seal to prove the same. But far be it from me to attest to my honesty – I would be a biased witness.'

The Duke laughed.

'We like your wit, Knight. You should have been a Fool.'

'Far safer to be Knight than Fool, Duke Nicolaus. When a Knight's wit runs out, he still has friends and gold; when a Fool's wit runs out, he keeps not even his head.'

I regretted the comment the moment it had left my mouth and inwardly cursed my impulsive honesty. Isadora stared at me, open-mouthed. But Nicolaus just laughed again.

'Insolence cannot go unpunished, Knight. Your punishment shall be to talk with each of our guests. Perhaps you can stir them out of their dull ways.'

THE EAGLE AND THE RAVEN

He waved on the next guests. I nodded a bow to him, and Astra led me away to the table of refreshments.

'Gendal, when did you meet Cara Rea?'

I handed her a goblet of wine and raised a glass myself. She nodded to an acquaintance and turned back to me.

'I cannot mind the occasion of our first meeting, dear Astra. But obviously fortune favours those who help themselves. Now, who should I meet first?'

'One whose pride will not be affronted by your cutting tongue, dear heart. I see little of the butterfly in you now. What made you bait our adored Duke so?'

I would not tell her how revulsed I felt by the opulence of the Duke's court when I had seen all the poverty in the Duke's lands, how I hated him for parading the Countess Ened as a prisoner of war at his party, and how my heart ached for the poor who struggled to survive in the city slums at the bottom of the hill while he lorded them from the safety of his castle at the top.

'He is a petty tyrant, a god of tin,' I replied.

'Continue as you are, and you'll find he is steel, not tin.'

Astra's tone and facial expression alerted me to the possible danger that my every word might reach him through her, distorted through her love of exaggeration.

'Even steel can melt. It can be hammered and tempered, bent or broken. All I fear is rock.'

'And who is of rock, that you learned to fear him?'

'Not him, but you, of course, my dear Astra. What lurks inside that clever head of yours? And to what lengths would you go to gain your goals?'

She glared icily at me. The glare transformed into radiant sunshine as a friend joined us and she introduced me.

Happy to do the Duke's bidding because it suited me, I did not dance for meeting and talking to the other guests. I wondered how to get to speak to Ened, but she was left in isolation on the dais, protected by the Duke and Duchess who refused me access to her. Instead, I worked my way around the hall, speaking to all who would speak with me. I learned Freeman Meyer loved fruit so much he ordered a wagon of fruit to be delivered each week. I learned how all the fashionable people rode out in their carriages on the Drive every afternoon because the Duke and Duchess loved to ride out then and they liked to be seen doing so too. I learned that the Duke always took a nightcap of best brandy in milk before sleep; the brandy being a regular gift from his chief of staff. And while I talked with others, I watched the Duke's son Sigfrid, fawning for the attention of fair-skinned, boyish-faced Count Erhart Huber who was from the neighbouring county of Aacheim.

When I tired of the courteous conversation and polite politics, I sought out a forgotten corner of the foyer for a few brief moments of quiet. To my dismay, Cara Rea followed me there.

'Why did you come here?' she demanded, scowling.

'To reunite me with an old acquaintance, Widow Astra. It seems she has improved her status since last we met.'

'What of your uncivil tongue?'

'Would you have me lie and fawn as well as plot? What is Countess Ened doing here?'

'The Duke's men captured her and Count Bertram when they went to bury Raban. She is a prisoner in the Duke's apartments. He is imprisoned in the storerooms.'

Her tone changed. 'So you will not accept my commission, though Waldstromdorf is only a short ride off?'

I glanced up to see Astra standing nearby, apparently not

noticing me.

'Were it but the next village, I would not accept. I am attendant on the orders of a higher lord.'

Cara Rea swept away with an air of contempt. Straightway, Astra came over.

'What was that about, dear friend?'

'The Cara would have a knight do low messenger work!'

Astra laughed.

'My proud Gendal, who has the neck to question my deeds! Can you not face even temporary demotion? To think I once admired you!'

'What? Is all your love now for yourself?'

Astra turned away, affronted. She turned coyly back and took my arm.

'I know I have changed in station since last we met, and you have every reason to suspect an inward change as well. It is true, I am not the same woman who married your friend, but that I cannot help. Times change, and we change too. But our souls do not change, even if we later choose a different route. Wisdom can come with age, as well as disillusion. And though I am not wise to stir up the past by keeping you around, I cannot forget my husband's debt to you, and I know that you are strong enough to hold me back when I seek to go too far.'

Warm fingers touched my arm. Icy fingers touched my spine. I caught the hand that strayed and kissed it formally.

'Madam, you are enchantment itself; but no-one lets a spaniel lie with a wolf.'

'You are no wolf, my dear.'

'Did I say I was?'

'The double-edged sword – ever your favourite weapon.'

'Aye, and sharp almost as the double-edged tongue. But enough of this. I must return to the ball. Who have I yet to speak with?'

I learned little more of practical use, a few items of interest, and much to confirm my presumptions. The men were handsome, the women glamorous. Soldiers danced well, generals better. Petty loves were given and taken; and all talked of the heart, the weather, and the latest purchases. Politics apparently did not sully these precious minds: they had no cause to consider it in their trivial rivalries. Never had I seen a more decadent gathering, for behind the painted faces hid brilliant and cunning minds. The entire court could have been rebellious, and I would not have realised.

I was wondering about my next course of action as I tried to engage in conversation with the taciturn Condottiero Giacomo Maladriuzzi. He was commander of the mercenaries who had ransacked the Iyver and run berserk on the Eiswald/Danuvian border. The Italian was a short, fat man with a red clean-shaven face and grizzled hair. He wore a red damask tabard embroidered with an eight-pointed star. His manner was powerful and abrupt.

Our struggling conversation was interrupted by Nicolaus, who stood up on the dais, enraged. The Duke shouted for the music to stop and held up a scrap of paper in his hand.

'Who is the perpetrator of this?' he roared.

The music stopped mid phrase and the dancing mid allemande. People whispered 'What?' in consternation.

'Here, Ministerialis! Read this!'

I strode through the guests to Nicolaus, my curiosity making me swift to do his bidding.

The paper contained a note written in the Danuvian dialect, in a disguised hand.

'It reads – I can hardly make it out – *Friends of Rabenwald, fly to me, the Raven.* What does this mean?' I asked.

Astra glanced sidelong at me. The other guests looked suitably horrified.

'I mean, I know Rabenwald bore you rebels,' I continued, 'but surely it would have no friends in this glittering company. And who is the Raven?'

Cara Rea spoke up.

'My vision of Rabenwald, which told me of Raban's son and the Advisor – I mind that this Advisor had a pale crow-like visage, and carried a black bag emblazoned with the letter H. Perhaps it is Hrafn, the northern raven of battle and bloodshed.'

Astra stole a second glance at me; but I looked young and ruddy-cheeked with my recent exploits, and my expression was innocent.

'Then this can only be the rebels' rallying call to war!' Nicolaus declared. 'Heralds, send messengers across all Danuvia. Warn the army of impending uprising.'

'But didn't you destroy Rabenwald when Raban died, Duke Nicolaus?' I said.

'Dead, but won't lie down,' said Cara Rea. 'Is that not a part of the north's legend of the raven?'

Chapter 12
A Risky Venture

As Astra's yellow and black carriage took us back the short walk to her home, she talked at length about the strange message found at the ball and speculated about how it had got there. Her arch gaze kept turning back in my direction, as if I had been the one responsible. I barely answered her as my thoughts went over the ramifications of having our plot revealed too soon. On our return, I pleaded tiredness to retire for the night, which she permitted.

Once in my room, I lay down to rest for a couple of hours. In the depth of the night, I rose again and donned my padded black leather gambeson, gauntlets, and long black cloak, and armed myself with my dagger. I left Astra's house by the servants' back entrance and slipped away unseen into the empty streets.

The hood of my cloak kept my face in shadow as I stole through the deserted byways, treading softly on the cobbles. Aunsberg slept. No-one heard the eagle's flight across the backs of the exclusive houses to the castle. As I went, I prayed. I knew what I wanted to achieve that night and was all too aware of how unlikely that was to happen.

My conversations with Friar Fadrique and the guests at the ball had given me a lot of information about the dispositions of the castle, including the Duke's residence and the store rooms within its inner walls. As I had expected, the castle's inner gates were shut and barred for the night. I hid in the shadows of a nearby building until the change of patrol squads on the Matins bell in the middle of the night.

The company of four soldiers coming off duty arrived early. They stood by the gate talking about the shift they had just completed. Their Italian accents told me they were some of Condottiero Maladriuzzi's mercenaries. At length, the Matins bell tolled in the monastery outside the city walls. One of the main gates opened, the one with the wicket door. The replacement patrol marched out in formation, but their hand over was lax as they were not expecting any problems. While they gathered outside the walls to discuss the night's events so far, I took my chance and slipped behind them unnoticed through the open gates. I ventured along the inside of the gatehouse tower wall to the right and hid in the shadows of a corner. The retiring patrol came inside, shut the gate behind them, and left the courtyard for their quarters in the south gatehouse tower.

I had already come far further than I had hoped for that night. As I feared Count Bertram's life was probably in more danger than Countess Ened's, I looked for him first.

The castle storerooms were in the south gatehouse tower, below the rooms occupied by more of the mercenaries. The spiral staircase serving the gatehouse had been built on the corner of the tower, standing out in the courtyard. Once the mercenaries had settled, I slipped in through the gatehouse tower door and felt my way along the short wall to my left until I found the staircase door. Around me, I could hear the heavy breathing of men who were fast asleep. The air was heavy with the odour of stale breath and sweat.

The wooden staircase door groaned a little on its hinges as I pushed it open far enough to steal through. I glided down the stone steps to the storerooms, fearing the movement of the door might have disturbed someone. No footsteps sounded behind me. I reached the bottom of the staircase and paused to control my rising tension with a prayer. My heart was pounding in my chest, my mouth was dry and my palms sweated. After several deep breaths, my body came back under my control.

The chamber into which the storage rooms opened was in near darkness. Just one small oil lamp lit the passage between the cellar doors. I picked up the oil lamp by its handle and searched for the cell holding Bertram. Each wooden cellar door had a small square window air vent, protected by wrought iron bars. Each cell looked to be filled with produce: barrels of oil and wine; sacks of wheat and oats.

A quiet, hoarse raven call arrested my search. I pressed myself into the shadows between two doors. When the call repeated, I answered similarly. A man's hand reached out through the bars in the wooden door beside me.

'Bertram?' I asked.

'Gendal?' he said, shocked.

'Are any of the other cells occupied?'

'No. The Duke's prisoners don't usually survive the day. My aunt must be protecting me somehow.'

'She told me you were being held here. I met her at the Duke's ball tonight. Do you know where the keys are kept?'

'They are hanging on the wall near the door to the staircase.'

'That's very lax. They can't be expecting any trouble.'

I found the bunch of keys and tried each one in the cell door until it swung open. Bertram emerged, moving stiffly after more than a week of enforced immobility. He was dressed in a grubby white shirt and long breeches, with buckskin ankle boots on his feet. While he stretched to get his muscles moving again, I unlocked all the other cell doors and left them open.

'Why are you doing that, Gendal?'

'You'll see. Do you have a plate or cup in your cell, you can bring me?'

He fetched a pewter dish. I explained my plan to get us out of the castle. Because the plan depended on our not being seen or heard, I wrapped my black cloak around Bertram to hide the whiteness of his shirt, and told him to move as quietly as possible. I replaced the oil lamp in its niche and led the way out of the cellar.

We crept up the stone spiral staircase to the guardroom, feeling our way in the darkness. Bertram entered the guardroom first, following the wall to his right towards the door. Just when I thought he had made it safely through the room to the entrance, his foot kicked against something, knocking it across the floor. The men around us sprung awake.

I threw the keys and platter down the stone staircase.

'It came from the storerooms!' I said in Italian.

The mercenaries stumbled about in the darkness trying to find a torch or lamp to light. I slid along the wall past them and out of the door before they could see their way. We heard them clatter down the spiral staircase as we slipped round the gatehouse wall to the main gates.

I undid the wicket door in the main gate and let Bertram out of the castle first. Before I could follow him out, a rough hand grabbed my left shoulder and spun me round. It was the soldier who should have been on guard duty at the wicket. Before he got a better hold of me, I punched him in the groin. Then I followed Bertram through the wicket door and drew it shut behind us.

We ran across the cobbled square outside the castle gate, into the byways at the back of the large houses along The Drive which circled the castle. I led Bertram down the hill via alleys and wynds. We emerged at length in the Nedauf quarter. There I looked for Friar Fadrique, but though I found Rope Walk, I could not locate the ruin Fadrique had shared with me the night before. I concealed Bertram in a similar ruin nearby.

'How can I thank you?' he asked me once we were safe.

'Thank God, and some lazy soldiers,' I said. 'Mercenaries are never as thorough as the land's own men. They will not be so lax tomorrow.'

'What of Ened?'

'Thanks to our noisy departure, we cannot go back for her. I will plan for her rescue at a later date. She looks reasonably well, living in the Duke's apartments under the watchful eye of Cara Rea. She should be safe enough, meantime.'

'How are things going at Rabenschloss while I've been away?'

My heart warmed to Bertram, hearing him ask after his wife and his people before he thought of his own situation.

'Your generals have worked wonders. The castle is secure once again, and the arsenal is full of arrows, pikes, and spears. Sir Rehlein is doing well as your Regent in your absence. But he needs you back there as soon as possible.'

'And I dearly want to be there. The biggest torment of my captivity was that I could not lead my people at this time. The other torment you have allayed, to know that Ened is safe.'

'What happened, that made you get caught?'

'We were ambushed by mercenaries two days after we left Rabenschloss, on the bridge between Danuvia and Eiswald. I think the soldiers expected us. They knew I would be looking for my father's remains.'

'They may have set it up as a trap to catch you. It had surprised me that Thiemo had slipped through their net.'

'But we did tonight.'

'We are only halfway. We may have escaped the citadel, but we still need to escape the city. That will take some daring too.'

'How do you think we can do it?'

'I'm not sure yet, but I will find a way. I must leave you here for a while, but I will come back later today. So lie low here and draw as little attention to yourself as possible.'

I left him in the ruin, with my cloak wrapping his body to hide him as he tried to snatch some sleep. My black gambeson helped conceal me in the shadows as I headed back up the hill towards The

Drive, though I missed my cloak for its greater ability to hide me in the shadows.

For the second time that night, a soft hoarse raven call arrested my flight. I pressed myself into a doorway, looking out onto a small cobbled square. When the call repeated, I answered similarly. A man passed, returned, and stood with his back to me, silhouetted against torchlight on the far side of the square.

'Raven eagle?' he whispered.

I drew my dagger and pressed its tip into the small of his back.

'Who calls on Rabenwald's messenger?'

'A crow.'

He turned his nervous face toward me. In the dim light, I recognised the saturnine features of the Duke's chancellor. I sheathed my dagger and drew the ally into the shadowed porch.

'Welcome, friend. What made you seek me out this night?'

'I seek allies in my secret fight against our noble Duke's tyranny. When I collect the taxes owed to him, I betray my own countrymen into the foulest depths of poverty and degradation. Nor does he gain aught with his coffers full after he's paid his henchmen their 2000 marks fee; but each coin is another person ruined.'

'Your secret fight will soon be more open. Already unrest stirs up in Danuvia. The plains folk are rising to aid us, not their lord.'

'But what will that give us? It is our system we must change, not our lord. Who would protect us with Nicolaus gone?'

'When battle breaks the condottieri's rule and delivers Nicolaus into the victors' hands, you will see that a nation can defend itself better than in thrall to a strutting glutton whose only claim to extortion is his thinning blood.'

'But when Nicolaus is threatened, his cousin The King of Rome will come to save him.'

I laughed. 'Louis may style himself the King of Rome, but he has not yet been elected Imperator. He is dissipating his power with his generous electioneering, giving lands he does not possess to those who promise to support him. He would not not risk the ignominy of civil defeat.'

'But you carry the Imperator's token! Are you not beholden to him?'

'I serve the one true Lord, Jesus Christ, who has commissioned me to fight for the poor and needy, to fight for the future so that children don't have to beg in the gutter to be fed; to fight for the new order, where every person has food and clothes and a bed, and the right to choose how they are governed.'

The chancellor clasped my hand.

'When the Raven goes to battle, a thousand plainsmen will drop their ploughs and run to join the fray to fight against their oppressor,' he promised. 'Many in the Duke's army will tear off their uniforms and turn on the leader they should defend. Have no fear when battle trumpets sound. The poor of Danuvia with be with you.'

We embraced and turned to go our separate ways across the small square into the quiet stillness of the night.

'Halt! Who goes there?' demanded an Italian soldier.

Two mercenaries leapt out from the shadows with drawn swords to block our paths.

Our weapons leapt into our hands for the fray. I rued having only my dagger and no cloak for the scrap. The padded leather of my gambeson saved me from serious wounding. I fought close to disadvantage the sword arm of the soldier attacking me. As I tussled, I could hear the chancellor struggling against the other soldier: their steel blades struck sparks on the cobbles when they over-cut.

Our desperation proved too much of a match for the two

mercenaries. They ran off, not wishing to risk their lives when their tactic of surprise had failed to win them the encounter.

I turned and embraced the chancellor once more. He was panting rapidly, his breathing shallow.

'Thank you, friend. Fair paths till battle days.'

'Till battle days,' he said, and stumbled off across the square.

I smelt blood on my cloak and touched its stickiness where his arms had hugged me. He had been badly wounded in the scrap. I dared not help him without endangering us both. I hurried back to Astra's house to clean off the tell-tale marks of the night's exploits.

Chapter 13
Escape from Aunsberg

'Have you heard the news, dear Gendal?' Astra asked as we broke our fast next morning.

We were eating little pancakes sweetened with honey, in a morning room on the upper floor of of her house. The sun shone pleasantly through the casement window, casting her in a flattering golden light.

I had slept late and had only just heard the call for breakfast. Not wanting to arouse her suspicions, I had quickly thrown on my brigandine over my shirt and breeches to join her. Her eyes noted the shortcomings in my appearance: my untidy hair, and the cuts in my shirt and breeches.

'Count Bertram has vanished from the castle,' she said. 'They say a flock of ravens stormed the gatehouse and spirited him away.' She could barely suppress a smile as she said this.

'And do you think so too?'

She smiled archly.

'Did you have a pleasant moonlit walk, Gendal dear?'

'Was there a moon last night. Astra? The only lights I recall are the candelabra at the ball. And now, alas, I have an announcement to make. I must leave Aunsberg.'

'But why? You have only just arrived.'

Astra tried to look hurt, but her scheming eyes gave her away. I returned her arch smile.

'I have a commission.'

'For whom would you ride after so short a rest? What work is of such import?'

'I have a consignment to deliver to a lord. More I dare not say.'

'When will you depart?'

'Straightway.'

'What a shame you cannot stay longer, dearest Gendal. I planned so much to show you.'

'I shall look forward to that next time I come this way. You have been most kind. Thank you for your welcome, and your hospitality.'

I rose from table and bowed to her before leaving the morning room to pack. It did not take me long. Astra joined me as I loaded my saddlebags onto my horse in the yard at the back of her house.

'Do you need directions to the South Gate?' she asked.

'No, friend, thank you. The North Gate is my exit, and I have no time to lose.'

'That is no easy gate to leave by. The South Gate is quicker – you can ride round the city walls and still gain time.'

'You forget I ride a good horse, Astra, not your awkward carriage. Still, thank you for thinking of my welfare.'

She gave me directions to the North Gate. As we embraced in

farewell, I felt her slip something into my pocket.

I mounted and rode off on Finstar, heading east along the Drive. It was good to be back on my horse: I trusted him so much more than I could Astra and her sham tears. Once we were out of sight of Astra's house, I turned off The Drive and the road to the North Gate, and headed downhill through the side streets towards Nedauf. By mid morning I was back in the ruins of the slums.

The streets in this poorest quarter of the city were now busy with people struggling to make a living from others as poor as themselves. Some ignored me, some tried to beg from me, some offered to sell their produce to me.

I turned down Rope Walk and found the building where I had left Bertram. The ruin was deserted, but a quick search among the debris turned up my half hidden cloak. I shook off the dirt and packed the cloak into a saddlebag. Then I sat and waited, fearing what might have happened to Bertram while I had been away.

As I sat, I took out the item Astra had slipped into my pocket. It was a letter with only my name, Guide Gendal, as the address. The seal was that of a family Astra did not like.

I opened the letter. It read, 'Our family is at one with your cause. We would know more. Please visit us tonight at the sign of the goat. PVR.'

I was not sure whether the note was genuine, but knew I must reply, and must get rid of both letter and reply before I tried to leave the city. I took out quill, ink and paper and wrote a brief note in response.

'Thank you for your support. Alas, business calls me away from Aunsberg. We have no set plans yet. You will know when the time is right. Then act. G.'

I sealed my letter and addressed it to PVR at the sign of the goat.

Then I resealed the letter Astra had given me, carefully matching the seal's edges. I copied the style of handwriting used in my name, to address the letter to Astra's house.

Four children were begging in the street outside my hovel. When I called one over, several came. They had big eyes, gaunt features and distended stomachs, and grey rags covered their thin bodies.

'Lads, I want you to run me two errands,' I told them.

They saw my clothes and swarmed round me, clamouring with shrill voices to be the one I chose. I divided them into pairs and gave each pair a letter with strict instructions about where to deliver it. I told them the contents were love letters and gave each pair a penny with the instruction to deliver the letters as quickly as they could.

They raced off up the street. Once they had gone, Friar Fadrique emerged in the ruins of my refuge and pulled me back from the doorway.

'Was that wise?' he asked with a wry smile on his lined, well-worn face. 'They will pocket the money and throw your letters away, or worse still, give them to the soldiers and earn two pennies more.'

'Let them: at least they are no longer on me.'

'I see.' He laughed and nodded. 'Did you fall out with the Widow Astra that quickly?'

'No: I heard your cooking is good, and arranged to meet a friend here for lunch.'

He laughed more deeply. 'Your friend is at my other premises, further down the hill. Come with me.'

The friar and I walked down Rope Walk side by side with my horse beside me. I was alert the whole time, half-expecting a betrayal, an assault, or a trap. We turned down a short alley and entered the back of the ruined building I had slept in two nights before, the day I had arrived in the city.

'Welcome once again to Casa Mia,' said Fadrique. 'Sadly, lunch is off, but at least I can reunite you with your friend.'

Bertram emerged from the shadows, wrapped in a torn and filthy blanket. He looked as if he had had a sleepless night. His drooping eyes were smudged with shadows, and his black hair and beard looked matted and untidy.

'Bertram, what are you doing here?' I asked.

'The mercenaries came looking for me. This good friar helped me hide from them.'

'Friar, I might have been, though good was never added. But you were right that I helped you to hide.'

'Why, Fadrique? Why are you helping us?' I asked.

'I see you as a kindred spirit, Gendal. I have heard a lot about you around town since we last met. Some of it may even be true. And if it is, you need to leave here before the city gates shut tonight at sunset.'

'What are they saying?'

'They say how you disguised yourself to attend the Duke's ball, how you fought four of the Duke's men and left them dead in the gutter, how you were betrayed in Leander's tavern and you escaped by using your great wits. And how you turned into a flock of ravens to spirit Count Bertram away from the castle dungeon.'

I smiled. 'Yes, some of it may even be true. But how can we leave the city when the Widow Astra has laid a trap for me at the South Gate?'

'I think I know a way.'

Fadrique outlined a daring plan, in which he played a prominent role. It required meticulous preparation, and would put us all at great risk if we roused suspicions and got caught. It solved the problems of the mercenaries looking for a lone traveller or two together, and the distinctive appearance of Bertram, my horse and all my gear.

'You plan is good, Fadrique,' I said: 'But why would you put yourself in such danger for us?'

'You have seen the starving children begging on the streets. You have seen the poor suffering while the wealthy squander their riches on trifles. You have seen a despotic rule enforced by Italian mercenaries because the state army refuses to commit such barbaric acts of cruelty. I joined the Friary to serve Christ among the poor, like those starving children, the destitute, and the oppressed. But the Friary chooses to serve Christ by forcing a rigid heterodoxy on all. The Friars support the status quo, and they are equally as cruel. I prayed to be shown a different way to serve my beloved Jesus. Now God has thrown you two in my path. You also seek to fight injustice, and cruelty, and spiritual abuse. That is why I happily place myself in danger for you. All I ask is that you take me with you and find some small role for me in your cause.'

I saw tears prick his eyes as he talked, welling from his compassion for all those who suffered, and at last found reason to trust him.

'We have the perfect role for you, Friar, should we escape Aunsberg and get back to Rabenwald.' said Bertram. 'What would you have us do?'

Fadrique asked for money to purchase an unusual list of items, which I gave him. He took some time to make the purchases, and the wait made me feel uneasy once again. But when he finally returned to our ruined shelter, no soldiers followed him. His full arms carried paniers, some grubby clothes including a black friar's habit and sandals, a large piece of canvas with needles and thread, more grimy blankets, a block of chalk, some food and a small wax capsule.

THE EAGLE AND THE RAVEN

Fadrique set Bertram and me to work grinding the block of chalk to powder while he went back out to find some poles. He returned with four rails, which he bound together to make two long poles. He roughly stitched the canvas between the two poles to make a travois litter large enough to carry a man.

Next, we turned my black horse into a grey. We rubbed the powdered chalk into his mane and coat, creating dapple circles by gently patting chalk in with a small round brush. Finstar snorted with the chalk dust blowing around his nostrils as we worked. The ruse turned him from a sleek, well-groomed knight's steed to a shabby-looking work horse.

I put Finstar's saddle back on the horse, and Fadrique somehow attached the travois poles to his girths. He tied the panniers over the saddle to disguise it. I buried all my possessions in their depths. He filled the top of the panniers with some of the blankets and the food.

Because of Bertram's distinctively tall appearance, we gave him the role of an invalid, dressing him in the grubby clothes and daubing mud on his face like pustules. While he lay on the travois wrapped in some blankets, I carried the other ends of the travois poles, dressed like Fadrique in a black friar robe and sandals. The blankets over Bertram also concealed my swords, close at hand should we need to defend ourselves.

We made our way towards the South Gate, with Fadrique leading my horse, who only tolerated this because I walked behind him, helping to carry Bertram on the litter. As we went, Fadrique shouted, 'Unclean, unclean!' and Bertram groaned as if suffering from some awful disease. Everyone we passed kept to the other side of the street.

A queue of travellers waited at the South Gate when we arrived shortly before sunset. Fadrique's cries of 'Unclean' and Bertram's groans quickly got us beckoned to the front. Although the soldiers had orders to question and search every traveller before they left the city, they only gave us a cursory inspection. One guard pulled the blanket from Bertram's face, saw the pustules of mud on his cheeks and forehead, and scowled in revulsion. Then Bertram bit open the wax capsule in his mouth. Blood oozed out between his lips.

The guard turned away in disgust and ordered us to leave the city at once. The other soldiers cleared the gateway of travellers as we passed through, to ensure Bertram's contagion did not infect anyone other than us monks carrying him.

And so we passed through the South Gate to freedom.

Chapter 14
A Meeting in the Woods

We followed the road down and across the Danuvian plain, keeping up our appearance as two friars and a packhorse carrying an invalid on a litter. Fadrique and I kept swapping places, as Bertram's weight was very tiring on our arms. We even let the litter drag as a travois when there was smooth grass at the side of the road. Most of our journey was through fields cleared from the forest, but the further we travelled, the fewer the fields became and the denser the trees surrounded us.

Several parties of people were journeying towards Aunsberg in time to enter the city before the gates shut at dusk. They could not avoid passing us and kept to the other side of the highway to keep their distance from our contagion as far as possible.

We neared the next village as the sun set. Before entering, we hid in a forest glade so that Bertram and I could change back to our true identities. Fadrique groomed the chalk out of my horse's coat and mane while I repacked my saddle bags and Bertram took the travois to pieces.

'This is where I say goodbye to you both for now,' said Fadrique once we were ready to travel on.

'Have you changed you mind about throwing your lot in with Rabenwald?' asked Bertram.

The friar laughed. 'Oh, no. I will get there soon enough, with the price of a donkey. But you are fugitives. I will slow you down.'

I laughed and gave him eight schillings.

'Make sure it's a good one. I'll need to sell it again afterwards.'

'We will make sure the Children of the Raven welcome you when you arrive,' Bertram promised.

Fadrique walked off to the village. We followed him on foot, leading my horse. I was wearing my trusty brigandine, and Bertram covered his shirt and breeches with my black cloak.

We stayed the night at the half-timbered village inn, enjoying an evening meal of rabbit and dumpling stew. The accommodation was basic, with all eight travellers staying there that night sleeping in the one common room on canvas-covered bedframes, not unlike the litter we had dismantled in the forest. I slept well, being used to such establishments. Bertram hardly slept at all, as he would normally have paid for the privacy of his own room.

After a tasty breakfast of gruel next morning, I went out to buy a mount for Bertram and came back some time later with a reasonable riding horse with saddle. She cost me five marks, despite my best attempts to haggle and bring the price down.

As Bertram and I mounted our horses in the courtyard of the inn to leave, a young man hurried across to us from the gateway. He had served us ale the night before and had made us feel welcome without asking too many questions.

'If you are fleeing from Aunsberg, strangers, the troops are close behind,' he warned, pointing in the general direction of the city road on the far side of the sprawling inn.

We thanked him and rode away, turning left out of the courtyard and down the village main street.

Bertram was a skilled horseman, but his mount was untried. I could not risk taking him across country when a fall's delay could mean our capture. Instead, we turned south-east along the Groshe highway. Once we were back in the forest, we turned down the Waldstromdorf road, concealing our course among the trees.

The villagers must have held back our pursuers, for we made good time and reached Waldstromdorf unhindered. The market day village thronged with stalls and their customers, farmers and their livestock. We mingled with the crowd. asking about the easiest way of reaching Rabenwald's north-east face. Then we followed their advice and took the south-east road out of Waldstromdorf.

By this time, Bertram was getting the measure of his horse. The mare was older than I would have liked, but biddable and without vice. We took the chance to ride cross-country, and left the road to cut across the fields to the track heading south west out of Waldstromdorf. Behind us, the mercenaries raced down the road we had left, following our false trail.

The track took us back into the thickest part of the forest. Branches reached up and closed above our heads, blocking out the sky. We rode down the dim byway for some time. Bertram's horse proved skittish in the shadows, shying at mice and falling leaves. He had to work hard to reassure her and keep her moving.

'How long must we ride through this gloom, Gendal?'

'Till we reach the foothills, about dusk, God willing. Then we take to Rabenwald's woods. Take heart. These trees are friends to the poor.'

'What are they to the rich?'

A wild man dropped onto our path ahead. Bertram's mare shied and threw him.

'Leave it!' the man ordered me, raising his knife.

He was short, lean but strong, and his ginger hair and beard grew free as the forest. He wore brown breeches and a green tunic, and carried a longbow and a quiver of arrows on his back.

I looked up at the treetops around me and saw human silhouettes among the branches. Bertram got to his feet and caught his mare's bridle. He rubbed her chest to reassure her.

'Who are you, travellers?' demanded the wild man.

'I am Knight Gendal and this is my squire. We are riding for Rabenwald with the Duke's men on our tails. We tried to shake them off at Waldstromdorf.'

The man sheathed his knife.

'Welcome to my home, Gendal. We knew from old you would run this way from the hounds. I have a message for Count Bertram of Rabenwald.'

I knew from his comment that he knew the true identity of my squire, but took care not to look in Bertram's direction.

'As that is on my way, I'll take your message to the Count, and for nothing.'

'We knew from old you would. Tell him the free men of Danuvia offer their support.'

'Need I tell him you only offer, Silvio? He would accept even outlaws to his side. You gentlemen of the forest, he will welcome gladly.'

Silvio frowned and then laughed heartily at this.

'Tell the Count we will watch Rabenwald till the beacon calls us. Now, follow me. We woodmen have safe and secret paths which will take you and your squire to Rabenwald more swiftly than your stumbling path brought you here.'

Silvio led the way along dark tunnels through the undergrowth and grassy glades not marked on any map. True to his word, he brought us to Rabenwald's base a good hour before sunset. When he realised we had reached land we recognised, he slipped back into the forest without farewell.

'You have some strange friends, Gendal. Thank heavens that wild man didn't know who I was,' Bertram said once he was sure Silvio and his men had gone.

'Oh, he knew who you were, Bertram. He didn't let us tell him, so that he could say in all innocence, no, I've not heard of him.'

'And you would have these criminals fight beside us?'

'They have useful skills that I would rather have on our side than the Duke's. Trust them for what they offer. They will not respond to your command.'

We rode on up and across Rabenwald's bracken-covered side towards the forested slopes that concealed the castle.

Chapter 15
Count Bertram Returns

The Rabenschloss drawbridge dropped and the portcullis raised to admit us. Bertram and I rode into the courtyard, grateful to be back in the safety of the castle walls. People crowded round to welcome us, their faces lit by the flaming torches in the wall sconces. As we dismounted, Rehlein marched through the throng to challenge me.

'So you condescend to return, Gendal! I have a matter to kill with you! Why did you destroy our one advantage by warning Nicolaus of our rising?'

He saw Bertram but did not recognise him as he was still wrapped in my cloak, and scowled.

'Who is that?'

Bertram pulled back the hood and cloak to reveal his black hair and broad face. The crowd gasped in surprise and then cheered for joy.

'Do not be too harsh with your friend, Sir Rehlein. Knight Gendal freed me from a prison cell last night. Let's eat and drink and rest awhile. We can talk business later.'

Rehlein's scowl turned into a broad grin. He strode across to Bertram and hugged him in welcome.

'Praise God you have returned, Count Bertram! And all in one piece! We had such fears for you.'

The two men walked through the throng towards the Lesser Hall. Hands reached out from the crowd to touch Bertram as he passed. I handed our horses to the care of Page Barthram, and followed them into the Lesser Hall. The two Rabenwald generals, Aldwin and Walther, joined us there.

Though the evening meal had finished in the Great Hall, the kitchen staff quickly brought food and drink to us: game pie, fruit from the orchards and malty beer. After we had eaten sufficient, Bertram brought our conversation round to business.

'You have worked wonders in my absence, gentlemen. Never did I expect to see the portcullis in place as well as the drawbridge, and in so short a time.'

'Both Aldwin and Walther have excelled in carrying out your orders, Count,' said Rehlein: 'They had no need to refer to my authority in their tasks while you were away. But I exceeded your instructions and crave your forgiveness for that. When you did not return and five days became a week, I sent out your spies on your behalf.'

'There is nothing to forgive. If you had not sent out the spies as I had planned, I would not be here tonight. For Gendal would not have gone to Aunsberg and learned enough to rescue me.'

Bertram described his experiences since he had left Rabenwald with Ened: their capture by the mercenaries, their separation in the castle at the Duke's command, his dark lonely nights in the cell not knowing what was to become of him, my daring rescue of him, and our perilous escape from Aunsberg and Danuvia with Fadrique's help.

I then related my part of the story: Leander's betrayal, Friar Fadrique's befriending, Widow Astra's hospitality, and my attendance at the Duke's ball, where I had met Duke Nicolaus himself and his henchman the Condottiero Giacomo Maladriuzzi.

'I also saw Countess Ened there, on the dais with the Duke and his wife, and Cara Rea. Astra told me Nicolaus had thrown the ball to celebrate Cara Rea's arrival. The Duke is a superstitious man and her magical powers are a comfort to him.'

'You saw Ened? Then she is not a prisoner in the ducal apartments?' Bertram said. The frown on his face alerted me to his fears about his bride.

'She was not there from choice, Count. And no-one was allowed to approach her. The Duke ordered me to speak to everyone present, but not to her.'

'Was she – well?'

'She looked healthy enough for someone in her position. But she did not look happy. And if looks were daggers, Duke Nicolaus would be dead already.'

Bertram sighed and sat back, his tension eased. Rehlein took up the questioning.

'If you were able to speak to everyone present at the ball, Gendal, why did you drop that note? All our spies have come back early because the Duke took heed and sent out his troops to find the rebels. Our one advantage of surprise has gone.'

'I assure you, that was not me. I suspected the Widow Astra, though it might have been Cara Rea.'

'Cara Rea?' Rehlein looked aghast. 'If she is against us, we are doomed.'

'My father Raban's will warned us my aunt's methods may seem unclear,' Bertram said.

'All is not lost,' I said. 'The Duke's reaction has warned the plains folk of our resistance. The crueller the soldiers become, the more the people will side with us. Even the free woodmen have just pledged us their support. All our allies wait only on our beacon to rise up and join our forces.'

'What matters that when the Duke's forces flood the plain, beating all life out of them?' Rehlein said.

'What, and destroy his one source of revenue? Nicolaus is not fool enough to murder the hands that feed him,' I said.

'Nay, he is not fool but mad! And you are too, if you see such an error as our advantage.'

'Now is not the time to place blame, Sir Rehlein,' Aldwin said. 'We need to plan for the situation as it is, not waste our time on what ought to have been.'

'The question we should be asking is, is this the right time for us to take up arms?' asked Walther.

'Or is there something else we can do to avoid the God-forsaken holocaust of war?' I added.

'Gentlemen, we are tired, and for some of us it has been a very long day indeed,' said Bertram. 'I suggest we all get some rest. Let us meet here again tomorrow morning, after I have had the chance to inspect the walls and everything else you have achieved in my absence.'

We did as he bade and went to our separate quarters. I checked on Finstar in the stables and then took the secret passage from the Lesser Hall down to the cave chamber below the castle. Rehlein followed me. I looked up from lighting a small fire in the hearth to see him coming down the narrow staircase.

'Cara Gendal, what has happened to you?' he asked: 'You have changed.'

I sighed and sat at the table, but longed for my bed. Rehlein sat opposite me. His face was full of reproach.

'I have always thought of you as one of the *pacifici*, the peacemakers of St Matthew's Gospel. But you rode out with the Children of the Raven to sow the seeds of rebellion and war.'

'I did ride out to sow the seeds of rebellion in men's hearts, Rehlein; but not the seeds of war. Too many of my friends have died in battles past to moulder long forgotten in some ignoble hole, for me to advocate recourse to arms. Too many lands I loved as fair, have been torn to ruins in that foulest tyranny of man. I do believe the many can overturn the power of the few by peaceful means as well as by conflict.'

'Did those friends of yours who died suffer the doubts that torment me now? I came here to die an honourable death, trusting my service would take me swiftly to paradise. But now I doubt that.

What if the priests are wrong?'

'If they are, they have perpetuated the longest living fraud known to man. And no dissatisfied customers have ever been able to come back and complain.'

Rehlein snorted a short laugh.

'There is that in it. But it would take more than wit to overcome this inner doubt. Do other men not feel this, or do none of them dare admit their fear of death for fear of being called heretic? Yet it is the very essence which can turn brave men to cowards.'

'He is no coward who acts bravely despite his fear and doubt – he is the greatest hero.'

'But now I cannot act.' Rehlein sighed. 'What if we die in this, some strange land's civil war? What if life's short dream ends for us in some ignoble death, fighting someone else's battle? Show me the way, Guide. I am frightened in this autumntime. To live but once is not enough in a world which wastes so many lives.'

He paused, looking deeply into the fire. I waited for him to continue, which he soon did.

'And yet, I sometimes wonder if this whole creation is no more than a dream, a diversion to amuse a bored god doomed to face eternity. But had I thought myself to cheer, would I have chosen this sordid waste where generations of people made in God's image, crawl like ants across the stubborn earth to live and die in sad futility? Would I have created this hard world where none are happy except those who excel in wrongdoing? Would I have created life in this frail form and placed myself in it? Do I play games with myself, or does God play games with me?'

'God gave us free will, Rehlein. God only orders our lives when we invite God to do so. Do not place the guilt on God when events have human causes.'

Rehlein sighed again.

'Tonight when you returned, Gendal, and brought Count Bertram back with you, I realised how glad I was to hand the reins of Death's horses back to him as the true coachman. I had had this conceit, to become a great leader and greater Imperator. I saw this as my training ground, an opportunity to test my skills. But the realities made me realise they were the idle fancies of a fool. I love these hard-working insular people I have come to know here and respect. I did not want to send them to their deaths.'

'Theirs is not a blind feudal obedience, Rehlein. If they march out to fight, they fight for family and willingly choose to go.'

'That makes it all the harder. Yet I cannot back out now. I have committed myself to avenge the murder of the ostler and his wife at the Iyver.'

'Aye, Rabenwald bewitched us into its web long before we winded its plot.'

Rehlein left me, looking better for having expressed the fears and doubts he had felt despite my having listened more than counselled. I stumbled to my bed and fell into a deep, dreamless sleep.

I did not know what hour it was when I woke at last in the dark chamber. It felt like late morning because I had slept so well. I took the stairs up to the Lesser Hall, expecting Bertram to be deep in battle plans with Rehlein and the generals, but the hall was empty. I went out into the courtyard to cross to the Great Hall in search of food, and saw the four men up on the battlements inspecting all the work that had been done in Bertram's absence. When they had seen that to their satisfaction, they came down to inspect the armoury and all the preparations for battle. I finished my breakfast and returned to the Lesser Hall, where they joined me soon after.

'I trust that you have all slept well,' said Bertram. 'My heart is so encouraged by all you have done in such a short time.' He was wearing the Raven surcoat over his shirt and breeches once again, and radiated energy and power.

We gathered round the table to begin our council of war.

'Last night, Aldwin advised us to concentrate on planning for our situation as it is. I have to ask, what can we do about my wife, Ened?'

'I have an idea for that,' I said: 'It would require some brave and astute volunteers to act as spies. I would go myself, only now I am too well known in Aunsberg.'

'What do you have in mind, Gendal?' Bertram asked.

'We send our volunteers to Aunsberg disguised as merchants. They bluff their way into the castle. They wait until nightfall to find Ened and free her.'

'How will they leave the castle after? The gate keeper won't be as lax a second time.'

'Cara Rea left some bottles of her Greek Fire in her store chamber. They can use that to distract them.'

'We could instruct our volunteers to assassinate the Duke at the same time,' said Aldwin.

'That could be dangerous, to have two separate tasks. There would be a much greater risk of discovery,' I said.

'But if they succeeded, we would not need to face the Duke's forces afterwards. The reason for our rebellion would be gone,' Walther said.

'This has to be Count Bertram's decision,' I said: 'It is the Countess Ened who will be placed in danger by giving them this second task as well.'

We looked at Bertram. He looked undecided.

'Knight Gendal, you spoke to Duke Nicolaus at the ball. What was he like?'

'The Duke is a hard and merciless man. He flaunts himself with other women before his wife Isadora. He thinks of nothing but himself: all else is eclipsed by his greed. He does not know how to lose. Though he sees plots everywhere, he cannot imagine his people could succeed in overthrowing him. This Christian even believes that eating from gold plates makes himself immortal!'

'Yes. He took great joy in humiliating me,' Bertram said. 'When the Italian soldiers handed us over to him, he paraded me in chains. He mocked my helplessness by threatening to dishonour my wife.'

Hatred flashed in Bertram's eyes. His face grew dark as he remembered the injustices he had suffered.

'Yes,' he said again: 'We will instruct our volunteers to kill the Duke as well as rescue Ened. I must thank you for that plan. Let's ask if anyone will volunteer for the sortie.'

He made to leave, as if our discussions were over. Rehlein stopped him.

'Count Bertram, we cannot rely on this plot as our only tactic. The likelihood our men will succeed in both tasks is very poor. What else can we do to try to stop armed conflict before it begins?'

'I have another suggestion,' I said. 'Nicolaus enforces his despotic rule using mercenary soldiers. None of the plains folk support his cruel methods. Even his own Danuvian soldiers and taxmen baulk at them. If we could eliminate the mercenaries, Nicolaus would topple, and we would virtually have won.'

'But how can we remove the mercenaries from the field without fighting them?' Aldwin asked.

I held up a gold piece.

'They would give him their lives for his money. They will save their lives for ours.'

Bertram paced the room, reflecting on the suggestion. In the pause, Rehlein looked across the table at me.

'Do we know who controls the mercenaries, Gendal?'

'Condottiero Giacomo Maladriuzzi. I met him at the ball. He enjoys a good living on the backs of his men. He never goes out without a guard.'

'He was the one who handed me over to the Duke,' said Bertram. 'He is short and fat, with a red face and white hair, and a stubbly beard with a greasy look.'

'I've seen him!' Rehlein said: 'He stayed the night at the inn in Eiswald, after Gendal carried Thiemo's message to the Iyver. He was the one who told Gendal not to go.'

'No wonder Thiemo went into hiding afterwards,' I said: 'He had walked straight into a trap.'

'Though I am loath to reward such a man, how much gold do you think would buy this Condottiero and his army?' Bertram asked.

'A fair sum more than the fee Nicolaus paid, which I believe was 2000 marks. And it will take skill in the bartering,' I said.

'How much can you raise here?' asked Rehlein.

'That's about as much as we have in our coffers,' said Bertram. 'What price, so many lives, when I cannot hope to find more?'

'I may be able to help,' said Rehlein. 'I will need to send a letter north.'

'This is not your war. Why would you do that for me?'

'Because the person I'll ask also has a complaint against Duke Nicolaus.'

They exchanged meaningful looks which I did not understand but presumed related to their aristocratic code.

Bertram thanked him and then involved us all in deciding the content of the letter to Maladriuzzi.

'I'll offer to meet the Condottiero in Dornholz. That's not too far from here,' Bertram said.

Both Aldwin and Walther gasped in horror.

'Don't give him the opportunity to ambush you again,' Walther warned. 'Far better to send any one of us here rather than yourself.'

'And would he even risk coming when it is so close to our stronghold?' Aldwin said. 'Direct him to the Wolfholz Tavern, well beyond the east face of Rabenwald.'

'But that is miles from here. We would have no support from the plain.'

'Yes. Thus will he trust us more and fear us less' said Walther: 'He should not fret until we bring him to the Castle, and then he will soon settle when he sees our money.'

'You would bring him here?'

'He will also see the repairs to our castle walls and know we are ready for a fight. That will encourage him to agree,' said Aldwin.

Bertram heeded his generals' advice and asked me to scribe the letter he dictated, for one of us to take to Maladriuzzi. It ran:

To the Commander Giacomo Maladriuzzi, Rabenwald greets you. One would speak with you in private, and invites you plus one other to an unspecified meeting place. An you accept, reply through the bearer of this invitation. A Guide shall meet you and your companion two days after the date of your reply, at the Wolfholz Tavern at sunset. No harm shall come to you. Bring only yourself and one companion, lest the Guide chooses not to appear. Count Bertram.

Bertram signed the letter with a flourish.

'What if Maladriuzzi declines our offer?' he asked.

'Then he would be a fool to make loyal men of mercenaries,' I replied: 'Condottieri, by nature, avoid face-to-face battle. His men would lynch him if they learnt of such a refusal.'

Bertram sealed the letter and held it up as a proud achievement.

'And now, who do I give it to, to take to the swine?'

'I will take it, as you and Gendal cannot,' Rehlein offered. 'I can recognise the man, and my family connections will keep me safe in Aunsberg. May I also suggest that Gendal and I are the people who meet him at the Wolfholz Tavern, with Gendal as your chief negotiator. And we should take some seasoned fighters with us in case the Condottiero's party is larger than we've stipulated.'

'Certainly, Sir Rehlein,' Bertram said, and handed the letter to him.

Our meeting ended. The generals went to find volunteers for our rescue mission and assassination attempt. I called on Mother Agatha to make some herbal potions. Then I drew plans of the castle and the city to help the volunteers. Rehlein returned to his room to write his letter and prepare for the morrow's journey to Aunsberg and the Court of Duke Nicolaus.

Chapter 16
Spies Briefing

Aldwin and Walther brought three volunteers to the Lesser Hall later that afternoon. They bowed to Count Bertram but showed me no courtesy and watched me with suspicious eyes. They were tall, thickset, muscular people, with hard yet handsome faces, and wore wool singlets and trousers. The woman Nyze and one of the men, Cunrad, were dark blond; the other man, Gawin, had brown bushy wool-like hair and beard.

'Why do you distrust me?' I asked them with a directness that dismayed Bertram, but they appreciated.

'You are Rabenwald's betrayer in Aunsberg,' Nyze said with accusing eyes.

'That, sister, I cannot disprove, except to say it was not so. You alone can decide whether you'll trust me enough to enact my plan.'

'Count Bertram, does it have your blessing?' asked Gawin.

'I do not know the details, Children,' he replied. 'But I have full faith in Knight Gendal as the one who rescued me from the place you now go to, so I urge you to find the same. Speak, Gendal.'

I uncovered the map of Aunsberg which I had drawn for them to take. They had not seen a map before, and only Nyze could read letters at all. As country folk, they had had little learning, and it took time and patience to teach them how to understand the symbols I had drawn. Once they had begun to grasp how to read the map, I moved on to telling them about their mission.

'While the Duke fusses with arms and men to prepare for rebellion, we shall attack elsewhere,' I said. 'Your tasks will be hard to carry out, if not impossible. If you fail you face certain death. If you choose to back out now or at any time, no-one will condemn you.'

'An it is worth the risk, we shall not shirk,' said Cunrad. 'What are we to do?'

'To rescue Countess Ened, kill Duke Nicolaus and send his family into exile.'

The three volunteers stared at me in disbelief.

'No, I have not taken leave of my senses. My stay in Aunsberg may have been short, but I learnt a lot of useful information at the ball and elsewhere which will help you.'

THE EAGLE AND THE RAVEN

I continued, pointing out the places I referred to on the map as I spoke to give them more practice reading maps.

'As you can see, the palace is built on the highest point in the citadel. It is ringed by this avenue, a wide cobble street called The Drive. Here the Duke rides with his wife in a white and gold carriage almost every afternoon, at about three hours past noon. His courtiers also like to ride there in their carriages at the same time – it is a fashionable afternoon's entertainment. The townsfolk often line the route to cheer or curse their masters. Troops watch in readiness for trouble. The palace is left with few guards then as attention is elsewhere.'

I placed an incomplete plan of the castle on top of the map. Again, as I talked, I pointed out the features to help them understand the drawing.

'More detail, I could not gather in my short time there. But this should be enough to help you find your way. The Duke's apartments are set in the north-east curtain wall, above the great hall where the ball was held. The servants' workrooms are next to these, in the basement and the floors above, here to the east of the castle. The stables and armoury are to the south, and the kitchens stand out on their own in a block against the north curtain wall.'

I gave the three volunteers time to study the plan of the castle and ask questions about it. They found the plan easier to understand than the map because of their experience of coming to Rabenschloss, which had a similar construction built on a smaller scale. When they felt confident about the layout, I continued.

'Several doors connect the servants' workrooms with the ducal apartments – those in this plan are on the ground floor. The ducal suite is on the first floor; the children's bedchambers are on the second floor. These apartments are guarded night and day.'

I poured out mugs of beer, which Cunrad and Gawin accepted. The woman filled her mug with water from a pitcher.

'A pack of dog-like fawners follows Nicolaus all his waking hours, but he shakes them off at night to sleep. He has a soothing drink of brandy in milk brought to his room by a servant who shares his bed if no court lady will oblige. The servants and his wife Isadora put up with this. Isadora sleeps in another room, and their four children each have a chamber leading from here, on the second floor. Cara Rea also sleeps in a chamber around here on the first floor: her door has no crest carved in its panels. Countess Ened is being held in one of the other rooms in this suite; but we don't know whether her room is on the first or second floor.'

We digressed into a brief discussion about the possible layout of the ducal apartments. I filled my mug with water from the pitcher and slaked my thirst while the others talked. Then I moved on to the plan.

'Your first problem will be getting into Aunsberg. I suggest you buy a wagon of fruit on your way there. At the city gate, say the fruit is for Freeman Meyer. He orders a wagon of fruit every week, and they are often delayed or arrive together. So the guards should accept your story with this forged chit. Be certain to deliver the fruit to Freeman Meyer, mind. The soldiers may well watch your early progress in the citadel. That cross near the palace on the map is the Meyer residence.'

'We have apples, pears, and late plums from Rabenwald's west slopes, which we can take,' said Cunrad.

'Even better,' I replied. 'Once free in the city, hide yourselves and the wagon in the ruined Nedauf Quarter at the bottom of the hill. Your next step is to acquire three surcoats from the Duke's Danuvian soldiers.'

'That is not a problem,' said Aldwin with a wry smile. 'We already have four Danuvian Guard uniforms in our armoury.'

'When they came to sack our castle after the Imperator granted our lands to the Duke, we took rear-guard action in revenge,' Bertram explained.

'Excellent: you can smuggle the uniforms into Aunsberg under the fruit,' I said. 'At three after noon, line the streets with the Danuvian Guard near the castle gates. After the Duke's ride, enter the palace grounds with them. Slip away into the gatehouse south tower before the troops go into formation in the courtyard and get redeployed to castle duties. You can hide in the storerooms below the mercenaries' quarters.'

'You're very unlikely to be disturbed there,' said Bertram: 'I barely heard or saw a person from one day to the next, when they used one of the store rooms for my cell.'

'Come evening,' I continued, 'leave the gatehouse and cross the courtyard to the Great Hall. There, Nyze, you need to change out of your mail and tabard into a servant's uniform, which is a russet dress with a white apron. I am not sure where these are stored: probably in a cupboard in the basement.'

'That's common dress around here,' said Nyze. 'I'll wear my own and put the chain mail over it.'

'You'll look like a big, fat sausage,' joked Cunrad. I realised they were brother and sister.

'Gawin and Cunrad, after the evening change of guard, you must remove the two guards at the Duke's bedroom door and take up guard duty there yourselves. Salute the Duke when he goes to bed. When the servant comes with the Duke's nightcap, remove her and give the cup to Nyze to take in to the Duke. Nyze, put this phial of poison in the cup and take it in to Nicolaus. Mother Agatha made the poison: it should send him gently into a sleep he will not wake up from. Just make sure he drinks it.'

'And if he refuses?'

'Find some other way to kill him. Get Cunrad and Gawin to help if you must. When he is dead, Gawin should go to Cara Rea and tell her the Duke is dead by Rabenwald. Tell her to order Isadora and the children to the King of Rome for their safety. Ride with them to escort them out of Danuvia. Nyze and Cunrad, you find Countess Ened and give her the clothes of the servant who brought the nightcap. Then try to bluff your way out of the castle through the wicket gate in the main door. If the guards challenge you, smash these bottles of Greek Fire on the ground to distract them while you make your escape. Cara Rea left them. There are enough for one each.'

I handed them each a small stoppered green glass bottle.

'This is a challenging mission, but if you succeed, you will save the lives of all your brothers and sisters here in Rabenwald,' said Walther.

'And if you fail or are betrayed, try to send us word,' said Aldwin.

We discussed and refined the details of the plan until each of the volunteers felt confident about their tasks. They finally left the chamber to make their preparations, as the evening meal was being served in the Great Hall. They took the map and plan with them.

Bertram sat back in his chair and drank a deep draught of beer.

'Poison? Such a dishonourable weapon,' he said.

'Better one death than entire armies,' Aldwin said.

'Mind, secret plans are not for breaking early,' I warned.

'I agree,' said Walther. 'This whole plot is riddled with danger. Don't build up the Children's hopes, when they are so likely to be dashed.'

'You are right,' said Bertram. 'Let us breathe no word of this until we hear whether our three brave warriors have succeeded or failed.'

Chapter 17
Rehlein's Ride

Rehlein set out for Aunsberg the following day. Although he left after the spies had set off with their wagon of fruit, he soon overtook them. He told me later that he made good time across the Danuvian plain with the help of the maps I had drawn for our sortie forces. By early afternoon, his road had brought him to the deforested region of fields surrounding the city and its neighbouring villages.

As he neared the village of Haahof, he saw a black friar walking south towards him. Knowing there was no Blackfriars' monastery in the vicinity, he reined in his horse and dismounted to talk to him. The friar had a striking face with deep lines and a bulbous nose.

'Are you by chance, Father Fadrique?'

'No, son. I am Friar Fadrique. Who is it who is asking?'

'Bertram's friend. He got back home to the castle and sends his thanks.'

'What of Gendal?'

Fadrique's question told Rehlein the friar was who he claimed, someone he could trust in a region of the potentially untrustworthy.

'Our friend Gendal is safe there, too. I have a task for you, if you would like to help them further.'

'I already have a task, to get to their castle as quickly as I can.'

'Come with me and I will buy you a horse.'

'But I can't ride.'

'You'll have the rest of the day to learn.'

Rehlein led Fadrique back to Haahof, where he bought him a placid old piebald mare from the farrier there. Fadrique's normally calm expression turned to alarm when he sat on the mare. It turned to pure terror when the mare moved. Rehlein ignored his protests.

'Friar Fadrique, I need you to learn how to ride this lovely old lady by the time I come back here. I will have a message for you to take to our friends in the castle, which will be very important for them.'

'With the Lord's help, I will try.' Fadrique screamed when the mare moved again.

'Don't worry, Sir,' said the farrier who had sold them the mare. 'My son will help him find his seat.'

Rehlein left Fadrique to his riding lesson and rode on to Aunsberg. He arrived about an hour before sunset. He had changed his travelling surcoat over his chain mail for the white surcoat bearing his full coat of arms. This gained him immediate entry through the south gate.

He rode up the street through Nedauf, observing with distaste the political mismanagement which had left such swathes of the poorest quarter of the city in ruins. The needy clamoured round him as he rode, their thin, ragged arms reaching for his alms. Their desperation showed him how vital it was for Rabenwald's revolt to succeed.

The castle gates opened for Rehlein without challenge when he reached the cobbled square. Duke Nicolaus met him in the courtyard to greet him as he dismounted. A gentle breeze blew the Duke's long, greying brown hair from his long face. Nicolaus was wearing an elaborately embroidered royal blue doublet and breeches and elegant, over-embellished court shoes. His arrogant manner and overstated dress told Rehlein he was trying to live up to his station.

'My humble court is honoured to receive you, Lord Rehlein of Harzland. What joyous reason has brought you here to our lovely city?'

Rehlein handed the reins of his horse over to the castle ostler to stable and turned back to answer Nicolaus.

'I sought a resting place on my way to visit my cousins, the Schwarzenbergs, and found myself near here. Your fine dances and masquerades are famous across the Empire.'

'Yes, our court prides itself on its evening entertainments. Let us hold a ball tonight, in honour of your arrival.'

'That would be delightful.'

Nicolaus provided Rehlein with a comfortable bedroom in the ducal apartments for his stay. He gave him the place of honour at his table for the elaborate evening meal. They were joined by Nicolas' wife Isadora and Cara Rea. Rea was so surprised to discover Rehlein's true status, he feared she would give him away, but the meal passed without incident.

Rehlein attended the ball in his crested surcoat over shirt and breeches, as he had not brought court robes. His understated clothes made the Duke's apparel look all the more showy when they sat together on the dais with Isabel, Countess Ened and Cara Rea seated behind them.

Rehlein watched the milling guests, looking for the people I had seen there. When he saw Giacomo Maladriuzzi in the crowd, he asked Nicolaus if he could escort Isadora onto the dance floor. As Rehlein was his honoured guest, Nicolaus not refuse the request. Rehlein danced with the Duchess and then offered to dance with

Cara Rea. She refused, much to Nicolaus's displeasure. He offered Rehlein a dance with Ened instead.

Rehlein accepted the invitation and led the awkward prisoner onto the floor for the next circle-and-pair dance. The bright music and the moves of the dance prevented them from making conversation. He managed in one pass to warn her, 'You will be rescued,' and in a second pass, 'Be ready to escape'. When the dance ended, he escorted Ened back to the dais but stayed on the floor to dance with some of the other ladies present. Astra soon claimed a dance from him, but her coquettish questioning produced few answers.

When a dance ended leaving Rehlein near Maladriuzzi, he stepped back from the dance floor to rest a space. He made polite conversation with those around him as he drifted towards the Condottiero. He wondered if the Italian would recognise him from their stay at the inn at Eiswald over three weeks before.

Maladriuzzi was too interested in pursuing the business opportunity to associate the golden knight with that escapade. He saw Rehlein as a prospective new client and approached him with a fluent sales message. They discussed the capabilities of Maladriuzzi's army at length. Those around them soon tired of their business talk and turned their attention back to the music and the dances. Rehlein clapped Maladriuzzi's shoulder and turned his back on the dance floor. The move blocked Nicolaus from seeing him pass over the letter from Rabenwald. Maladriuzzi stowed the letter away equally deftly. Then Rehlein moved on to look for another lady to take onto the dance floor.

The ball was still in full flow at midnight, when Rehlein sought permission from his host the Duke to retire after a long day. Nicolaus and his company left the ball with Rehlein. They ascended to the ducal apartments above the hall. Behind them, the party became a little wilder but soon quietened again and was over before the next hour.

Rehlein stretched out on his bed, too alert to the possibilities of danger to sleep. In the silence after the ball had finished, he heard a sound at the bedroom door. He went over and picked up a letter which had been pushed under the door. When he opened the door, the person who had left the message had gone.

The letter was addressed to him by title alone and had been sealed with the eight-pointed star device of Maladriuzzi's army. It read, *I shall meet you there in two days' time. GM.* It was the confirmation Rehlein required to get to sleep.

He woke early next morning, aware of the sounds of horsemen preparing to leave the castle. He looked out of the window onto the cobbled courtyard, to see Maladriuzzi's departure with a cohort of ten mercenaries. The Condottiero looked up at his window as if aware of his attention. He darted back so that he would not see him.

A servant girl clad in a russet dress with a white apron, brought Rehlein a tray of breakfast foods: porridge, fruit, bread, cheese and a herbal tea. He instructed her to warn the Duke he would leave shortly to continue his journey to see his cousin, and to pass his thanks on to the Duke for his hospitality should the Duke not be available to see him before he left.

The Duke did not appear. The only face at a window in the ducal apartments to watch him leave was that of the pale, dark-haired Ened.

Rehlein left Aunsberg by the North Gate. He rode some distance towards his purported destination before he doubled back on byroads to return to Haahof and Friar Fadrique. He found the reluctant horseman still struggling to ride in the farrier's field.

'At least the Friar doesn't fall off any more,' said the farrier's son.

Rehlein tipped him for his patience and ordered Fadrique to mount up. They rode south a short way out of the village. The Friar sat like a sack of turnips and flapped when his mare broke into a trot, but seemed secure enough on her for the journey.

'Now you are ready, Fadrique, I want you to ride as fast as you can to Rabenschloss. It is important that you take this message to Bertram, for Gendal's life might be in danger otherwise. Tell him: Giacomo Maladriuzzi is even now on his way to the Wolfholz Tavern. And his ten best men ride with him.'

Fadrique repeated back the message to Rehlein, who nodded.

'Now ride!' he ordered, and slapped the mare's rump.

The mare cantered off down the road, with Fadrique crying out in fear as he struggled to hold on to her saddle. Rehlein said a prayer for him and for Rabenwald, and turned his horse's head to ride north once again.

Chapter 18
A Secret is Discovered

After the communal evening meal in the Great Hall, Bertram leaned forward on his table and beckoned me across.

'I must introduce Page Barthram to the Luck of Rabenwald. Prepare your cell for our visit,' he said.

I hurried down to my cavern quarters, lighting my way with a flaming torch which I placed in a sconce to light the chamber. There was little to tidy, but as the cell always felt damp with the stream running through, I lit a small fire in the hearth for my guests.

Bertram descended the stairs soon after with his cousin Page Barthram. The lad was a skinny youngster of twelve, with his family's curly black hair and dark flashing eyes. Those eyes were wide with awe at the strange world he had never known existed under the castle until then. His head turned all around as he took in every detail while Bertram spoke.

'Barthram, I need to show you this, so that I am not the only person to know the secret besides our Aunt Rea.'

'Do you wish me to leave?' I asked, choosing not to reveal Cara Rea had already given me that information.

He shook his head. 'No. You saved my life. You are family too.'

Bertram tapped the catch in the niche wall beside the statue of the water goddess Danu and opened the secret door. He raised his torch so that we could all see into the gloomy chamber.

'There is the Luck of Rabenwald,' he said.

Barthram peered inside.

'What, that ancient bottle?'

'No: the table on which it stands. But should another ask you, say the myrrh in the bottle, for Rabenwald's safety and ourselves as her lords.'

Bertram told Barthram the same tale Cara Rea had told me, about Danu and Iyverid, the first Count of Rabenwald. As he spoke, the youngster inched closer to the door until he stood on the threshold.

'May I go in?'

'Yes, and take this torch with you. I will shut the door. See if you can find the way out.'

Barthram took the torch into the small room and looked all around the walls. Bertram closed the door behind him. He waited for some time before he opened it again. When he did, Barthram seemed undisturbed by the ordeal. The youth was standing at the table, looking at a book which had not been there before the door had shut.

'I could not find the way out, Sir,' he said. 'But I found this book in a little corner cupboard, so I brought it out to look at it. I thought the answer might be in there, but it's too hard to read.'

'That must be Cara Rea's book,' I said.

'Then it will have lots of answers, Barthram, but not the answer to the riddle I just set you. This is a secret chamber, with no way to open the door from inside. Never let yourself be shut in here again.'

'No, Sir. Shall I bring out the book?'

I saw Bertram hesitate and quickly spoke before he refused.

'Yes, do, Barthram. It would be interesting to know what Cara Rea chose to leave behind.'

The youngster brought out the book and placed it on my table. The Count glanced inside it with a casual air and soon shut it again. He was clearly more a man for action than learning.

'Why should this interest you, Gendal?' he asked.

'Any book interests me, because so much effort goes into the making.'

I inspected the volume. It was hand-sewn by a novice book binder, with leather covers and tawny pages of fine Andalusian paper.

'Ask yourself, why did Cara Rea choose to hide this there? It must be important to her, though she forgot to take it with her. Or perhaps, she thought it might betray her if it were found in the Duke's household.'

The two cousins leaned over to look again as I opened the book at a middle page and inspected the script.

'That doesn't look like Latin,' Bertram remarked.

'No. It is a Gallic coastal dialect I'm not that familiar with. It will make extending reading at least.'

'Aye? Then read it if you will. We must be away to our beds.'

Once they had gone, I settled on my couch to read the open volume. It proved to be a diary Cara Rea had written in her own fair hand. Her narrative described some exciting and difficult times in her journeys.

'But why should Cara Rea write a diary in a dialect different to her own?' I asked myself as I read.

I turned to the first page of the volume. The title read, *The diary of Marie, second born of Robert of Burgundy. Later Cara Rea.*

The inscription surprised me. It proved Cara Rea was no child of Rabenwald, but daughter of the southern Duchy of Burgundy. Yet Rabenwald called her sister to Raban.

Puzzled, I recalled our first meeting many years before. I could not remember Cara Rea mentioning her ancestors or homeland, beyond knowing she was travelling from Wales to Frankfurt. That had not surprised me at the time, as travellers are reticent folk to protect their safety on the road. I looked for the diary account of our meeting but found no mention of that or even of our dangerous journey through Flanders at the time of the battle of Courtrai. This was puzzling, as we had met less than three months after Rea had assumed the Cara's broad-brimmed hat. I looked through the diary to see how she had achieved that professional honour, and found a strange entry out of keeping with the rest of the diary.

Cara Rea De Rabenwald died in my arms, yearning for her homeland she had been travelling to after her years of study. She had charged me to take home the news of her death after seeing her buried. Now I wear her badges of office as promissory sign. I carry her record of her life and work as proof to her family of her death. I can scarce believe her land still holds an earlier faith than Christianity, and such faith hangs so much on a table!

The entry made me uneasy. I moved on through the pages, seeking her record of arriving at Rabenschloss with the news of the death of Raban's sister. I found the entry about four months later.

At last, my destination! But my reception is not what I expected. Rabenwald mourns its Count, Bertrand, the father of Cara Rea. When I arrived at the Castle, the people greeted me, saying, "See, Cara Rea returns unsummoned to mourn her father." Raban greeted me by Rea's name and said how much my travels had changed his sister. If I were to reveal the truth now, it would greatly disappoint these superstitious folk. And I could also gain an honour here, albeit a poor one, when I have lost Burgundy forever after being driven out for my alchemy.

Where would Cara Rea's real loyalty lie, when she had renounced allegiance to her native land, to assume the role of Raban's sister, Bertram's aunt? Into what trap had I sent the three spies? I feared that a woman who swapped standards once would do the same again for the same reason; especially when more power beckoned as the Duke of Danuvia's advisor as aunt to the Count of Rabenwald.

I sat by the fire for some time, rethinking all my stratagems in the light of this new information. It looked highly unlikely that the spies heading to Aunsberg would come back alive. The weight of sending them to their deaths spurred me into physical action. I left my deep refuge and climbed to the heights of the castle walls.

Dawn silhouetted the black horizon against a faintly greyer backcloth. Somewhere in the forest shadows beneath, a wolf howled in the drizzle-laden wind. Behind me, within the castle walls, the Children of the Raven slept, released for a while from their hard days' labours.

The castle bore proud witness to their dedicated work. Once more, its walls were all intact. The new day would see the rebuilding of the damaged roof with clay tiles rather than thatch.

I climbed up to the crenelated battlements over the gateway and looked down at the causeway, the Castle's only visible link with the rest of Rabenwald. The drawbridge was raised again for the night. Beside me fluttered the red and black raven pennants of Rabenwald. I stood, inspired to pride.

'Who goes there?'

'Knight Gendal.'

The sentry spat on the ground as I passed.

I quit the battlements for the stables, to check my horse. Finstar nuzzled me affectionately as I ran my hand down his legs to his hooves.

'Thinking to make your break afore time?' asked the stable hand.

'Nay. Shortly I will ride on the Count's business, when my horse will be a vital friend.'

I went down to the Great Hall. The kitchen staff were setting out breakfast there. I picked up some bread and cheese and took them with me back to my cave.

Bertram was waiting impatiently in the chamber for me when I arrived.

'At last, Gendal! Have you heard aught of Sir Rehlein?'

'Bide awhile, friend. So far, Rehlein has had time only to arrive and return. Maladriuzzi will have him wait around awhile. The pool before the falls does not look fast. What of Rabenwald? Its Children's work is well done, but they still mistrust me, for something I did not do.'

'I have tried to placate my people, but they hear naught of it. Now the Castle is all but finished, they call for battle.'

I sighed and turned away. I sensed the pressure on Bertram was from the generals, Aldwin and Walther, rather than the people.

'Then let them have battle plans,' I said. 'But do not use them yet, not until we know the outcomes of all our other strategies. Promise me that.'

'I shall try, but I cannot promise. How long will they need to wait?'

'A week at most. Maladriuzzi will not hold back long to line his pockets a second time.'

I sat by the ashy hearth and picked up my longsword, half-unsheathing it from its leather scabbard.

'Alas, my Spanish beauty; once more, men must run to wet your blade for life and liberty. How apt the raven symbol of Rabenwald. See how thoughts alone drive armies to the grave.'

'Freedom is a different cause,' said Bertram. 'She is not just some thought. And she gains power only by battle, whether by the word or by the sword.'

'Aye, and how she changes face once she has that power.' I paused and took the plunge. 'Like Cara Rea.'

'Cara Rea? What do you mean?'

I sensed how difficult my revelation would be for Bertram and tried to soften the blow by introducing the subterfuge in a more gentle way.

'Tell me, Count Bertram: what was your aunt Rea like before she went away to train with the Celtic church?'

The young Count's dark face broadened with an affectionate smile.

'I was still a child when she left – not yet Barthram's age. Aunt

Rea was my second mother. My real mother died in childbirth having me. After Rea went, Mother Agatha took her place. I'll never forget my aunt's long black hair tickling my cheeks, and the motherly smile on her face as she bent over my crib. I thought she was our goddess Danu come to life.'

'Yes, that's how I remember her. I escorted her on her way back here from Wales for her safety. We landed at Bruges and crossed Flanders on the trade route to Frankfurt, where we parted company. She wanted to rest from the road and finish her journey the following spring. When I left her there, she was well.'

'What do you mean by that?'

'Bertram, what did you think when Cara Rea returned at the time of your grandfather's death?'

'I thought it was a miracle, like everyone else. After so many years away, my aunt should come back just then, when we needed her.'

'And you had no doubts?'

'Well, I did think she had changed. I thought it was because she had been away in foreign lands for many years. I was a grown man of twenty then – I thought I had mis-recalled her as a child. What makes you ask these questions?'

'The night we met at the Iyver, Bertram, you addressed Cara Rea by name. When I reminded her of our common past, she had no recollection of me. Yet we had travelled together for many months, and I had saved her life more than once. Had she been the real Cara Rea, she would not have forgotten that.'

'Are you saying the woman who came back is not my aunt, Raban's sister?'

'I wish it were not true. I dare not tell Rabenwald, but you must learn of it. Place no further faith in her. She is an impostor: the disgraced daughter of the Duke of Burgundy, who hid here to avoid being executed as a witch.'

'Nay! This is invention! Where did you come by this?'

'It's in her diary, that book on the table, which Barthram found in the secret chamber. I had thought of her as Rabenwald's ally in Nicolaus's court. But now I fear greater power has already tempted her to betray us. She must have been the one who dropped the message at the ball. And now our spies are in jeopardy, and I cannot warn them.'

Bertram threw open the leather cover of the diary with a thud to show his disbelief. He went to the page I had bookmarked and struggled to read the passage written there. I translated some words for him but let him piece together the meaning himself. Emotions chased across his face: anger, fear, and a deep distaste. For a while, his body slumped as if in defeat.

After some thought, his manner became more alert and his body straightened. A fire now lit his eyes which I had not seen before.

'Alas, Gendal, you have not slept this night, and yet I need you now and fresh. While I take this book to show our generals, you measure your couch till noon. Then I shall wake you to join us as we discuss what Rabenwald must do next.'

Chapter 19
Battle Planning

Page Barthram woke me at noon and took me to the Lesser Hall, where Bertram was talking with Aldwin and Walther. Bertram was in a serious mood after spending the morning discussing battle tactics with the two generals.

They unrolled the map I had drawn of Danuvia to aid us as they reviewed their morning's discussions with me.

'The mercenary armoury is deadly. The sword is no match against the crossbow,' said Aldwin. He looked particularly hawklike that day, and his chestnut hair and beard were even more unkempt than usual. 'At this stage, it would be wise to plan as if our ploy with Maladriuzzi fails.'

'Yes,' Bertram agreed. 'That's why our main force should fight from some wooded tor, that the trees might hamper the arrows' flight. It would also give our men the advantage in close combat with a foe that has run up a hill.'

'We should use spears and pikes too,' I said: 'There you have arms quick and cheap to make, good against cavalry, and unexpected when our men have not used them before.'

'Pikes take more training to handle than we have time for,' objected Walther. His long black ringlets of hair hung about his fleshy face in greasy lanks to his shoulders, making him look unusually disreputable.

'What if they besiege us on the tor?' Aldwin asked. 'We would have no food or water.'

His intention to fight with his men impressed me.

'Nicolaus cannot afford a slow war, General. The serfs would rise up and attack his troops from the rear, out of sympathy with the oppressed as we take a stand against his tyranny. Nicolaus cannot risk any but a swift kill for victory.'

'We are almost at the end of the battle season too,' Walther said: 'Winter will soon be upon us, when it would be hard for us all to keep our men.'

'Have you chosen the tor for the campaign?' I asked.

'We have a list of possible sites, with two clear favourites,' Walther said: 'Baerhuegel, which is not far from here, and Dernfels.'

'Let us ride out after lunch to inspect the different sites and make our choice,' Bertram said.

It was a beautiful September afternoon. The sun was warm, and the trees were still in full leaf before the autumn fall. It was a joy for our party of four to ride out in the fresh air again after spending so much time inside the castle walls.

We rode downhill along the river to Baerhuegel first. This large wooded tor was about a mile from the castle, making it easy to supply during conflict, and close to the security of the castle if our forces needed to retreat and fall back. The river skirted its base to the west, making it easier for enemy forces to attack from the northwest. The slopes on that side were heavily wooded and would require some tree felling for our forces to see the enemy advances.

We rode back uphill onto Rabenberg and took the path east to Rabenmoss and the crest of the hilltop cradling the bog. The path was high enough above the tree line for us to look down across the wooded slopes to the Danuvian plain. A chequerboard of forests and fields spread out to the misty horizon in the far distance. Closer by, we could see the treacherous gills cutting down the sides of the mountain to the plain.

One by one we discounted the other possible sites, until we looked down on Dernfels, the suggested site furthest to the east. I saw at once why the generals favoured this hillside over the rest. The tor was much larger, and could easily accommodate our forces along its rounded summit. While forest covered most of the hill, a gale had once blown down a swathe of trees with shallower roots on the stony north side, and a stream at the base of the hill had swollen to a marsh in that area. The back of the hill dropped to a saddle which connected it with a ridge to the south, making it a spur of Rabenberg. If our forces needed to retreat, they could easily fall back over the saddle onto the mountain to disperse across Rabenwald and, if necessary, flee further south into the Alps. Its only disadvantage was that it stood some fourteen miles from the castle by roads that troops and supplies could use.

We rode down the ridge onto the Dernfels spur and inspected the site at closer quarters. Though a lot of work would be needed to prepare a camp for our forces, it would be far less than the work involved in preparing Baerhuegel.

'So it is agreed,' said Bertram as we rested our horses awhile: 'We make our preparations to fight here, on Dernfels.'

All three of us nodded.

'What tactics do you propose for the actual battle, Generals?' I asked.

'We fight from the tor and let the enemy come to us.' Aldwin said.

'Their men will tire toiling up the slope towards our archers and be picked off by their arrows,' said Walther. 'Then our main force and side phalanxes will close around them with swords and halberds to box them in so that they must fight or fall back into the marsh.'

'Perhaps we could also make use of the tactics used by the Spanish guerillos,' I suggested. 'The Children of the Raven are skilled in woodcraft and hunting. You could create a special reserve force to act against the enemy while our army musters on the tor.'

'I have not heard of this new style of warfare,' said Walther, frowning.

'It is not new. King David in the Bible used such tactics. The men work in small teams, harrying the enemy's military columns by picking off the soldiers at the back and those who leave the security of the camp. They can ambush their supply trains and make sorties to torch their tents at night.'

The generals flushed indignantly.

'But that is cowardly! Contrary to the rules of war,' said Aldwin.

'Would you have us fighting like Silvio and his vagabonds?' said Walther.

Bertram frowned. 'When Nicolaus usurped Rabenwald, he fought contrary to the rules of war. I see some value in Gendal's suggestion.'

'Nicolaus's cheap action does not give us the right to behave like rats too,' said Walther.

'My God! You are a desperate people!' I cried: 'You have no time for chivalry, no place for honour. This is civil war: people rising up against their masters with axes and scythes. Do not ask them to obey the rules of warfare. They will destroy you too.'

Bertram touched my arm to caution me.

'Honour is not simply good manners, friend,' he cautioned.

'Aye? And what is honour when you are dead? You plan war. That is dishonourable to both man and God. We are all made in God's image, so when you take a life, you destroy a part of God. If you must stoop low, at least stoop low enough to win. Nicolaus would have now't of your honour were our positions reversed.'

There was an uncomfortable silence, which Bertram broke.

'Let us return to the castle, gentlemen, where we can discuss our strategies further.'

'As long as there is no more mention of "special reserve" forces and cowardly deeds,' Walther said.

I mounted Finstar and turned his head to ride down the hill towards the road our troops would take to get there. The others mounted and followed me. Little was said on the way back to the castle.

We crossed the drawbridge into the courtyard to find our sentries gathered around a friar on an elderly bay mare.

'Who are you? Who sent you here?' the sentries shouted at him.

Their clamour was frightening his horse. She turned round in circles, looking for a way to escape. Then the friar's eyes caught sight of Bertram and me.

'Gendal! Bertram!' he cried in joy.

'Friar Fadrique!' I replied with equal joy.

'My other saviour!' Bertram said. 'Here, men! Help the Friar from his horse. Can't you see he's not a horseman?'

The sentries, who had heckled Fadrique, now gathered round him to hold the mare by her bridle and help him down from her saddle. We dismounted too and went over to embrace him.

'Well, you told me I'd get a warm welcome, but I didn't think it would be that hot!' Fadrique joked.

'I didn't think you'd find your way here so soon,' Bertram replied. 'What happened? Come and have something to eat.'

We entered the Great Hall as the makings of the communal evening meal were being set out. I brought the Friar some bread and cold meat and a mug of beer as he sat with Bertram and the generals at the top table. Fadrique devoured the food as if he had not eaten for several days. When I offered him more, he refused.

'Your kitchen is certainly better than mine, Gendal,' he joked. 'I wanted to get some food in my belly before you throw me out, when you hear the message I was told to bring you.'

He placed eight schillings on the table and pushed them over to me.

'I didn't need to spend your money, Gendal. I was about to acquire a donkey when a man with a face like the sun came up to me.

"Are you Friar Fadrique?" he asked me. When I said I was, he said Gendal had sent him and he had a job for me. He wanted me to deliver a message here as soon as possible. He couldn't, as he had to travel on to deliver another message before he meets you at the Wolfholz Tavern. And he gave me that horse to speed my journey. But I've never ridden a horse before in my life! I don't know how I stayed on such a massive brute!'

All four of us laughed, to think the friar found the old mare so frightening.

'Then you've done well to get here so soon, Fadrique,' I said.

'What is Sir Rehlein's message?' Bertram asked.

The friar gave him a double look before answering, after hearing the status of the person who had sent the message.

'Giacomo Maladriuzzi is even now on his way to the Wolfholz Tavern.' Fadrique took a breath, and added, 'And his ten best men ride with him for Rabenwald's hide.'

Anger flashed through me. I sat down to control it, knowing anger makes for poor decisions. As Maladriuzzi had not gone alone, I should not ride to meet him. But with the generals hungry for battle, I needed to strike a bargain with the Condottiero as soon as possible, before they forced Bertram into military action.

'Here is your adherence to the rules of war!' I growled, glaring at Aldwin and Walther.

Fadrique looked at them and saw what manner of men they were. 'Is that not what you wanted to hear?' he asked, feeling the tension that separated us.

'No, but you have done right in telling us,' I said. 'Knowing the truth of the situation will help us plan better.'

I turned to Bertram.

'Count, give me three good woodsmen to surprise Maladriuzzi's ten and enforce the conditions of our letter. There could be no better time to follow King David's example than now.'

The inner conflict of the decision played across Bertram's face as he wrestled with the conflict between the generals' opinion and my request.

'All right, Gendal: you shall have the men. Walther, send Johannes, Ulrich and Gotfrid to meet us in the Lesser Hall for their instructions.'

Walther left the Great Hall to do Bertram's bidding. His face was grim.

Chapter 20
The Rendezvous at Wolfholz

Our party of four rode out of Rabenschloss, heading for Wolfholz early next morning. I was wearing my leather gambeson with skullcap helmet, riding boots and gauntlets. Johannes, Ulrich and Gotfrid wore chain mail with plain white linen surcoats and a form of unadorned leather bascinet helmet which they found more comfortable for riding. We all carried longswords in our saddle scabbards and daggers sheathed on our belts.

The three woodsmen warriors spoke with none of their generals' respect for honour in battle. Their chief weapon was a bitter hatred for Duke Nicolaus and all he stood for. They were ready to do anything to free their homeland from his thrall.

We rode hard from Rabenwald's foothills, travelling east along the edge of the plain through forest and field. Our quest to surprise Maladriuzzi's cohort of ten relied on all speed. In another day, he and they would expect us.

We arrived in the Groshe region soon after noon, and split into pairs to look for Maladriuzzi's party. Ulrich and Gotfrid turned left at the crossroads to follow the road from Aunsberg. Johannes and I turned right to follow the road towards the Wolfholz Tavern. We travelled through deep forest, riding two abreast so that we could talk as we rode.

'Thank you for sending out the party to rescue my daughter, Ened,' Johannes said.

'Who told you about that?' I asked, recalling how the generals had agreed not to let anyone know about the plan.

'My son-in-law. Bertram wanted me to know you are doing all you can to bring her home. I have kept it to myself.'

A wild boar dashed out of the trees at that moment and ran under my horse's hooves. Finstar shied in surprise and threw me. I fell with a cry. Johannes' horse bolted into the undergrowth.

The boar turned on me. I struggled to my feet and reached for my dagger, but found the scabbard empty. The weapon lay on the ground, too far to reach. I turned to face the boar with empty hands.

He was a handsome brute: his bristled head would have graced the finest table. The scars on his side bore witness to a seasoned fighter. He turned at bay, tusks gleaming, red eyes glinting in the patchy sunlight. I stood my ground in fear, thinking I would have little chance against him, but hoping I could leap behind a tree out of his course at the last moment.

He lumbered forward. His momentum took him quickly to a gallop. My fear heightened as he closed. I heard his pounding trotters tearing up the turf; I smelled his steaming breath.

An arrow whistled past my ear as I dived aside. The arrow hit the boar squarely between his eyes. He crashed down on me, dead.

His heavy bulk pinned my legs to the leaf-littered earthy track.

Johannes ran back to help me. He rolled the dead boar aside so that I could stand.

'A close one, that,' he said: 'How did you save yourself?'

'An archer saved me. I must thank him.'

Johannes looked at the arrow and shook his head. 'That is a woodman's arrow, and they can be a wild sort. Silvio only saved you to catch his lunch: the boar's carcass is all he needs in thanks.'

I whistled for my horse. Finstar returned to me, nuzzling my neck as if consoling me after the danger I had faced. I mounted and rode on with Johannes down the track towards the Wolfholz Tavern, praising God for my lucky escape.

We stopped to rest in a glade in the thinning forest about two leagues from our destination. We waited there among the trees beside the track for Ulrich and Gotfrid to join us. While the horses grazed near us out of sight of the track, we lay back in the rough browning bracken. The scent of the leaf loam beneath us was sweet and the soughing breeze rustling through the branches above sent me to sleep.

The muffled sounds of horses' hooves woke me again. I lay still, my hand resting on Johannes' forearm to caution him not to move either.

Along the track rode Maladriuzzi and his group of mercenaries, now only seven. I wondered what had happened to the other three. The soldiers were clad in chain mail and helmets, their white surcoats emblazoned with the eight-pointed star symbol of the mercenary army. The Condottiero rode in the centre of the column, a riding cloak wrapped around his face and body to conceal his identity. They looked a vicious bunch.

Like us, their party stopped in the glade for a rest. The men dismounted, and one came into the undergrowth near us to relieve himself.

I watched in awe as Johannes quietly rolled over onto his feet and slipped through the bracken to where the man crouched. The sounds of the forest masked the gentle chink of his chain mail as his dagger arm reached up and across. He slit the soldier's throat from behind and caught his body as it fell to place it quietly on the ground.

Johannes crept back through the undergrowth to me and beckoned me to follow him to our horses. Despite my leather armour, I could not hope to move as silently as him but tried. We crawled through the undergrowth to our horses and rode off as fast as we could through the trees.

We headed north and doubled back through the woods onto the track about four leagues from Wolfholz. Before we risked leaving the trees, Johannes made a bird call like the marsh snipe. When the call was repeated some distance away, he beckoned me forward onto the track. Ulrich and Gotfrid joined us there. The three men hugged each other and clapped my shoulders in greeting.

'You did well there, to reduce their number from ten to eight,' said Johannes.

'We found a use for those Danuvian caltrops,' Ulrich said. 'When they hobbled two of their horses, Maladriuzzi ordered the other soldiers to ride on with him. We soon dealt with the two men they had left.'

I noticed the spare swords and chain mail in their saddle packs, but said nothing.

'I dealt with a third,' Johannes replied with a sly grin: 'That's reduced the odds a bit.'

'Four to seven. Still not ideal,' Gotfrid said. He gave me a sideways glance which suggested he counted me out.

THE EAGLE AND THE RAVEN

'It's time we went to the Wolfholz Tavern,' I said. 'May I suggest we enter in ones and twos, like travellers, to keep them off their guard.'

My three companions gave me broad grins and brought out rough travelling cloaks from their saddle packs. I put mine on too, a cheap hooded cape of woven brown wool. Over the cloak, I hung the ribbon holding my old Company of Messengers seal in a prominent way, as if I had but newly become a journeyman.

'Let's go,' said Gotfrid, and cantered off down the track with Ulrich.

Johannes and I followed them at a gentler pace. The sun was dropping towards the horizon as we reached our destination.

The Wolfholz Tavern stood by a bridge on a bend in the river, a tributary of the Danube, where the track we followed crossed the main highway from Ulm to Innsbruck. The sprawling coaching inn was a half-timbered building of brick, wattle and daub, with large stables round a sizable courtyard because of its use as a staging post for carriages. Forest crowded down the slopes at the back of the inn, but a couple of fields stood to either side of the river on the flat floodplain.

As Johannes and I neared the bridge, we saw two travellers ride through the arch into the courtyard. We waited out of sight on the far bank of the river, listening to the sounds coming from the inn: a servant girl welcoming them, their horses being led to a stable, a door shutting as they went inside. For a few moments, I was able to reflect in peace. Then it was my turn to join the party.

The servant whose voice I had heard earlier, greeted me as I walked into the tavern with my pack over one shoulder and my longsword slung from the other. She was blonde and slight, and her peasant blouse and skirt were neat and clean. With a smile, she asked the stable lad to quarter my horse. She kept behind the bar of the busy inn herself, to stay out of the way of twelve merry travellers who had crowded round the fire to sup beer and howl hunting songs. The other servants helping her had to put up with the indignities thoughtlessly dished out by the coarser guests.

'Have you come far, messenger?' she asked as she poured me a beer.

'Aye. I have to meet someone here shortly. I may have to wait here a day or so until he comes by.'

'You're very welcome. We have a good company here today.'

I scanned the travellers' faces and saw Ulrich, Gotfrid and Maladriuzzi among them. Quieter than the rest, the short, corpulent Condottiero meditated sourly in a corner, hunched in his riding cloak to hide his expensive woollen clothes. His jowled face looked belligerent. He could not smile but only sneer, and his hog-like eyes were lit by a cunning gleam. His appearance alone would have made me mistrust him.

I went to sit down with the company, fearing Maladriuzzi might recognise me from the ball. When he beckoned me to his table, I moved to sit closer, but kept my face in the shadows.

'Are you the guide I await?' he muttered, as though he held me in the greatest contempt.

'I don't think so, sirrah. The one I came to serve has lost his way, and I have to wait on him here. What is your guide like? I may have passed him on my path.'

'I don't know. We haven't met. Probably a rough highland type. Not the sort to trust.'

'Is anyone, sirrah? Nay, I have met no-one of that ilk.'

I sat on, sipping the hoppy local beer as I listened to the company's banter. Then I polished my boots with a handful of the straw scattered over the packed earth floor. By bending low, I could see who else was bearing arms among the legs below the tables and chairs. When I sat up again, I accidentally knocked over a stranger's goblet. He stood up in anger.

'Refill my drink,' he ordered in Italian.

I gazed at him with a blank look of non-comprehension. He repeated his command. When I did not obey, he slapped my face with his leather gauntlet. I touched my stinging cheek.

'Sirrah, you have drunk too much. For your sake I shall ignore your challenge.'

I could tell Gotfrid and Ulrich thought me a coward not to take up the challenge at once, especially when our plan was to single out Maladriuzzi's ten and despatch each separately. They need not have worried.

The stranger struck my other cheek. I could not refuse.

I withdrew my longsword two inches behind the cover of the table. My move was visible only to the stranger, a tall young fiery eyed Italian with long black hair. He now wore a sackcloth tabard rather than the mercenaries' eight-pointed star surcoat over his fine light chain mail: a sign that he was downplaying his skills as much as I was mine. He nodded and beckoned with his head to the door. I nodded and stood up to follow.

We left the company, shedding our cloaks in the porch. A servant followed us outside, open-mouthed. I led the way along the river bank, wary of this drunk mercenary who was not quite beside me. In the clearing between the trees and the riverbank, we turned to face each other. I scanned the ground for tripping hazards as I drew my sword.

The mercenary produced a fine Italian blade and stood on guard, confident of his dexterity. His stabbing sword was a good three inches longer than my double-edged longsword. He held his weapon one handed, his left arm balancing the weight in his right. In contrast, I held my sword with both hands, to give added strength and distance to the power of my slashes. We touched blades and circled, our eyes locked on each other, each awaiting the other's first move.

He broke to attack first, stabbing forward when he thought my attention had been distracted. I raised my sword, easily forcing his blade up my own and away, before returning with a counter-swing which jarred against the join between his blade and hilt. That first exchange unsettled him a little. He realised the ale he had drunk had made him underestimate my skill.

We circled further in our face off. I let him start each attack and easily parried whatever he aimed at me. He mocked me as we sparred, hoping to spur me into an error, but I was not the green youth he had thought. I concentrated only on his movements, not his words.

I over-judged a cut, and his answering blade scratched the side of my leather armour. Angry with myself for such a slip, I swung my longsword back across and somehow cut his sword out of his hand.

He backed off and reached to draw his Rondel dagger from his belt, but stumbled on the uneven turf. Before he had freed the dagger from its scabbard, I swung my sword high across the front of his shoulders. My blade half-severed his head from his neck. His body dropped to the ground, pumping out scarlet arterial blood. I stabbed my longsword into his chest in a final coup de grâce. Its point sheared through the rings of mail.

I retrieved his weapons and cleaned them in the river with my own. I dragged the mercenary's body into the woods for the wolves to take care of the corpse. Then I checked there was no blood on my own clothes, and covered the blood on the ground with leaf mould from the forest.

When I returned to the inn, I stowed the mercenary's weapons with my saddle in the stable. Then I picked up my cloak and wrapped it round myself again before strolling back inside to continue my drink.

Maladriuzzi observed me with shrewd eyes. When his soldier did not return, he spoke, his voice low.

'I could find a place for you to serve in a private army, messenger.'

'Thank you, sirrah, but no; I cannot yet. I am bound upon another master's business.'

'Trustworthy too! Should you seek work when that is done, seek out Maladriuzzi. He shall find a place for you.'

I nodded my thanks and raised my cup to drink.

Gotfrid stood up, talking loudly about his lame horse. A mercenary followed him out to the stable. After some minutes, Gotfrid returned alone. He said the man who had accompanied him had decided to ride on.

In entered Johannes, shortly after that. His wild hair and expression made him look as if he had ridden hard to escape danger.

'Rabenwald marauders are coming through the woods!' he cried. 'We must stop them before they sack the town!'

He ran back outside and unsheathed his sword. Five mercenaries leapt up and left the inn after him, buckling on their weapons. Ulrich left by another door to join Johannes as he turned on the mercenaries in the courtyard. Johannes' turn so surprised them, he felled the first one with a dagger uppercut to his throat, severing his windpipe and splitting an artery. As the other mercenaries turned on Johannes, Gotfrid and I came out behind them and shouted to make them turn back to face us.

The four mercenaries found themselves surrounded. They turned at bay, their backs towards each other for protection. They wielded their swords and daggers with professional skill. We would be hard pressed to better them.

The man I faced was tall and lean, and well-seasoned. The tricks he used against me with his stabbing sword took all my concentration to evade.

'You bastard bog dweller!' he snarled at me in Italian.

I recalled that moment, weeks before, when I had heard that same voice say much the same, before I had fallen into the bog at the Iyver. Fury surged through me as I recalled what those men had done to Hans and Anna. This man was one of the fiends who had inflicted so much suffering.

I gripped my longsword tightly in both hands and swung it with such fury that it dragged down and broke the mercenary's finer Italian blade in half as he lunged forward to stab me. I swung my blade back across and broke his wrists before he could recoil. Then, completing the figure of eight movement, I changed my grip on my haft and slashed him across his exposed neck. He fell to the cobbles.

I turned to help my three friends. Johannes and Ulrich had despatched their rivals, but Gotfrid was on his knees before his foe. The mercenary cut across his neck. As Gotfrid dropped to the ground, we attacked the mercenary from three sides. He fell dead across Gotfrid's body.

For a moment, the three of us still standing, just stood there in the courtyard, panting heavily after our exertion. When we had recovered our breath, Johannes and I stripped the dead mercenaries of their weapons and armour and loaded them onto their horses. Ulrich struggled to help us with the task.

'I must take Gotfrid's body home,' he said, a tear in his eye.

'I will help you with your brother,' Johannes replied.

While I lost the bodies of the dead mercenaries in the woods, Johannes helped Ulrich lift Gotfrid's body onto his horse and secure him. When I returned, Ulrich had mounted, ready to return to Rabenwald.

'Ulrich, take the mercenaries' horses and their booty with you, too,' Johannes suggested: 'Then Gendal and I can concentrate on the two that are left.'

Ulrich agreed, vacantly. I left Johannes securing the horses in a string for him to lead, and returned to the inn, hooding myself in my rough cloak again. When I strolled in alone, Maladriuzzi regarded me with a wary sneer of a frown.

Then entered Rehlein by the main road door.

'I am looking for Giacomo Maladriuzzi. I was told he might be here.'

'That is he,' said the taverner, nodding towards the Condottiero.

'Come into the light, whoever you are,' Maladriuzzi ordered.

His one remaining soldier stood ready to face up to Rehlein, his hand upon his sword.

Rehlein stepped into the light coming through the window behind Maladriuzzi. Just like Fadrique had described, I saw his face shine, haloed with the gold of his hair and beard. The Condottiero drew back from him in recognition.

'Prince Rehlein, what are you doing here?' he asked.

I gaped. It had never dawned on me that this friend I had travelled with over so many miles had such an exalted status.

'You are to ride with me,' Rehlein said.

'And if I choose not to?' Maladriuzzi asked.

'Then I shall assist your departure,' I said. I drew back my hood and took up the same stance as his one remaining soldier.

He looked at the two of us, and remembered. I knew from his expression that he remembered me not only at the Duke's ball but also the two of us, at the inn in Eiswald. He blustered to hide his discomfort.

'What is this, that knight plays the messenger and prince becomes the guide? Messenger, you lied to me.'

'No, Giacomo Maladriuzzi. I just waited till the one I came to serve fulfilled the conditions of his invitation. My message is this. Travel on alone with Prince Rehlein and you shall have safe conduct. Refuse, and…'

I withdrew my sword three inches and re-sheathed it. Maladriuzzi lumbered to his feet and left with my friend. I blocked his soldier bodyguard from leaving with them.

Chapter 21
The Meeting with Maladriuzzi

After Maladriuzzi had left the tavern with Rehlein, the taverner spoke to me as I paid our bar bill.

'Are you and yours of Rabenwald?'

'Aye, and of the Raven,' I replied.

'Then we are right pleased to have had you come by here. When will you rise up against the Duke?'

'When anger breaks through restraint. I would give it but a week, a fortnight at the latest. You will know, when the horn sounds and the beacon is lit.'

'We shall watch and wait, messenger. Groshe is with Rabenwald. The Grosha will run to fight by the Children's side.'

THE EAGLE AND THE RAVEN

We embraced. I beckoned to Maladriuzzi's bodyguard to come with me. We saddled up and rode with Johannes, taking the route Rehlein and Maladriuzzi were following, but keeping a short distance behind them. Ulrich took a more direct route, fetching his brother Gotfrid's body home.

Evening was already bringing the shadows of night to the long forest trail Rehlein took. Being untrustworthy himself, Maladriuzzi could not trust another's pledge. He forced Rehlein to ride slowly because his suspicions made him fear what might lurk behind every bush. I feared his wealthy appearance might attract Silvio's attack; but the one solitary woodsman we saw let us pass unhindered with a nod of support.

With the light failing and still some distance to go, Johannes and I overtook Rehlein and Maladriuzzi to set a quicker pace, bringing the bodyguard with us in our vanguard. We led them a more direct route to the castle than originally planned, to ensure we could still just about pick our way along the path before the full darkness of night. Seeing the bodyguard in front seemed to cheer the Condottiero: his pace increased to match ours so that he could keep up with him.

When we finally entered the forest paths around the castle. I left Johannes riding at the front of the group and cantered off to the castle to warn Bertram of our special guest's imminent arrival.

The Count followed me down to my apartment, where we could talk as I changed into the court robe Maladriuzzi had seen me wearing when we had first met at the ball: the long white belted surcoat with my device, the butterfly over the spread eagle in tawny brown on dark brown.

'The meal has been prepared for Maladriuzzi,' said Bertram. 'Why must he eat with us? His fear will not let him enjoy the food, nor shall I for dining with a cur.'

'We must learn all we can about him. I do not trust him an inch. Has Rabenwald found the money yet?'

'We have found what we can: it's in the cassone in the Lesser Hall. But we have not heard from Sir Rehlein yet, about how his negotiations have gone. All we know, from what Ulrich has told us, is that Sir Rehlein met you at Wolfholz and is escorting the Condottiero here now.'

'Let us hope Rehlein was successful there, too. No mercenary will fight with only half his fee in his pocket. His employer might die in battle, or get captured and use the balance to pay his ransom.'

Page Barthram came down the stone staircase to tell us Rehlein and Maladriuzzi had arrived with Johannes and the bodyguard. We returned to the courtyard to greet our guest as the party dismounted. Aldwin and Walther were already out there, keen to see what the Condottiero looked like. They escorted the bodyguard to the Great Hall to eat from the castle's plainer fair. Bertram and I took Rehlein and Maladriuzzi to the Lesser Hall to negotiate over a more splendid meal.

The nights of encroaching autumn were making the Lesser Hall cold. As well as the tapestries on the walls, curtains now hung over the windows and doors to lessen the drafts. Torches lit the food-laden refectory table near the fire.

Maladriuzzi handed his cloak to Page Barthram and turned to speak to Bertram. He saw me behind Bertram's right shoulder and took a deep breath to regain his composure.

'So my messenger was none other than the famous Knight Gendal. You must have some special plan for a ministerialis to take a station beneath an apprentice.'

'We do,' Bertram agreed. 'But first, let us eat. You will be hungry after your journey.'

We invited our guest to rinse his hands in the laver and sat down with him at the table. Bertram sat at the head, with Rehlein opposite him at the other end, on a watching brief and there mainly to reassure Maladriuzzi. The Condottiero sat on Bertram's right, and I sat opposite him on Bertram's left. An excellent meal was set before us: broth from the bounty of the forest, with freshly baked bread, venison, and fruits from the orchards.

Bertram ate little, pushing each plate aside after two mouthfuls. Maladriuzzi ate little more, only that which convention demanded, but not enough to risk falling foul of the feared poison which was not there. Only Rehlein and I ate well: after the experiences of years of travelling, few things turn our stomachs when we are hungry. The meal finished with the delicious steamed honey pudding that was a speciality of Rabenwald. As I ate it, the tension in the atmosphere became suffocating. Respecting my companions' feelings, I refused a second helping. A serving woman refilled our mugs with beer and placed the flagon on the table before leaving us so that we could turn our discussions to business.

'You are not such barbarians that you are fattening me up even more for sacrifice,' Maladriuzzi jested, woodenly.

'Had that been our plan, you would not have reached the woods,' I replied.

He nodded. 'You have taken great measures to bring me here alone but for my one aide. Why all your trouble? And why am I here?'

I threw a bag of gold on the table. Then I rose to lift the lid of the ornately carved cassone which stood by the wall, revealing more coins.

'Business, Commander,' I replied. 'Your army's one loyalty is to gold. Are you interested in Rabenwald's mint?'

Maladriuzzi thought on a space.

'You would have my men turn against Duke Nicolaus? My price would be high. And Rabenwald cannot trust my motives or my word.'

'Aye. But I'm sure your men would prefer being paid twice over for doing nowt than risk their lives for half as much.'

'You have a point, Knight Gendal. What say you, Count Rabenwald?'

Bertram's nostrils flared.

'I little like business, Commander. The smell of this repulses me.'

He emphasised his words by crossing to the laver to wash his hands again.

'So you are a pawn in the Count's hands, Free Imperial Knight Gendal,' Maladriuzzi mocked, reminding me of my allegiance to the Imperator alone.

'When it suits me, Commander. Do you accept Rabenwald's offer?'

'We have not mentioned prices yet. Six thousand.'

I turned away with a look of patient scorn.

'That is six times the fee Nicolaus paid. Even the Imperator would baulk at such a sum. You know Rabenwald must refuse.'

'So ye are not desperate men after all. What is your offer?'

'Nicolaus's price. A thousand,' I bartered, knowing it was two thousand.

'He would triple that to keep us.'

'Don't be so sure. Two thousand five hundred. And that is our final offer. Your forces will be paid more than twice over for now't.'

'Fair enough. On behalf of my men, I accept. Where is the

money?'

'Here is half for you to take back with you. The rest will arrive when we have proof your army has orders to suit Rabenwald.'

'Part payment? What money-lender would finance this down-trodden backwater? Have you minded that you might all be dead before the gold is found?'

'Your one order is easy enough to rescind, Commander. But that will not be necessary. Just as you will not be harmed here despite Rabenwald's dislike for you.'

Maladriuzzi reflected on the offer before responding.

'You have a way with you, Knight Gendal. I will take Rabenwald's gold and await the balance. Till then, my men shall be seen to do Nicolaus's bidding. After the balance arrives, they will obey orders that benefit Rabenwald. What are your plans?'

'Those I am not permitted to reveal, Commander.'

'If you mistrust my intentions, I go back on our agreement now. How can my men help Rabenwald if I do not know what you intend to do?'

I looked at Bertram. He smiled to reassure us both.

'I do not confide everything in Knight Gendal, Commander. Rabenwald will be ready for battle in nine days. We will challenge Nicolaus at Baerhuegel in the foothill marches. Our position will enable us to fall back here to Rabenschloss should we weaken, and if we prevail, we can drive Nicolaus's forces into treacherous lands known well only by the children of Rabenwald. We have also imported some martial techniques to make the fight more interesting.'

'I believe you also have supporters in Danuvia. What of them?'

'When our beacon is lit, they will fall to and attack the enemy from the rear. Surrounded after a tiring march, Nicolaus's forces cannot hope to win.'

'A shrewd plan! I am glad my men will play no part in it.'

Maladriuzzi raised his beer mug and toasted Rabenwald with us.

Our business concluded, Bertram took Maladriuzzi to his quarters for the night. The Condottiero planned to leave first thing the following morning, saying the Duke would notice if he were away too long.

'It is unusual for me to seek enlisters in person,' he explained.

When our host and our guest had gone, Rehlein clapped my shoulder and embraced me.

'That was well done, Cara Gendal!' he exclaimed.

'Thank you. But it has not been my best day's work. I do not trust Maladriuzzi's intentions. He is a foul man.'

'Count Bertram's false battle plans at least were well described.'

'That was one of Rabenwald's proposals, but another found better favour. Now tell me, how did your journey to Aunsberg go? You look so strong, so confident now. Have you also sorted the problem that was causing you such sorrow?'

A cloud passed across Rehlein's face.

'No, not yet. One day, God willing, I shall find some way to redress the wrong done to me.' His face brightened. 'But in the meantime, this caper is giving me such sport.'

'This is not a game, Prince Rehlein. Nine mercenaries and our ally Gotfrid lost their lives this day. The only good that came of it is that I fought the soldier who committed the outrage at the Iyver and avenged it for you.'

Rehlein's expression told me he had heeded the rebuke.

'Thank you, Gendal, for releasing me from my vow. That shall not change my course of action.'

'Have you found the additional funds?'

'Yes. I have arranged for them to be brought here. I was only able to secure five hundred gold coins, so you did well to haggle the price down. They will arrive in a few days, with an escort provided by my second cousin, Sinter. He will then arrange for them to be sent on.'

'Then at least we can keep our side of the bargain.'

'Whether or not that odious man keeps his.'

The next day, Rehlein escorted Maladriuzzi, his bodyguard and Bertram's treasure chest down into Danuvia. He was supported by a cohort of eight Children of the Raven. They ensured the Condottiero reached the dukedom safely before abandoning him there with his bodyguard and returning to Rabenschloss.

Chapter 22
Cunrad Returns

A great shout of excitement filled the castle courtyard the following afternoon, as a horse-drawn wagon crossed the drawbridge. The Children of the Raven had been working hard, preparing the battle site at Dernfels and organising supply routes, supplies and encampments for the campaign. The noise outside brought Bertram and the generals out of the Lesser Hall. Rehlein and I came down from Rehlein's chamber. Even Friar Fadrique came out of the kitchens, where he had happily hitched up the sleeves of his habit to help the cooks prepare the evening meal.

The wagon was the same one that had left Rabenschloss ten days before, laden with fruit and driven by the three spies. Only two people had come back on it: the young woman in her russet servant dress and bonnet, who was holding the reins, and the blond young man Cunrad, who lay under a blanket in the back of the wagon, motionless.

'Call for Mother Agatha!' cried the young woman. I had expected to hear Nyze's rough tones, and was shocked to hear Ened's confident voice.

'Ened!' Bertram cried. He ran to her side and swept her off the wagon's running board.

They hugged each other passionately, surrounded by the crowd in the courtyard. We all cheered.

Then Ened pulled back a little.

'Cunrad is in the cart. He's badly injured. He's the only one who survived. Please, send for Mother Agatha!'

'Page Barthram has already gone to fetch her from her cottage in the woods,' Rehlein said.

Bertram tenderly picked Cunrad up in his powerful arms and carried him into the Lesser Hall. I ran ahead and swept our maps from the refectory table so that he could lay Cunrad there. Fadrique ran to the kitchens to fetch salt and boiling water, bowls and clean cloths.

'What happened?' Bertram asked Ened as she put a cushion under Cunrad's head to make him more comfortable on the hard wooden board.

'Some of it is not easy to tell,' she replied. She saw Rehlein enter the hall with the generals and turned to him.

'I must thank you, Prince Rehlein, for honouring me with a dance at the Duke's ball. Your simple words: *you will be rescued* and *prepare to escape* gave me hope.'

Bertram gave Rehlein the same double look as I had done on learning the true status of his former regent and present advisor.

THE EAGLE AND THE RAVEN

'I wished I could have done more,' Rehlein said.

Ened sat beside Cunrad and looked up at Bertram.

'The Duke tried hard to destroy my hope. But after that dance, I did prepare. I spilt food on my day gown, so that they would give me a dress the servant girls wear while they had the gown cleaned. I thought it might be easier to escape dressed like a servant. The hope of escape made me pay more attention to what was happening in the Duke's apartments and the castle courtyard. When Cunrad, Nyze and Gawin came to rescue me, I heard them in the passage.'

Mother Agatha hurried into the hall with Page Barthram and went straight to Cunrad's side. She acknowledged the rest of us with the shortest of nods before she tended to her patient. Her cool hand touched his forehead. His eyes flickered open.

'Tell Count Bertram, we failed,' he croaked: 'The Duke is still alive.'

'Bertram is here,' she reassured him. She looked up and asked, 'Can someone hold Cunrad's hand? He is in much pain.'

I sat beside him and gave him my right hand. His fingers closed tightly over mine. Mother Agatha started cleaning his wounds with a brine made from the salt and water. He turned his face towards me: it was taut with pain so severe he could only speak in short, breathless gasps. His fist clutched my palm so strongly my fingers went white.

'What happened, Cunrad?' I asked.

'It all went, as you said, at first,' he replied. 'We delivered the fruit. We dressed as soldiers, we entered the castle, we took the place of the guard, at the Duke's bedchamber.'

He gasped a cry as Agatha cleaned a deep wound with the brine. His hand clutched mine more fiercely for a moment, and then relaxed a little.

'Nyze took the Duke the poisoned drink. He did not like her dress. It wasn't right. He told her to drink his cup. She obeyed, to save us. The poison was not kind. She ran to Gawin in agony.'

Mother Agatha's hands shook. Some blood-stained water spilled from the basin she was holding. She set the bowl down and continue to treat Cunrad's wounds.

'A soldier heard her. He ran to help the Duke. He killed Gawin, before I could reach them. I stopped him.'

'What about Ened?'

'Ened?' he repeated, his concentration fading. 'I found her room. I killed the guard outside. I unlocked the door. Then I heard Gawin. I couldn't save him. Ened helped me down the stairs. When the other soldiers came. I threw the Greek fire. It got us through the gate.'

Cunrad's eyes glazed. I patted his left cheek to rouse him again.

'Did Cara Rea see any of you before Nyze took Nicolaus the drink?'

'Not Gawin or me. But she let Nyze hide, in her rooms, that evening.'

The effort and the pain were too much for Cunrad. His grip relaxed and his head rolled to one side as he fell unconscious. Mother Agatha sent Page Barthram for more supplies from the kitchen.

Bertram scowled at me across Cunrad's wounded body.

'You promised me your poison would be gentle!'

'And so it was. The poison I asked Mother Agatha to prepare would have snuffed Nicolaus out gently while he slept. It could not have caused such agony.'

'Aye? Then it is only as we suspected. Cara Rea recognised them and warned Nicolaus to strengthen her own position.'

'Nyze would have trusted her too, seeing her as our ally. Perhaps she told her of the plot, and Cara Rea took the opportunity to replace my potion with something far more evil.'

The generals' faces hardened to hear of Cara Rea's betrayal. They had not spoken much so far as they were absorbing all the details of the coup's partial failure before they drew their conclusions.

'So Cunrad unlocked your room, and you came out, Ened. What happened next?' Bertram asked.

'I went into the passage and saw the guard getting the better of Cunrad,' Ened said: 'So I took Gawin's dagger and stabbed him in the neck to stop him. Then I helped Cunrad down the stairs to the servants' quarters. We got out into the courtyard before they could stop us. Some soldiers tried to block our way to the main gates. Cunrad gave me a glass bottle to throw at them. I smashed it on the cobbles. Their screams as it burst into flames! They couldn't put it out.'

'That would be Cara Rea's Greek fire,' I said, remembering how it had burned on the bog when Bertram and I were fleeing from the Iyver the morning after we met.

'It kept the soldiers busy enough for us to escape through the wicket gate. Cunrad guided me through the streets, down the hill into a poorer area. We found his horse and cart where he had left it, in a disused yard. I took care of him and the horse as best I could that night. Then I drove the cart through the South Gate next morning, with Cunrad hiding under the covers, trying not to make a sound. Luckily, there was a receipt among the covers. The soldiers thought I was just another peasant girl returning home after delivering a load of fruit.'

Bertram was sitting in the curved wooden chair at the head of the refectory table. He looked deep in thought, his chin resting on his right hand. Rehlein and the generals gathered round him. I still sat by Cunrad, holding his limp hand.

'What should we do now?' Bertram asked us all. He asked the question wearily, as if he already knew the answer and only sought our confirmation that it was the right way to go.

I was conscious of a distant noise coming from the courtyard outside. It was the sound of angry voices, growing louder. The murmur swiftly grew into a clamour, as more and more people protested against the betrayal.

'Rabenwald must go to war,' said Walther, his fleshy features flushed with anger.

'Yes,' agreed Aldwin, his hawkish face looking like flint. 'Tell the men to prepare to march. Send the watch to finish the beacon. We start out tomorrow, to take up our positions the following dawn.'

'Is there nothing else we can do first? Some other attempt on Nicolaus, perhaps?' Rehlein asked, looking at me.

'Not now, friend. The news of Cara Rea's betrayal is already out. You can hear the angry cries in the courtyard.'

'No-one can hold back the Children of the Raven now,' said Bertram with deep regret. 'Sound the alphorn! We go to war!'

Chapter 23
Final Preparations

Bertram was furious with Page Barthram for having told the kitchen staff about Cara Rea's betrayal. He saw it as the slip which was precipitating our rush to arms.

Rehlein heard Bertram's voice berating the lad in the next room as he sorted his battle gear in Cara Rea's chamber. When he heard Bertram's door open on Barthram's dismissal, he came out and caught up with the lad.

'I believe Knight Gendal has something for you, page. Come down to Gendal's cave with me.'

Barthram could not refuse the prince, though he longed to run off and shed the tears brimming in his eyes. Rehlein brought the lad through the Lesser Hall to my cavern chamber, where I too was sorting my possessions in readiness for battle.

I saw the lad's pinched face and tear-filled eyes, and invited him to sit at the table with me. He sat hunched, trying to look as small as possible in his shame. Rehlein sat on a chair near the fire, out of our immediate vision.

'Made a mistake?' I asked.

Barthram nodded. 'I didn't realise. We were just chatting in the kitchen, when I went to fetch more cloths for Mother Agatha.'

I nodded. After a pause, I asked, 'Would you make the same mistake again?'

'He's blaming me for making our men go before we're ready.'

'He is upset, Barthram, because he does not want to see any of us die. But in truth, you are not responsible for others or their reactions, only your own. Just as you are not responsible for Duke Nicolaus's deeds or the future Imperator's decision to grant this land to Danuvia. Let this be a lesson for you to keep your own counsel in future.'

The lad nodded. 'But now Count Bertram refuses to let me ride out with you tomorrow. He says I must stay here with the children and the old ones and those too sick to fight.'

Rehlein spoke from his seat beside the fire.

'I don't think that is a consequence of this, page. You are Count

Bertram's heir. Should he die before Ened bears him a son, you will become the Count in his stead, just as he replaced Raban. He dare not risk your life on the battlefield as well as his own.'

'Do you think he is treating you as a child too, to stay here?' I asked.

Barthram nodded again.

'Then think again, young man. The Count has rather given you two tasks of great responsibility. Firstly, you are the one charged with the duty to light the beacon tomorrow evening, to warn our allies in Danuvia and beyond to rally in support of us. Secondly, and more importantly, in Count Bertram's absence, you will be his regent here: defending the castle, protecting Countess Ened and leading those still here with you.'

'But I have no sword.'

'That I can remedy for you.'

I brought out the sword I had taken in the duel at Wolfholz Tavern and placed it on the table between us. It was a fine Italian blade, sheathed in a plain, workmanlike scabbard.

'A few days ago, I won this sword from a man who challenged me to a duel, confident in his skill. My sword proved him wrong. Remember that when you go to draw it, Barthram. The blade is light and short. With a few hours' training, you should be skilled enough to defend yourself and this castle. Take it, try it.'

He picked up the scabbard and drew the sword. After inspecting its fine blade, he stood up and waved it the way he thought experienced sword masters handle their blades. Then he remembered me, sheathed the sword and sat back down.

'Thank you, Knight Gendal. I won't forget your warning.'

'Page, go to my chamber now, and I will join you shortly,' Rehlein said: 'I have a small matter to discuss with Gendal. Then I will show you how to handle that fine blade of yours.'

Rehlein watched Barthram leave by the stairs to the Lesser Hall and sat with me at the table.

'That was a good thing you did for that lad, Gendal.'

'I have been where he was, thinking all the world's woes came about through my own mistakes. Then I was able to rectify them again, after going through the fire of adversity. He does not have that time to learn.'

'That is true. We could both be dead this time next week, fighting someone else's battles. So I must settle my affairs on the eve of this campaign.'

It seemed odd to hear Rehlein talk of death in such a way, at that moment when I had never seen him more alive. He looked me squarely in the face.

'If aught should happen to me, Cara Gendal, I charge you as the messenger Gendal: your first duty, above this land, is to ride to Harzland with this letter and this ring.'

He handed me a sealed letter and the Hart seal ring of his family.

'There, seek out my brother Prince Oscar and tell him of my fate. He will think it fitting that such a fool as I should die heading another land's rebellion. I was widely condemned when I left, but fear not: they shall welcome you honourably in my name. They may even offer you my castle as fief for your trouble – no-one in my family likes its non-existent ghosts.'

I gazed at him. How tall and strong he looked in the torchlight, a natural golden prince among men. It was hard to recall him only a few weeks before, a depressed drunk slumped on a tavern floor.

'Oh, Rehlein. Don't scorn the route that brought you hither. For it has brought you back to life.'

I stowed away the ring and letter in the saddlebag I planned to leave in the cavern chamber. Then Rehlein and I climbed the stairs back to the main castle. We found Count Bertram arguing with Friar Fadrique in the Lesser Hall.

'There is no priest on Rabenwald, so you will have to do, whatever faith you choose,' Bertram said: 'The men would commend themselves to God in His war, to help Rabenwald win.'

'No war is God's war!' Fadrique replied: 'All killing is Devil-inspired destruction. No-one can return a life stolen by death!'

The friar's defiance shamed me. Like him, I believed life to be a gift from God, so to take a life was to sin against God's holy laws as written in the Ten Commandments. Those excuses I argued to myself: that I killed only in self-defence in a culture where violence was the currency of the times, that the Friar's habit protected him in a way my civilian clothes could not; were only my attempts to justify the unjustifiable.

'Then ask God to bless them and keep them safe!' Bertram pleaded. 'Please, Friar, there are men outside, wanting to pray to God. Can you not help them pray?'

Fadrique sighed. 'Yes, I shall come. To bless those who tomorrow shall march proudly side by side to battle and to death. As God's child died for the world, so shall they lay down their lives for Rabenwald. A long sleep might be a good promise for them after this fretful dream.'

We followed Bertram into the Great Hall, which was filled with the Rabenwald army: some two hundred men together with their wives and children. How pitifully small the number looked to me at the start of such a desperate campaign.

The people fell silent as Bertram and Fadrique mounted the dais to address them. Rehlein and I stood at the back of the hall to listen. Each man and woman sat prayerfully, but each face was flushed with the expectation of battle. Their proud determination fired Bertram: he stood inspired to greatness before them.

'Children of The Raven, this is our last night of peace before the start of a fateful day. Tomorrow begins the day when we march out to defeat Duke Nicolaus. Tomorrow, each one of you will hold the fate of Rabenwald in your hands, when at last you can avenge all the injustices of the past. The Raven lives! Once more its silent wings will take to the sky; and all our enemies, aye, even the wolf, shall fear its coming, for they know it means Death! Let us pray to our God for strength, for courage, and for victory.'

Friar Fadrique raised his arms in blessing over the gathering.

'O Lord, Thou knowest thy children here rise up only to overcome injustice. Be with them in this long, dark hour. Strengthen their bodies and their hearts in the fray, and lead them on to vanquish their enemies; that Rabenwald and her children might once more be free from the cruel sway of despotism. Inspire their leaders, guide and protect these soldiers. And for those who must heed the final call, accept them into Thy glorious Kingdom. The blessings of the Lord our God be upon us all, and keep us safe to serve You in all we do. *In nomine patris et filio et spiritus sancti*; Amen.'

Chapter 24
The Raven Marches Out to Battle

Our column assembled in the courtyard next dawn. Count Bertram and his standard bearer Ditwin headed the column, with Rehlein and me behind them and ahead of our Generals Aldwin and Walther, all mounted. The portcullis raised, the drawbridge dropped, and the Children of the Raven marched out to depose Duke Nicolaus. We were cheered off by the handful who were unable to bear arms: the old and feeble, the infirm and the very young. They stayed behind under the leadership of Page Barthram and Countess Ened.

Our foot soldiers sang ancient battle songs to speed the miles we would cover that day. Their hearts yearned to fight, making them set out at too fast a pace for the distance. Aldwin and Walther enforced a slower gait upon them. The generals were tight-lipped, grim-faced, silent. They knew my doubts about Maladriuzzi and had pessimistic expectations of the campaign ahead.

Above our heads fluttered Rabenwald's standard, the black raven on gules scarlet, against an early autumn back-drop of black ravens wheeling against an ochre-grey sky. The damp air drifted misty ribbons from gushing becks to mask the plain-ward path. Untroubled by the mist, we marched down into the foothills in swift safety.

As we cleared Uhrturm, the last foothill to the plain which is also known as The Sentinel or Watchtower, a Knight rode up to us. He was dressed in studded black velvet similar to my brigandine. Behind him rode two standard bearers, one carrying the Sun pennant on argent of Sinter Schwarzenberg, and the other the argent flag of truce. Behind the three stood a force of five hundred fresh, experienced and well-equipped soldiers.

I reached cautiously for my longsword, but Rehlein stayed my hand.

'So the Brothers of the Sun rally to my request for men, which accompanied my plea for gold,' said he aside to me. 'My second cousin Sinter Schwarzenberg is a cruel cur. He must see some fine booty from this war.'

Sinter dropped his right hand, and the Sun standard dropped

with it. Bertram signalled for the Raven flag to drop also in an acknowledgement of friendship.

'I hear you have a pretty war game to play against Nicolaus and Maladriuzzi, which you have no hope to win,' said Sinter.

'Aye, we have; and no time to dawdle on the road this day,' Bertram replied.

'Then let me join you. I have a score to settle with Maladriuzzi for deceiving me some years back. And I have a bone to pick with Nicolaus for killing my best hound.'

'I am glad to accept you to our side. Let us forward. We can talk on the road.'

Our journey paused while the Brothers of the Sun fell in with the Children of the Raven. Sinter paired with Rehlein, and I moved forward to pair with Bertram. The two standard bearers led the column from the front. While we waited for the foot soldiers to reassemble, Sinter joked with Rehlein.

'Who was that cadaverous bag of bones who rode beside you, cousin?' he asked, gesturing to me.

'That is Knight Gendal, my best friend, so mark your words, second cousin.'

'What, won't you call me bastard prince while we are allies, young buck?'

The two laughed and clapped each other's shoulders. Then Sinter appraised me with dark flashing eyes, hawk keen. His long brown curls were nearly as dark as his spangled doublet. His severe angular face smiled in youthful impudence.

'So you are the great Knight Gendal, famed across this fair empire, God's own earth. I see you wonder why I join you here. My father, Rehlein's great uncle, has an ever-open mouth. When food and wine don't pour in, a garbage of words pours out. He is a chatty fellow. He has told the world of your exploits and put the fear of God up Nicolaus. It is all invention, of course: the poor man is dotardly in his old age. He sees my second cousin as a demigod with whom only heroes can consort.'

Sinter turned back to Rehlein. 'Oh, cousin, you have been away too long. Your family needs you. Your brother longs to have you home. Then we can stay with each other and go hunting again, as we used to when we were lads. Though battle is such fine sport too. Do you think otherwise, Knight Gendal?'

His face turned back to me. He must have heard my snort of disagreement.

'Is that really of interest to Prince Schwarzenberg?' I asked.

He laughed. 'And a wit, too! What a great journey this is proving to be.'

After our forces had reformed, we rode on along the broad track through the trees through the foothills on the edge of Rabenwald. A mile further on, a horseman rode out from among the trees onto the curved track ahead.

'Hold! Who is that blocking our route?' Bertram warned. His short sword was in his hand.

The unkempt horseman was clad in green and brown. His standard was emblazoned with the Oak. I recognised him and stayed Bertram's hand.

'Hold, friends: here are my allies.'

I heard Sinter sheath his sword behind me, after Bertram had sheathed his.

'But there is only one,' Sinter mocked.

'Look up in the treetops,' I replied

'Does Knight Gendal mix with brigands and outlaws?' Sinter asked.

'Aye. They make good company.'

Our column halted. I rode up to the woodsman standing in our path.

'Greetings, Silvio. I am Knight Gendal. What brings you on this road?'

'We heard Rabenwald's alphorn and are rallying to your call,' he replied. 'I am John O' The Woods, who people call Silvio, leader of our small but valiant band.'

'We are right glad to see you, John Silvio. Will your band ride with us, or will you take your own paths to the battleground?'

'We will make our own way. Then we can reconnoitre the land for you. And we can send out scouts and sortie parties to assist your men.'

'Thank you. Your special skills shall be of great use to us. We ride to Dernfels to encamp and fight from its spinneyed tor.'

'To Dernfels, then.'

We clasped arms, and Silvio vanished into the trees. I returned to my place beside Bertram, and our force moved forward again.

'So we will not have the pleasure of their company,' said Sinter.

'Aye, we have,' I replied: 'But your sharp eyes shall not see them, unless they choose to be seen.'

'I would rather I did not see them at all. Still, the more at the party, the merrier it shall be. Cousin, what strategies have you planned?'

Our column reached Dernfels late afternoon. Walther's teams lit fires and set to work in the kitchen to feed our hungry soldiers. Some of Sinter's men erected a pavilion in the trees on the hilltop. Here, our leaders assembled to review my maps and outline our plans. Then we settled for a quiet night, knowing Nicolaus could not hope to arrive before that time the next day, however hard he ran his men.

We posted sentries to watch for spies, but the night passed without incident.

The following morning the camp bustled with men carrying out work details. The woodsmen foraged for food to supplement our supplies. The soldiers cut branches and saplings to make pikes and build palisades. Count Bertram, Prince Rehlein, Prince Sinter, General Walther, and General Aldwin met in the pavilion to hold a council of war. I also attended the meeting with the two standard bearers, ready to carry out their instructions.

'What numbers of troops can we expect Duke Nicolaus to mobilise?' Bertram asked.

'His personal Danuvian army is about two hundred strong,' Aldwin said. 'He can claim military duty from another eighteen hundred, but they are scattered across the Danuvian plain and are not skilled fighters. It will take time for them to arrive here after he summons them.'

'He may call in some political alliances,' said Sinter. 'At least his cousin has refused to support him. They say the King of Rome is unable to finance another army. His regular forces are defending the north east borders.'

'Nicolaus will have to depend on his mercenaries,' said Bertram with a wry smile.

'I don't trust Maladriuzzi to act in our best interests,' said Aldwin, voicing everyone's doubts. 'Have we heard back from him yet?'

'No,' said Bertram.

'He should have received the balance of the money by now,' said Sinter: 'I sent it as soon as we made camp.'

'Then he should have sent us confirmation that the deal is on,' said Rehlein.

'He should also be on his way here now with his company,' said Sinter. 'Send Knight Gendal to intercept him on the road and find out his intentions.'

'Won't his soldiers be travelling with the Duke's?' asked Bertram.

'No,' said Walther: 'The mercenaries will make far better time than the Danuvian forces.'

'Gendal?' Bertram called to me.

'I am on my way,' I said.

I left the pavilion, saddled Finstar, and rode away from the tense atmosphere of the military camp.

It felt a relief to leave the clamour behind and canter along the empty tracks through the woods again. Though I needed to travel with all speed, I knew I would also need my horse to be fit again for the morrow and therefore did not push him hard.

Shortly before midday, and two hours after I had bypassed the Wolfholz Tavern, I was nearing the edge of the forest when a woodsman dropped out of the trees in front of me. He looked a wild man, with clothes made of sacking and a tangle of long unkept mousy hair. I reined in my horse and stopped to speak to him.

'Show me your rings!' he ordered, and held up a German-bladed dagger to support his demand.

I drew off my left glove to show him my eagle and butterfly ring, and the Imperator's eagle. He nodded and grinned, his yellow teeth showing several gaps.

'Gendal! I have always wanted to meet you. What brings you here, when your friends are preparing for a pitch battle over by Rabenberg?'

'I am looking for the enemy forces.'

He laughed. 'We've had some grand sport with them. The

Duke's at least. They are taking the east high road. The bastard mercenaries aren't so green. They're taking the westerly track, with their best men at the rear of the column. They're about two miles from here.'

'Can I intercept them, Jack o' the Woods?' I asked.

He roared with laughter at the name. 'That's my brother. I'm John.'

I laughed with him. 'Yes, I've heard the woods are full of Johns.'

He laughed again and pointed back along the way I had come.

'Go back a league or so, and you will see a path between the trees to your left. That will bring you out just a little ahead of them.'

I thanked him and followed his directions. The path he mentioned looked little more than an animal trail, with trees crowding in around my horse. I had to keep my stirrups tucked in to avoid catching my feet on the branches. With little daylight coming through the canopy above, Finstar moved slowly, testing each hoof fall before planting it securely on the littered ground. It took us so long to follow the path, I feared I would come out too late to intercept the mercenary force. My fears proved groundless. When the path finally emerged onto a wider track, I could hear the rhythmic footfalls of a force of men marching towards me, about a furlong away.

I hid among the trees, waiting for the force to come by. A cohort of twenty cavalrymen headed the column. One of them carried Maladriuzzi's banner of the eight-pointed star. Behind the cavalry, rode Maladriuzzi himself with his bodyguard beside him. His infantry of a hundred and fifty soldiers marched behind. Thirty more cavalrymen rode at the back of the column.

I waited until Maladriuzzi was level with me. Then I rode out from the undergrowth and joined his side. His bodyguard leapt to his defence, drawing his sword to protect the Condottiero from me.

Maladriuzzi recognised me at once. He ordered the guard to sheath his sword and shouted to the column to halt for a brief rest.

The cavalrymen dismounted. The infantrymen sat down along the track, glad of an unexpected break. Once the soldiers' attention was elsewhere, Maladriuzzi spoke with me. We were the only two still on horseback.

'Knight Gendal,' he said with a sigh, as if he tired of the way I kept appearing in his life.

'The Raven sent me to ask your intentions,' I said.

A smile played on his face as he looked down at his hands. They rested on the pommel of his saddle, loosely holding the reins.

'Yes, the balance has arrived. On our signal, during the thick of battle, my men will flee from the field, leaving the Duke's forces to fight the Raven alone.'

Only after he had said this, he looked up at me, with that strange wry smile still curling his lips.

'We shall make camp with the Duke and his allies about two leagues from your forces,' he continued: 'Today and tomorrow are our travelling days. The day after that, we will engage.'

I questioned him but learned no more and only wore his patience thin. The meeting had not reassured me. I rode off again down the track heading southward, unconvinced of his true support. Behind me, his men formed back into their column and set off again.

I rode back to Dernfels. A look-out had been posted on the edge of camp. He let me pass. It was early evening and the men were queuing for their supper. I rode up to the pavilion and tethered Finstar outside. As I dismounted, my gauntlet fell to the ground. When I bent down to pick it up, I could hear low voices through the canvas pavilion walls. I turned to adjust Finstar's saddle, while centring my attention on the whisperers and their conversation.

'General Walther does not agree to it, cousin,' said Rehlein.

'Then command him, Prince. How can you hope to win back a principality when you cannot even give an order serfs will obey?' Sinter replied.

'He thinks me a coward.'

'Let him think that. What worth is the opinion of one puffed up little general spawned from a peat bog, against the honour of our family, the peace of your dead father, and your lost heritage? Are you fool enough to risk even your life for this paltry mountain?'

'You are, to but settle a score and avenge a hound.'

'Do not think I came here of my own volition. It was your great uncle, my father, who sent me, that he might live to see his favourite nephew rest easy in his grave. You and your brother were not the only ones to hear your father's dying request. Others, like my father, were present too nearby.'

'Then why did they not step in when he betrayed me?'

Walther and Aldwin walked back up through the tents to the pavilion, the sentry having alerted them to my return. I followed the generals inside. Bertram joined us soon after. As I reported my exchange with Maladriuzzi, I quickly forgot the strange conversation I had overheard.

'Maladriuzzi confirmed the balance has arrived,' I said: 'He told me he has ordered his men to flee in the thick of battle and so weaken Nicolaus. His men will encamp about two leagues from us, with the Duke and his allies. Today and tomorrow are their travelling days. They plan to face us the day after tomorrow.'

Bertram and the Generals were pleased with this report. But Rehlein could tell from my expression that I was not convinced.

'What is wrong, Gendal?' he asked.

'Do not trust Maladriuzzi. He smiled strangely when he gave me his pledge to help Rabenwald.'

'I don't think that toad knows how to look any different,' Sinter joked.

They discussed the probable effect of Maladriuzzi's planned move and agreed our men should not pursue the fleeing force. Rabenwald would stay safely on the tor, and leave freedom-seeking Danuvia to rise up and destroy the Duke's forces from behind.

Chapter 25
The Battle of Dernfels

We took our stations at dawn on the day of the battle. Many of the men had not slept well, but those who like me had already made peace with our God, woke refreshed. I watched from the front line, gazing across the undulating, mist-hung land.

From the spinneyed tor to the heathland plain, stretched a short, steep, rough common slope dotted with gorse and bracken. A marshy stream curved through narrow fields around the base of the hill, useful to hinder a heavy enemy onslaught. The Duke's attacking forces would have to wade through the muddy stream and run up the steep slope through our rain of arrows. When they reached our palisade, they would face our pikes, our poleaxes, and finally our swords.

On either side of our main force, small phalanges of our troops waited, ready to strengthen a weakening line or to rout the enemy at the end of the fray.

The air was charged with the tension of the waiting men. They stood, alert, unmindful of the thin drizzle which lightly wetted their mail and weapons. Ears strained to hear the distant marchers. Eyes scanned the wooded bluffs for movement. A raven circled overhead, wings stretched out on the bitter breeze. My horse stamped impatiently, his harness ringing. The man beside me fingered his prayer beads.

Our two scouts galloped in, warning of the enemy's approach. Shortly after their report, the plain resounded with the regular marching steps of a large force. As the enemy troops massed below us, Bertram's adjutant, Ditwin, summoned me back to the pavilion.

'Where have all these men come from?' I asked him.

'First reports say that with Duke Nicolaus' Wolf standard, fly the standards of the Falcon, the Boar's Head and the mercenaries' Eight-Pointed Star. Prince Sinter says that is an uneasy alliance. The Falcon and the Boar are bitter enemies most seasons, and grudging allies at best. The Count instructs you to return to the pavilion for your safety.'

'I shall mind my safety when I must,' I replied, placing my hand on the pommel of my longsword.

I was better dressed for battle than the men around me, with my light mail suit and my armoured brigandine jacket. Many of our fighters had no armour other than quilted cloth or stiff tanned leather, or pieces of chain mail taken as booty in other campaigns.

The adjutant saluted and returned to the pavilion. I rode along the line to encourage our brave, impatient men.

The enemy forces filed into formation on the far bank of the stream. Messengers darted between their columns. An ornate pavilion was erected behind their lines. Their statement of patient force did not trouble our soldiers. The men around me jeered, speculating on the spoils they would find when they took the enemy positions. It seemed Rabenwald no longer wanted only to free itself, but to sack Danuvia as well.

A buisine trumpet sounded in the enemy camp. A cry went up and the first three ranks of the enemy crossed the stream. They ran steadily up the hill. Seconds stretched as General Walther waited for them to come into range. Then his voice rang out, followed by our alphorn. Our arrows rained over the common, felling the sortie force. The few who got through fell foul of our pikes.

Immediately, up started three fresh enemy ranks, advancing steadily into our arrow fire. I realised Nicolaus's intentions and rode back to our pavilion. A page took my horse's head for me to dismount. I hurried inside to where Count Bertram and the two princes had gathered over my map, moving counters for men.

'Count Bertram, the enemy makes us waste our arrows. When they are spent, Nicolaus will send up his main forces,' I warned.

'No matter. We can make more,' said Bertram.

'Not in the numbers our bowmen are using and the short time they take to use them.'

'Can we retrieve those that missed their targets?' asked Rehlein.

'No. The enemy advances again too soon.'

Bertram nodded and turned to Ditwin. 'Tell General Walther to order his men to be more thrifty with their arrows.'

The young man nodded to him and hurried out.

I joined the three leaders around the map. Sinter moved some of the blocks representing the enemy forces.

'Nicolaus seems to be playing into our hands,' he said.

'Is it a feint?' I asked. 'His men move with disciplined timing, as if they know this is his battle.'

I moved some of the blocks to correct the enemy dispositions.

'They are encamped across the beck from us, on the other side of that hawthorn dyke.'

'So he has a certain confidence,' said Sinter.

'That will be with his four allies,' Rehlein replied.

'Four?' I asked, alarmed. 'I thought he had but three: Maladriuzzi's Eight-Pointed Star, Asher's Falcon, and Erhart Huber's Boar's Head.'

'There is Tilo's pack of Hounds as well,' Sinter said.

I ran from the pavilion and rode to the back of the tor. Cantering up the steep slope onto the saddle of the hill, rode a line of ten spear and lance-bearing cavalry followed by thirty infantrymen under the green standard of the Hound. I raced to Aldwin for help. He was stationed on the east flank, also on horseback.

'The back of the tor! The Hound's forces are storming the saddle with cavalry and foot soldiers!' I shouted.

Aldwin sent eight mounted lancers to create a defence there, followed by twenty infantry armed with pikes, axes and swords. He rode with the lancers and I followed with the infantry. The men fought beside us on the hillside to push the enemy back down the slopes.

The battle engulfed us. My shield and longsword leapt to my defence, and then, in the heat of the action, to attack. The advantage of my height on horseback helped me disable several of the foot soldiers who saw my brigandine and thought to win a fair prize.

Our rallied force soon put the Hounds to flight. They retreated swiftly, their surprise spoilt. Aldwin slapped my shoulder as we watched them disperse. We rode back to the pavilion side by side to report the incident. A page took our horses as we hurried inside.

All seemed calm in the pavilion. Sinter still fought with counters while Bertram and Rehlein watched.

THE EAGLE AND THE RAVEN

'My, my, dear Cara: your brigandine is a trifle torn; and you'll have need of it tomorrow,' Sinter mocked.

Too tired to reproach him, I poured out a goblet of red wine. Aldwin was in a different humour and had enough energy to throw him a retort.

'Whose callow youths quitted their watch on the tor's back end? They nigh had us butchered!' he roared with invective. 'Only Knight Gendal saved the bloody day!'

'At least the hour was saved, so what matters that now?' said Sinter.

I felt how much the two men hated each other. In other circumstances, they would have fallen out with fatal consequences. I handed them goblets of wine to break their cock-fight. Aldwin drained his goblet and left the pavilion. I hurried out after to pacify him. He waved his hand to silence me.

'How I would that cur were Nicolaus's!' he spat. 'But fear not, Knight Gendal. Through this little scrap, we shall stay allies at least, though we could never be friends.'

He rode off to post his own sentries along the back ridge of the tor. I returned to my station behind our front line. The enemy was continuing its steady attack in series of three ranks. Our archers had almost spent their arrows. General Walther called over General Aldwin and his infantry to relieve them.

As our last volley embedded in the rough grass, Maladriuzzi's crossbowmen ran forward in two ranks halfway up the slope. Their front rank dropped for the rear rank to fire a volley. Then, as the rear rank crouched to reload, the front rank stood to fire a volley. Our infantrymen raised their shields and ran back behind the palisades for protection. Nicolaus then sent up his infantry under cover of his crossbow archers' fire.

The enemy forces came upon us. They tried to scramble over our pointed palisade walls while pikers, swords and axemen fought them back. The fighting shifted and surged around either side of the palisade. Our phalanges struggled to hold them back.

All around me, flashing blades cut through the air and drew blood. Once again, my longsword sliced flesh and armour to protect me from death. But we were outnumbered and out-skilled, and certain to fall.

When in from the plain ran a horde of Nicolaus's serfs, sickles and axes in hand to end their years of oppression. The battle slowly turned back in our favour. We gained back some of our ground.

Maladriuzzi's force gave way to our right. The battle frenzy redoubled with the new advance. The men of the Eight-Pointed Star fled back down the slope. Our men forgot their leader's orders to stay on the tor and followed them down the hillside.

'Don't chase them! Come back!' I shouted, to no avail

My voice was just one of many in the clamour of the fray. Foolish Rabenwald pursued the mercenaries down to the plain.

Behind them surged in the reformed troops of the Hound. Our men became surrounded in the marshy fields, equal in number but lacking in skill.

Now I understood Maladriuzzi's smile when he had promised to order an unexpected retreat. He had known our poorly trained troops would follow. As untrustworthy as all his kind, the Condottiero had taken a little more of Nicolaus's money to ensure the battle would end the Duke's way.

Anger swept through me, intensifying the battle fever which had driven me before. Shouting at the foe as had all my northern ancestors, I swung my longsword in a rage, fighting over the bodies of my allies until it seemed I fought the host alone. I saw the armoured Prince Sinter fall, and then fiendish Johannes; and raged more viciously to seek revenge.

Finstar stumbled, almost throwing me. Instinct alone kept me in the saddle as I looked down, and saw Rehlein Hirschman's surcoat on the bloody ground.

At that moment, a Hound horseman picked a fight with me. He almost won, as the shock of seeing Rehlein's body had dulled my senses. Instinct alone made me jab my longsword at him. The lucky blow caught him askew. He fell from his horse and under Finstar's hooves.

I looked again at Rehlein Hirschman's surcoat. The armoured body lay awkwardly beneath it, helmet awry with a broken neck. Grief mingled with my anger as I turned back to face the foe.

On the hill behind me, the alphorn sounded once more. The signal played was the long, repeated note we had hoped never to hear – each man for himself.

The enemy encircled me. I fought desperately to break through, but the harder I fought, the fiercer the battle raged about me.

At last, a gap appeared. Swinging my sword to right and left, I heeled my horse and galloped through the melee to the open hill beyond. Three horsemen gave chase, following me west into the woods. I tried to lose them among the trees, but Finstar stepped on a sett and threw me. I lay in silence on the ground, half masked by bracken, bruised and winded, hardly daring to breathe for fear the rattling brigandine plates would give me away.

The enemy soldiers cast round for me. One spotted the hole in the bracken where I lay and rode towards me. As I struggled to find the energy to fight again, two woodsmen ran past him, fleeing from the battle. He rode off after them and the other horsemen followed. My head fell back, and I lay as one dead on the peaty ground.

Chapter 26
Broken Goddess

Night's stillness chilled the air when I became conscious again. I staggered from my bracken hide and called to my horse. Finstar whinnied back. He had been grazing nearby. I threw my arm over his shoulder in gratitude and affection. His muzzle gently nudged me as I ran my hands over his coat. His hide had been wounded in many places, but most of the cuts felt superficial. I struggled onto his back and lay slumped across his withers.

Rabenwald's dwindling beacon still burned above us far up the hillside. It gleamed for me now as a promised haven between Dernfels and Harzland, the country I needed to go to with the message of Rehlein's death. No other refuge would be open to a fallen rebel two days' journey from Danuvia. I prayed as my horse stumbled towards the castle that Nicolaus would not follow too quickly to destroy the rebuilt remains of Rabenschloss.

Clouds obscured the three-quarter moon in the dark night sky. The shadowed way stretched endlessly into pre-dawn grey. At length, I stood at the edge of the precipice in the rain and gazed across the void to the castle's raised drawbridge. Rabenschloss slept, and did not see the battle-weary ally who pleaded voicelessly at her stronghold gates. I slid from the saddle and fell to the ground. Finstar nuzzled my shoulder to try to rouse me.

I woke again shortly after sunrise, as people placed me on a canvas stretcher. They carried me over the drawbridge, across the courtyard and into the Lesser Hall. Mother Agatha tended me as she had tended Cunrad, on the refectory table, stripping off my brigandine and chain mail so that she could clean my wounds with brine to stop infection. I fought against her ministrations with the urgency of the warning I needed to give.

'Forget these scratches, Mother Agatha. Tell the people Rabenwald's army has fallen at Dernfels. Even now Nicolaus will be riding this way. Cara Rea will have told them the secret ways into the Castle. Tell everyone to flee for the Iyver. At least that can still be defended.'

'No, Gendal: we cannot leave yet. We hold this place in trust for Count Bertram and the Children of the Raven.'

Her calm voice was meant to reassure me, but it only made me struggle all the more.

'Rabenwald is more than castle walls. The Children of The Raven mean more to Bertram than this resurrected ruin. You elders must take the young to some hide to ensure this race and its faith survives.'

Exhaustion overcame me. I fell back into a fitful sleep, disturbed each time Mother Agatha washed another wound with brine. Some of my wounds were more severe than I had realised. Through pain's distancing haze, I heard her praise my loyalty and ask me questions about the course of the battle. My disjointed descriptions tailed away as a fever came over me. I fell into a turbulent dreamworld which overtook sleep and consciousness with its hazed memories.

I was back in Halsanger, following the river that was red with blood, through the fields, towards the distant clamour of battle and the acrid smoke of fire. The citizens of Berren fought valiantly against their undefeatable foe. The enemy, soldiers of the forces of evil, were far better equipped in every way. When one fell mortally wounded, he rose again, immortal.

The battle was futile. The Halsanger volunteers were mown down with no hope of advantage. Yet more and more volunteers stepped forward to fill the places left by their fallen brothers and sisters, wresting weapons from dead hands to carry on the fight. They still saw some hope in defending their beliefs with their blood and their lives in that futile battle.

I knew then I had to end that battle somehow. Did that mean that I now needed to end this? In that otherworldly country beyond the Tarn of Mirrors, I had had to sacrifice myself to start the change that would end the war. Was that my commission here? But how can one person fight against the established world order and bring about significant change? And what weapons should I reach for to engage in that fight?

Then my dreams turned into delirium. I saw the statue of the goddess Danu come alive and step down from her niche into the stream that ran through the cave. She took my hand and led me downstream to my home in Sluthe Wood. There she turned into the Green Lady of the water and brought me through the Tarn of Mirrors to the gateway of heaven. But once again the gateway keeper Arzandel turned me away, saying, 'Your time is not yet.'

I do not know how long I took to surface in reality. It seemed an eternity, though Mother Agatha contradicted that. She had managed to persuade the few last Children of The Raven to leave the Castle. It had not been easy, for in the height of my fever, she had needed several people to hold me down, and all had feared for my life. Ened had wanted to take me with them, but Mother Agatha had refused, certain that if I were to travel while so unwell, the journey would kill me.

Instead, she had the others hide me in the castle's secret cave, and stayed on to care for me, telling them she would bring either me recovered or word of my death to the Iyver at my fever's end.

I woke with a start, acutely aware that I was wearing no clothes under the blanket which covered me. Mother Agatha left the fire and came to my bedside. She rested her cool, gnarled hand on my forehead and smiled.

'Welcome back to the land of the living, Gendal.'

'Where are my clothes?' I demanded, fearing she had seen me naked.

'Do not fret, Gendal. Your secret is safe with me. I have made some broth. Would you like some?'

The broth she gave me tasted delicious. Its goodness revived me, and my supping it marked the turning point in my recovery. Over the next three days, I ate better and gained strength. I got up and dressed and wandered around the castle, and forgot immediate dangers. I visited my horse, whom Mother Agatha had also been treating.

Finstar whinnied in greeting to see me again. As we hugged, I heard a distant alphorn sounding from the mountains at the back of Rabenwald: a pattern of short and long notes signalling to the Children of the Raven in the hills. I let Finstar out into the courtyard and ran to tell Mother Agatha about the horn, repeating the pattern to her as best I could remember it.

'That is good news,' she said: 'Our survivors have reached the alpine pastures safely, and Bertram and Ened are with them. When you are fitter, we can join them there.'

I returned to the courtyard to groom Finstar and clean his stable. The effort tired me far more than I had expected. It was a relief to finish the task and return to my bed in the cave chamber.

A couple of days later, Mother Agatha and I were talking about her skills as a healer, when her head lowered unexpectedly in what I realised was shame.

'Something grave is on my heart, which I must confess to you, Gendal.'

She paused, seeking the words to explain what was burdening her.

'Weeks ago, you asked me to make up a gentle poison to send Duke Nicolaus to sleep forever. I mixed a poison for you, as you asked. But I hate the Duke for having my son Raban murdered so cruelly. So the poison I mixed was anything but gentle.'

'Then Cara Rea did not betray Nyze?' I asked.

'She didn't. I did; and most cruelly. It was my fault the Children of the Raven forced my grandson Bertram to bring forward the battle before we had fully prepared. Because of my hatred for that one man, I have all but destroyed our whole clan.'

I sat for some time, praying for guidance about what to say in reply.

'Mother Agatha, hindsight can be a harsh judge. I am as complicit in your crime as you, because I was the one who hatched the plan to murder one man, hoping to prevent the deaths of many. I was the one who asked you to make the poison. Prince Rehlein rightly criticised me for that.'

'But at least what you did was for the good of many. In my hatred, I just wanted to avenge the past.'

'It was a catalogue of mistakes by many that brought us to this present pass, Mother Agatha. Nyze chose to wear her own dress rather than take one from the royal household, which caused Duke Nicolaus to be suspicious. The Generals drew the wrong conclusions about Cara Rea from Cunrad's evidence. Bertram did not try to control your clan when the crowd pressed him to go to battle. And our soldiers disobeyed his command not to follow when the mercenaries retreated from the battle.'

'Are you saying you forgive me?'

'It is not my place to forgive. But I believe our God always forgives us when we truly repent. Would you make that same decision again, now?'

She shook her head, and almost whispered, 'No.'

'Then you are more worthy of forgiveness than me, for in those same circumstances I would certainly propose the same plan again.'

The confession seemed to put her mind to rest, but my own conscience unsettled me.

The next morning, I was exercising Finstar in the courtyard, when I heard men shouting on the far side of the curtain wall. I put Finstar back in his stable and headed back to the Lesser Hall. As I crossed the courtyard, I heard the clatter of wrought iron hitting stone. A movement made me look up. A grappling iron bounced against the crenellated wall and fell back.

I hurried down to the cavern chamber.

'We have visitors, Mother Agatha. You are dressed all ready. Quick, make your escape up the stairs and over the drawbridge now. I shall follow behind as soon as I have dressed for travel.' I knew I had no hope.

'Who will open the gate for me? Let me help you dress.'

She helped me put on the clothes that lay to hand, over my shirt and braies: my chain mail and the brigandine I had worn in battle. Both were much marked, but she had made some repairs.

The sound of subterranean scratching silenced us. The sound came from the far side of the balanced stone door to the chamber's river entrance.

'We must prepare for travel,' Mother Agatha said. She did not say what we were both thinking: whether our journey ahead would be in this world or the next.

She mixed a medicine from the jars on the shelves while I packed my saddlebag with the rest of my few belongings. When I had finished packing, she gave me half the medicine to sup.

'This will strengthen you for the journey ahead. The rest I have poured into a phial to help you later, whatever that may bring. Be warned, the strength it gives you today will be taken in payment tomorrow.'

The medicine tasted bitter and gritty to drink, but what a change it made in me. Fire stole through my veins as I girt my swords to my side. I turned to leave by the stairs upwards.

A crash resounded through the chamber as invaders threw down the balanced door stone from its pivots. We turned, our ears ringing. In the open passageway stood Maladriuzzi. I turned back and saw eight of his mercenaries spew out of the staircase from the hall.

With both exits from the crypt blocked by mercenaries, I gave up ideas of escape and turned to defence. I swung the table round before us as a shield to protect us from physical attack.

Down the steps from the Lesser Hall strode Nicolaus, handsome in his unmarked battle dress, his armour gleaming, the wolf emblem snarling at me from his royal blue surcoat.

'So this is the hovel where my fine Eagle hides to mutter incantations of vengeance and bedevil me still,' he said.

He strode up to me and leaned on the table to study my appearance with cruel eyes. Mother Agatha's medicine had heightened my senses. I could clearly see the patterns in his irises despite the flickering shadows cast by the torches lighting the room.

I raised the phial to sup more of the medicine's potency. Nicolaus struck it from my grasp. It smashed on the flagstone floor.

'There is no easy escape for you, traitor. Well pleased am I to take you prisoner, who proved so valuable to the rebels.'

'Adversary, aye, but traitor, nay. Ask the real traitor, Cara Rea. I am Free Knight Gendal, Ministerialis to the Imperator. I answer only to him.'

'You demoted yourself in flying east, winged one. What made you change your golden plumes for the black feathers of the Raven?'

'I was given the commission to seek justice for the poor, to fight oppression, and to set the captive free. You oppressed the Children of the Raven, you stole what was theirs, and those you did not capture and imprison, you killed. That is what brought me hither, Nicolaus.'

'Fool! Do you court death?'

'I have no fear of dying: I have already tasted the joys beyond the grave.'

'It is a little late to play the hero.'

'Why? All people can be heroes who have nothing dear to lose. But you should fear death, Duke Nicolaus. Those people who rose up against you, lived lives that were brief, beastly and desperate. Your rule made their existence a sordid futility, a hell from which even nothingness would be heaven; and all to keep you in your usual luxury while they struggled to survive after the Great Famine. God will hold you to account for that.'

'Impudent dog! Men, seize this heretic!'

'Not without fight,' I cried, and drew my longsword.

The mercenaries leapt forward to take me. Two dragged the table to one side as three others set on me. I had no hope of winning and fought only to bring as many down as possible before I fell.

Nicolaus called off the men, realising my intent to die a hero. They disengaged and stepped back. I stood in the centre of the floor, panting after the exertion. Nicolaus walked up to me.

'So, Knight Gendal, you would demonstrate your death wish, knowing I would only take you alive.'

I recalled Rehlein's body lying among the fallen on Dernfels and felt that same hatred and desire for vengeance which had led Mother Agatha into sin.

'Unless you lead me hence, Nicolaus, I shall not leave this cave alive; and you must take me first.'

'On point of honour! You shall be my prisoner of war! To sword, infidel!'

I lifted my longsword again and turned to face the Duke. He held a fine Italian blade much lighter than my Spanish friend. We circled cautiously. The mercenaries moved into a ring to line our fighting pit. They excluded Mother Agatha. She pressed against the wall by the statue of Danu, her face resolute.

Nicolaus lunged towards me. I engaged with a two-handed block, my blade parallel to my body to sweep his blade away. He attacked, I parried, he feinted, I swiped, he countered; all the time watched by the silent soldiers. Nicolaus leapt forward, his sword drawing blood. I swung my longsword across beneath his guard. His chain mail deflected my awkward strike. He responded with a remise of attacks which forced me back.

I realised the medicine which had restored my fever-weakened body, was interfering with the instinct that kept me alert to my combatant's second intentions. With such poor swordsmanship, I could not hope to avenge Rehlein's death before I died too. With nothing to lose, I threw the last of my energy into a frenzied attack.

My enraged swings at last put fear in Nicolaus's eyes. His long pin pricked me into greater fury. As my longsword hewed through all between us, he realised our unmatched weapons kept the outcome uncertain despite his greater skill.

He parried a blow with his sword's haft. The weapon flew from his hand, saving him. Maladriuzzi threw him his own sword.

Nicolaus fought closer to hamper my stronger strikes. I tried to keep back, but my staggers could not match his excellent footwork; nor did I realise his intention. The mercenaries moved aside as he forced me back until I pressed against the cold stone wall. When I tried to dodge aside, he put out his foot and tripped me. I fell heavily, winded, my sword flung away. Before I could recover, he was on me, his foot on my chest, his blade at my throat.

'An excellent fighter, as Commander Maladriuzzi warned me, despite your ancient sword,' he said. 'I claim your hatchet for myself.'

'An you take my longsword, take also his sister, lest her vengeance causes you regret, Nicolaus. Better still to kill me now while you can, lest I escape to continue the rebellion.'

'No. That would suit you, Knight Gendal, to return to your God before your natural hour. I cannot let that be. For all the suffering you caused me and mine, I shall give you suffering. In Aunsberg's deepest dungeon shall I keep you, where the sun never shines, till you learn at last to love the true Lord our God, and His wondrous gift of life. Then shall I kill you myself, when you scream to be saved.'

He released me to the soldiers and buckled my swords to his side. Then he turned to the statue of Danu.

'At last I can destroy this heathen idol!' he cried, and reached to take the statue from its niche.

Mother Agatha blocked his arm and tried to push him away. He struck the old woman so hard she fell to the floor. Then he crushed her neck with the weight of his foot until she breathed no more.

I gasped in horror to see such immoderate use of power. Even some of the mercenaries balked at the murder, recalling mothers and grandparents they had known.

'Such a heathen witch does not deserve to live,' Nicolaus said, to justify the deed.

He threw down the statue of Danu onto the stone floor beside Mother Agatha's body. The goddess broke in two. He pressed the catch in the empty niche to unlock the secret chamber and opened the door. He took out the bottle of myrrh and smashed it on the pieces of Rabenwald's god.

'At last, the end of Rabenwald, her insularity, her sedition, her power, and her hope. Let all heretics and pagans beware! As completely as Rabenwald falls, so shall fall all people and lands not lovers of the One True Faith!'

Inflamed with self-righteousness, Nicolaus spat on the objects of his vandalism, and gave the order to leave.

Chapter 27
Imprisoned

Aunsberg's streets lined with a silent throng for Nicolaus's triumphant homecoming. Victory was debated but not sung because Nicolaus had not recovered the standards of the Sun and the Raven from the battlefield. People stared scornfully at me, his only prisoner: they would have preferred another martyr to the Count of Rabenwald's cause. They did not know that Rehlein Hirschmann and his cousin Sinter Schwarzenberg had died for that Count.

The Duke paraded me in chains on my black horse, stripped of my armour and wearing just my surcoat over my shirt and braies. He had wanted my horse for himself, but I had trained Finstar to obey only me, which made the prospect too troublesome for him. Nicolaus presented me in the city church and exhibited me slumped over Finstar's pommel in the Drive during the afternoon carriage ride. How true was Mother Agatha's warning that her medicine would steal the strength of next day. With weary eyes, I watched Astra pass in her carriage, her pensive expression hidden behind a lace veil.

An unlit, unfurnished castle cell swallowed me to rot on its damp stone-flagged floor. For many days, I only saw light and company when my jailor brought me food and drink. I tried to make him talk, but he kept silent. He would not venture near me and scuttled from my stinking cell when I tried to hold him back.

I used my enforced captivity to exercise and pray. Both needed much attention after the rigours of battle and its consequences. Recalling St Paul's prayers in prison, I thanked God that I was still alive, and prayed for all those I had met with, both friend and foe, both living and dead. I prayed for God to take control of my future. Then I worked to build up my physical strength again, to be ready for that future, whatever it might hold.

After more than a week had passed, Nicolaus himself came to break my silence. He brought me some food and drink too. The jailor stood by outside the open door, ready to defend the Duke with sword and torch should I be foolish enough to attack my captor. I had to shade my eyes from the brightness of the Duke's lantern.

'Your journey north from Rabenwald demoted you, Nicolaus. Or does local custom require Dukes to serve messengers?'

Nicolaus ignored my surliness, He placed the tray of food on the ground and lifted his lantern to study me. Though I was lounging on a clean patch of the littered floor, I was no longer the fever-weakened invalid he had captured ten days before. My efforts spent exercising my body during those long, dark hours were already showing in my physique.

'Stand up when your overlord enters!' Nicolaus ordered.

'You are not my feudal lord. I am a free knight who kneels to no ruler but the Imperator.'

'Then I need fear no reprisals for your cage. Or are you of noble blood?'

'Nay, so no hope for a ransom.'

'I disagree. The clothes you wore, the horse you rode, the weapons and armour you owned, show generous benefactors for one born a commoner. I asked Widow Astra about your past – if you remember, she entertained us with some of your exploits when we met at my summer ball.'

'The Widow Astra was always good at turning a slight incident into an epic tale.'

'She told me your swords were a gift from the princes you saved. The brigandine jacket that served you so well came from the Count of Ziegenhein. Your chain mail was a gift from the Bishop of Munster. And your horse was a gift from the Imperator himself, from his own stables.'

I struggled not to laugh at Astra's fabrications.

'What a remarkable memory she has!'

'I have written to them all, telling them of your recent exploits and asking them how I should dispose of you. I await their replies before the end of October.'

'Why? How long have I been confined here?'

'Eight days. As long as Bertram Rabenwald was here. But be assured, it will not be so easy to spring you from this cell. So take this food and eat. You eat well, at least.'

I took the tray and picked over the food. After a diet of porridge and broth and stale bread, it tasted very rich to my palate. The meats were too salty and the little honey tarts far too sweet.

'Does this food not tempt you? It is of the choicest morsels from my table.'

'And excellent it is too, but why do you bother with me?'

'I thought that time spent in this dark hole would give you a chance to reflect. Maladriuzzi has great respect for you, as one who wreaked so much havoc with so few men. And now that it is over – now that the Children of Rabenwald are raven pickings and Rabenschloss is in ruins again, now the false god is overthrown and the luck destroyed, now the Cara has turned traitor and the Count is dead, and you are in prison for your loyalty – and still I rule Danuvia: how do you feel?'

'Naught. I feel only as I felt before. Why have you come to pester me? Is your lovemaking so ineffective that you must make your mark on everything else to prove your manhood?'

Though my provocation hit the mark, Nicolaus chose not to react. He studied me for a while. I wondered if King Herod had looked at John the Baptist in a similar way.

'Prince Rehlein called you Cara, too. What did that title mean between you both?'

'Where I come from, across the seas and outside the Holy Roman Empire, there is a caste of advisers known as the Anam Cara: soul friends. The connection between a person and their true Anam Cara is deep. Cara Rea did not deserve the title she awarded herself. Prince Rehlein heard me talking about such advisors and liked to use it of me when he sought more than just a listening ear.'

'Cara Rea spoke much of the elemental kingdoms. Over which kingdom do you have power?'

'Air's kingdom, thought; which shall ensure I leave here

without having to plan my escape.'

Nicolaus laughed in disbelief.

'What magic power does thought give you? Can you fly?'

'Nay. Nothing in this world happens by magic. Even miracles have an explanation, though we may not yet understand how.'

'You discredit God.'

'On the contrary, God's power is often explanation enough for me.'

'Cara Rea made much magic with her strange waters and powders.'

'Then she pandered to you to increase her power. A true Anam Cara is no travelling entertainer that he must perform tricks to please his audience and pay his way. Nor would Cara Rea do such things without some far more political reason. Guard yourself against her.'

'Your warning comes too late. Even now, the woman who called herself Cara Rea rides for Burgundy to play politics there. Her elder brother the Duke is dead, and her younger brother argues with his nephews over the inheritance... It does not surprise you?'

'Naught would now. Aye, I knew Cara Rea was an imposter. And Count Bertram knew. I showed him the evidence shortly before we rode out to Dernfels. That was the turning point which spurred the Children of the Raven to rush headlong into the fight.'

'The Count of Rabenwald? The hero I slew myself?'

'Aye, Raban's son Bertram. But I am sure he is not dead, for you would have paraded his corpse with me on your triumphal return to Aunsberg. He will be living safely with his wife where you will never find them, until such time as the signs are right, when he will lead Rabenwald on at last to victory.'

'Never! I shall crush Rabenwald till the marrow runs from its bones. It will never succour rebellion again!'

'Rabenwald's spirit lives not in land or luck. It lives on exiled in other lands now. However hard you crush your people, you will never kill their desire to rebel. Indeed, the harder pressed they are, the more their hearts yearn to be free. Your schemes will always fail, because you seek your people's respect with violence which only makes them hate you.'

'It also makes them fear, which is as good as respect.'

'Nay: fear compels half the man, when in respect he would act with his all. If you would end rebellion, you must take over each man whole. By the sword you can only take his body and his life: you will never take his mind and soul as well.'

'I could not make a loyal subject of you by fear, but few live without fear the way you do. Though my people live in fear of me, they also know I protect them from warriors and ruffians and bad winters, which they fear far more. They complain less heartily than you give them credit for.'

'What blinds you and deafens you, Nicolaus? Is it your vanity, your greed, your ambition? Each of your serfs is like you, with an equal measure of hopes, fears, strengths, weaknesses, prides and sorrows. Each one kicks back when kicked, as you do, or holds back his response to some safer time. Hatred surrounds you, which is all of your own making. You do not honour God's image in every man. Yet you would call me heretic!'

'These are serious claims you make. Where is your evidence to back them? Or does your death wish make you play the outspoken fool?'

'Aye, a fool I am, but not the greatest. The greatest fool is he who does not realise his foolishness. He underestimates his foe, ignoring him, while his foe plots darkly and attacks in stealth, his attacks unrecognised until the final hour when the two face each other alone in the secret chamber. Then his enemy cries, "I challenge you!" and he falls back unprepared, not knowing his foe's weaknesses or strengths, when his foe knows all his own.'

'Are you claiming that fool is me?'

'That is the position you have placed us in, Nicolaus. For I do listen. I heard what the people were saying in Nedauf. I talked with the people in your court, at your command. I listened to the gossip in the best houses and the poorest taverns. I know your strengths and weaknesses, and those of your noble court which you really must not trust.'

'You seek to undermine my confidence in the people I trust most! Even now, here in your prison cell, you fight a rear-guard action against me. Name names; give details; cite proof.'

'As you wish. Your Chamberlain diverts funds from the household purse for his own use. Your Cardinal ingratiates himself with you to increase his stipend and obtain a fief for his family. The ladies of your court wrangle to depose the duchess, Isadora. She is not averse to smiling on Knight Othmar of the Falcon, who is buying the services of a rival Condottiero to win Danuvia for his new empire. From there. he intends to assail the Imperator. Your eldest son Sigfrid looks northeast to Erhart Huber, thinking the Boar's Head standard might win him an early inheritance. How glad they are that you plot only to destroy the Raven, for they need not hide their own plotting when you blind yourself to their greater sedition.'

'Those are serious claims. And your proof?'

'I am your prisoner. What proof can I produce here in this prison cell? Go seek the evidence yourself. Use your eyes and start to see. Open your ears and start to hear.'

'And if your claims prove true?'

I sighed, and recalled again the gospel tale of Herod's repeated visits to John the Baptist in his prison, before Salome demanded the prophet's head in payment for a dance. The story helped me understand how lonely Nicolaus felt. The ducal crown lay heavy on his head. His power had isolated him in a sea of flatterers. He hungered for honesty and sought it from me, just as Herod Antipas had sought honesty from John.

'Do not punish them, for your own negligence contributed to their plans. Devote a little more of your attention to your lawful wife, Isadora. If you would punish her treachery, Knight Othmar would avenge to suit his greed for this land. Instead, bestir Erhart Huber against Knight Othmar in such a way that they use their common border for battle, rather than Danuvia as the march they both covet to win. They little like each other, so such stirring would not be hard. Take greater interest in your first-born son, Sigfrid. Keep him at your side in all you do for Danuvia. Teach him how to rule. Tell him war may soon end your life, and Danuvia must not be left leaderless. He will mock your instruction at first, but with care he will soon come to side with you.'

'And my Chamberlain?'

'Take him aside separately and tell him if you find aught else against him, he will be punished, but you respect his skills and would have him continue in office, while warning that another might do the work as well. Then keep alert for someone who would fill his place. Regarding the Cardinal, you can do little against him when the Pope has such political sway, but make him feel uneasy at court, without actual harm coming to him or blame being brought back to you.'

'And my people?'

'Ease their tax burden and your army's heavy policing. Check that your excisemen do not line their own pockets in your name. Employ your people to rebuild Aunsberg: its ruins are dishonouring to a noble Duke. Go among your people in disguise: appreciate their lot and try to eradicate the causes of their grievances.'

Nicolaus considered my words. He looked up, as if he had sensed my eyes were on him.

'Think not that I shall follow such advice, Cara Gendal, for I see clearly how it is coloured by your revolutionary beliefs. You are a rebel still.'

'I am a Christian. I am called to seek justice for the poor, to defend the oppressed, and to set the captive free.'

'That makes you no less dangerous.'

'I did not seek civil war in Danuvia, nor did I hold you as my personal enemy. Rather, I fought against what you represented: injustice and cruelty and the abuse of power. I tried to solve Rabenwald's grievances by peaceful means, but that was not to be. Were you to repent and change your ways, as our good Lord requires of us, we are enemies no more.'

'Cara Gendal, do not be surprised when people disbelieve you.'

He left. That was the first, and last time Duke Nicolaus visited me in my cell.

Chapter 28
The Mischief Night Ball

I was roused from sleep some two weeks later by two of Duke Nicolaus's own Danuvian soldiers. They dragged me from my cell, up the spiral stone staircase and out into the bright late autumn sunlight of the castle courtyard. The intensity of the sun blinded me after weeks of being kept in darkness.

THE EAGLE AND THE RAVEN

My abrupt departure from the cell made me expect some sort of moot court and a summary execution. My fears proved wrong. The soldiers took me across to the ducal apartments above Aunsberg Castle's main hall and left me locked in a room that looked as if it had been Cara Rea's boudoir. A fire burned in the hearth, making the room wonderfully warm. The elegant canopied bed was draped in rose and cream damask silk. Matching curtains framed the window looking onto the courtyard. Bottles and jars of plants, powders, and liquids were housed in a cupboard beside a workbench table with a stool seat. On the table stood a jug of water and a bowl. I drank some of the water and used the rest to wash, a delight after so many weeks of living in my own filth.

I lay on the bed and wondered what had caused this change of circumstance. The comfort was such that I fell asleep again. I woke in a panic, fearing the beautiful bedroom had been a figment of a dream; but no, it was still there: the daylight, the warmth of the fire, and the soft damask bed.

A servant entered with a curtsey and brought in my saddlebag. She wore the neat russet dress and white apron uniform of all the female servants in the castle. One glance at her told me why Duke Nicolaus had been suspicious about Nyze's appearance, for the servant's dress was crease-free and made of a much finer linen.

'Would you like me to unpack your bag for you, Sir?' she asked with another curtsey.

I rolled off the bed to undo the straps. A lot seemed to be missing from the shape of the bag.

'Where are my other things?' I asked her.

'They are being washed and mended, Sir,' she said, and bobbed again.

'Thank you. I will see to it myself.'

She curtseyed yet again and left the room, taking the used jug and bowl with her.

As I unpacked the few items that had not required washing or mending, I heard the sound of horse hooves in the courtyard outside. I opened the casement window to watch.

A two horse litter crossed the cobbles from the gateway to the hall below. The litter was painted with the arms of the Imperator: the black spread eagle on yellow, with the King of Rome's blue and white shield on the eagle's breast. As the litter stopped, Duke Nicolaus came out to greet his visitor, an elderly man I recognised as one of the previous Imperator's most trusted envoys.

The visitor's presence made it easy to deduce what prompted Nicolaus to move me from my cell. In response to the Duke's letter, the King of Rome had sent his envoy to examine the claims made against me. Nicolaus did not want to be found mistreating one of the Imperator's free knights. He had therefore arranged for me to be treated more appropriately for a well-connected hostage of war.

Other dignitaries arrived throughout the afternoon: Knight Othmar, Count Erhart, and envoys from Prince Rupert, the Bishop of Munster, and the Count of Ziegenhein. I feared Astra's exaggerations were about to get me into trouble.

The courtyard bustled with activity as the day wore on. Musicians and mummers arrived, kitted out for a festival. When servants hung turnip lanterns around the courtyard as dusk fell, I realised what it was: October 31st, All Hallows Eve and the Night of Misrule. The ball would be the start of three days of festivities celebrating the saints and other believers who had gone before.

The servant returned to my room, bringing me food and drink. Behind her came two valets with my beautifully laundered and mended surcoat, shirt, breeches, and braies.

THE EAGLE AND THE RAVEN

'The Duke has sent us to help you dress for tonight's costume ball,' the older valet informed me with a little bow.

'Sadly, I don't have a costume.'

'This court robe you wore the last time you attended the Duke's ball will be suitable. We can bring you a mask.'

'If you would. Draw me a bath also.'

They went to prepare the bath for me. After years of bathing in rivers and lakes, I appreciated the luxury of immersing my body in pleasantly warm water in the barrel-like tub in the ducal bathroom. Soothing herbs had been scattered in the water, and gentle white soap and dainty brushes provided to wash off the grime. When I finally dressed in my long white court surcoat emblazoned with the eagle and butterfly, over my best shirt and breeches, I felt transformed.

Two members of the Duke's personal guard escorted me to the hall for the festivities. They ordered me to sit on the dais, in the place Ened had been forced to sit the last time I had been there. A valet offered me a choice of masks held on sticks. I chose orange to match the colouring of the butterfly on my surcoat. A wine waiter brought me a cup of mulled wine punch, sweet yet tangy and far too powerful to risk drinking too much.

Soon, the guests started to arrive. I recognised many from the previous ball. All the most influential townsfolk, including Astra, had gathered before the Duke's triumphal entrance with Duchess Isadora on his left arm. We all stood to show our respect. Behind the Duke came the envoys. He provided seats for them round about him on the dais, but kept the closest seat for his wife. All wore suitable masks. The only other deferences to costume were the choices of dark colours for everyone's robes. My white court surcoat made me stand out among them all like a bright lantern on a dark night. I wished I had thought to wear my black brigandine, but to sport armour at such a social gathering would have been thought very rude to my host.

The mummers entered, running and cartwheeling across the floor of the hall. The guests moved back and lined the walls to make space for them. They performed a humorous morality play about the perils of flirting with the Devil, using costume and mime alone to tell the tale. When they bounded off again, the musicians struck up in the gallery and the dancing began.

I realised my presence on the dais was only to satisfy the envoys I was alive and well, and amused myself by watching the courtly games playing out on the floor below. When Nicolaus stood up to dance with Isadora, the entire court stood with them as convention required, but everyone was clearly surprised. Their departure from the dais gave the Imperator's envoy an opportunity to speak to me.

'Our excellency, the Imperator has received a letter of complaint from Duke Nicolaus about you,' he said, his tone cold.

'What was the nature of his complaint, Sire?' I asked in reply, aware that the other envoys were listening to our conversation with great attention.

'He said you were responsible for leading the uprising by Count Bertram against the legitimate granting of Rabenwald to the Duke by our excellency the Imperator, your Lord.'

'What else did he claim?'

'He said you played a key part in the battle of Dernfels. He claims to have arrested you after the battle, in the cellars beneath the rebel stronghold at Rabenschloss. There he found you consorting with a witch who tried to stop him from destroying her demon god.'

'The woman was no witch, Sire. She was the mother of Count Raban of Rabenwald. Duke Nicolaus had Count Raban mutilated and then murdered, when the Count had visited him in peace to discuss the terms of the grant by our illustrious Imperator. Had the Duke not sanctioned that atrocity, I would not have become involved.'

'Why? Did you see the murder?' asked the Ziegenhein envoy.

'No. I was staying the night at an inn in Eiswald, with Prince Rehlein of Harzland, when a witness to the atrocity came to the door, asking for someone to take a message to the Rabenwald Iyver. I offered, as that is my trade, and the young man was injured and desperate. The Duke's mercenaries tried to stop me, but I got the message through, and told Raban's son Bertram he was now the Count. The mercenaries tried to stop us from leaving the Iyver next day. When I returned that night for Prince Rehlein, we found the Iyver sacked and the innkeeper and his wife dead. They had been so badly abused before they died that Prince Rehlein swore to avenge the atrocity.'

'Duke Nicolaus informed the Bishop that you had been plotting with the rebels, and even tried to have him assassinated,' said the envoy from Munster.

'I tried to end the conflict by peaceful means. When that failed, I tried to choose the lesser of two evils. When those plans also failed, I did not think it right to withdraw.'

'St Paul tells us God has placed our rulers over us by divine right. Do you go against that teaching?' asked the Bishop's envoy.

'Isaiah says the just purposes of government are the commendation of good, the punishment of evil, the maintenance of peace and the protection of the oppressed. *Woe to those who issue iniquitous decrees, who turn aside the needy from justice, and rob the poor of their right.* Daniel says God disciplines rulers who do not obey His commands. So any edict that contradicts God's commands must be disobeyed.'

'Where did you hear such idle fancies about Holy Scripture?' asked the Bishop's envoy, horrified.

'I studied theology at the new university in Toulouse. This was at the behest of our illustrious former Imperator, who granted me freedom to roam. Both Church and State seek to stamp out gnostic Catharism.'

The envoy almost choked to discover how the university I had attended was spreading religious learning outside the confines of the church.

Nicolaus returned to the dais with his wife Isadora, paying her such attention that tongues were wagging among his regular ball guests. After they had sat, the rest of us were also free to sit. The music started up again, and queenly Astra worked her way around the room to the dais. She curtseyed to Duke Nicolaus and waited for his permission to speak before asking if any of the envoys would like to join the dance. When they refused, she suggested I might like to join her on the floor. To my surprise, Duke Nicolaus agreed. But then it became less surprising, as he began a long discussion with the envoys once I had left their presence. I came to suspect the whole matter had been planned.

Buxom Astra looked magnificent in her deep crimson satins. She danced well, making up for my deficiencies. I felt as if I were in a parallel world and at any moment I would wake back up in the darkness of that lonely cell.

Astra handled her mask with coquettish style throughout the dance. When the music ended, she drew me to one side, in a place where I would be clearly visible to everyone on the dais.

'Hasn't it been a wet October? No wonder you're looking a little pale, dear heart,' she said.

'I haven't been out much recently. However, you look radiant,'

I replied.

'I understand you have been very naughty.'

'The envoys would agree with you. But it was all in the cause of justice and peace. Isn't this dance rather naughty too?'

'Oh, no. The Duke himself instructed me to ask you.'

'Mischief night indeed!'

The Duke signalled to the musicians to play a short fanfare. When the trumpet fell silent, he settled back in his chair to make an announcement.

'My people, I am right pleased with the outcome of our recent little skirmish at Dernfels. To celebrate the unification of my duchy, I have ended the emergency measures in Danuvia and lifted the curfew in Aunsberg. Tomorrow I will also begin the rebuilding of my city. Thus may all Danuvia rejoice with your Duke's rejoicing.'

The news stunned the gathering, including me. I had not expected Nicolaus to take up any of my suggestions. No-one cheered his announcement, and I did not have the gall to respond. To end the shocked silence, Isadora signalled to the musicians to play on.

I realised that Giacomo Maladriuzzi was standing nearby and turned to him. Even at this light evening's celebration, the heavy, red-faced Condottiero looked a shrewd untrustworthy military man.

'Does the Duke's announcement mean your army's services are no longer needed here, Commander?' I asked.

His smile was cat-like. 'Not at all. I see your master's envoy has spoken to you. If he has withdrawn you from the Imperator's service, my offer is still open. My Standard has need of people like you.'

'You need people like me? When your Standard reneged on your contract and turned the battle in the Duke's favour?'

'Such naivety! Did you never fall upon the reason for my smile when I accepted? Whichever way the battle turned at Dernfels, my force was on the winning side. So forget Rabenwald's fall. I know it was not your battle you fought, just as the battles we fight are not ours. Rather, think on my offer.'

'It shall be considered.'

He strolled off into the throng. I turned back to Astra, knowing she would have hung on every word of our conversation. She hid her expression with the skilful use of her mask.

'Dear Astra, was it your loyalty to the Duke which made you slip that letter into my pocket the last time I was here, as you told me to leave Aunsberg by the South Gate?' I asked her.

She waggled the mask in reply to censure my directness before answering with words.

'Gendal, I knew you were astute enough to foil such a petty ruse. I had to do it to show my "loyalty" to the Duke. Leander the innkeeper had made sure everyone suspected your new identity. Had I truly wanted to betray you, I would have done so when you came back from your midnight walk. The ruse earned me good credit at court, saved you, and alerted a family sympathetic to Rabenwald's cause. Ah, Gendal, you have the cunning of the road; but I have the cunning of the court, which can outwit the greatest general. Even Cara Rea.'

'You were wise to her tricks?'

'But of course. They were naught but schemes of wilfulness and power. Marie of Burgundy forgot to guard against Rabenwald's dialect: she thought it was the same as Danuvia's. Several of us realised she was a foreigner, not a native of Rabenwald. Between us, we pieced her story together from some off-guard comments she made. But none of us dared expose her to Nicolaus for fear of his displeasure. How do you like my plot to rid Danuvia of her?'

'What? Is her brother the Duke not dead?'

Astra laughed, peals of silvery laughter.

'The only messenger she could trust was you, Gendal, but her greed for power made her forget that. She will be furious when she returns home to a right royal welcome from her brother the Duke and the fire they will build for her.'

I laughed and clasped her hand. As I did so, I felt the point of a dagger press into the small of my back. I turned my head to look at the assailant, and saw the long, haughty features of the Chancellor. He was dressed in black velvet, like some sort of elegant fiend.

'Would you like to see your homeland again, Knight?' he hissed.

'What are my desires to you?'

'I would help you escape Danuvia.'

'Aye? What if I do not wish to go?'

'You'll be worm meat ere the week is out.'

'I must be a barbed thorn in your side. Leave me be, Chancellor. I dislike your tone.'

'Not as much as I dislike your face. Nor shall I leave without you. My coach awaits to take you to the border.'

'To cross the Duchy in the curfew hour?'

'Did you not hear the Duke? Are your ears already so filled and your head so stuffed with schemes to bewitch Nicolaus that you cannot take notice? Thanks to you, our land is no longer under martial law. Should you cry out, no-one will hear.'

'What of the Duke's guards posted to watch me?'

'They are here, waiting to escort you. Come! Your few things are already packed. Take Widow Astra's arm and walk out of the hall.'

I obeyed. The concealed knife pressed to my side ensured I did not make a disturbance unless I had a sudden yearning to be disembowelled. I stepped out into the courtyard, wondering what new schemes, what new betrayals were about to be played out on this mischief night.

Chapter 29
Kidnapped!

Astra and I walked out through the main doors into the courtyard, where we were flanked by a cohort of twelve Danuvian guards. At the foot of the entrance steps waited the Chancellor's coach, black against the shadows, its insignia painted out. Nicolaus's footman opened the door for me to alight. As the Chancellor escorted Astra back into the ball, I settled in the small corner of the coach left by the two soldiers sent to accompany me.

The footman closed the door and signalled to the coachman to go. He urged the two pairs of horses to trot on and the coach lurched forward into the chilly night. The cohort of guards marched with us: two pairs ahead, a pair on either side, and two pairs behind. Such elaborate arrangements warned me they were taking me to certain death. For why would the Chancellor squander money and risk his position to help me escape, when one simple act could end my meddling forever?

I sat back to plan what my next moves should be, dropping my head on my chest to give my captors the impression I sought sleep. With thought, it was obvious why Nicolaus had been happy for me to attend the ball in my white surcoat, when all his other guests wore dark costumes. He himself was the person behind this kidnap attempt, to dispose of me in such a way that the four envoys could not censure him. My situation was dire. I had no weapons, no armour and no allies. I prayed to God to send help for me, and planned to resist whatever way I could as circumstances unfolded.

The coach lurched to a halt.

A commotion outside alerted me. We had stopped at Aunsberg's south gate. The soldier next to me leaned across to shout out of the carriage window.

'What is happening?'

'We need to check who's with you,' said the gatekeeper.

'On whose authority?' demanded the soldier.

'Your master, and mine.'

The gate keeper opened the carriage door beside me and raised his torch to see my face. The flames were so bright, I could not see him in return. He slammed the door and stepped back.

'That's fine. You can pass! Open the gate.'

The two gate sentries lifted the bar and dragged the two gates open wide enough for the coach to go through. Barely had the wheels cleared the opening, they shut and barred the gates again.

The carriage lurched to a halt. The soldier beside me dragged me out onto the road. He held me in an armlock and raised his dagger to strike.

The coachman leapt down on top of us both, smothering the soldier with his cloak before he could make the fatal blow. Around us, other men rushed to join in the fight. They looked to be a crowd of well-armed ruffians, enjoying the chance to take on the cohort of Danuvian soldiers.

The coachman threw his cloak over my shoulders to cover my white surcoat and dragged me away from the fray. We fled about fifty yards along the city walls, to where two horses were tethered in the shadows. The coachman handed me the reins of one and mounted the other.

The whinny of welcome as I mounted my beloved black stallion, Finstar, brought a tear of gratitude to my eyes. I hugged his neck in relief and affection.

The coachman led me away down a path onto the highway. We rode as fast as our horses cared to go by the cold light of the three-quarter moon. After travelling a short distance south, we turned westward down the Groshe highway and later another road leading northward.

We rode for over an hour before halting. The coachman led me into a hay barn some distance from any village. A shadowy figure shut the barn doors as we dismounted, and then opened the shutters on a night lantern so that we could see. I discovered my coachman rescuer was none other than Count Bertram. His helper was Friar Fadrique.

Bertram laughed and clapped my shoulders in his joy at pulling off such a daring rescue. I hugged him and Fadrique in gratitude and relief.

'Count Bertram! Friar Fadrique! How? Why?' I stuttered.

Bertram laughed again.

'I had a debt of honour to rescue you, Gendal, after you risked so much to rescue me.'

'And I could not let the Count attempt that on his own,' Fadrique said.

'But that you're even alive!' I said.

'It was a bloody rout at Dernfels, wasn't it?' Bertram admitted. His face became grave. 'We lost half our fighting men there: mostly those who followed the mercenaries down the hill. One day, I'll avenge that. And Maladriuzzi will be the one who'll pay.'

'The last time I saw you was in the pavilion, fighting the battle

211

with Prince Sinter's counters.'

'We joined the battle when it was at its height. I saw your friends fall and you fighting like a madman in a rage to avenge them. I lost sight of you in the rout after our men followed the turncoats down the hill. Then, when I saw how the battle was going, I ordered Ditwin to take our standard from the field. After our alphorn called "each man for himself", I didn't see you again in the scramble of the retreat.'

'I fell from my horse in the bracken. When I came to, I found my way to Rabenschloss and warned your people there to leave.'

'Yes, they joined us in our alpine refuge, and told us you had turned up there. Mother Agatha had insisted they left you and her behind.'

'Sadly, she paid for it with her life, after she had saved mine.'

Bertram took a deep intake of breath and sat down on a heap of hay.

'What happened?'

'The Duke's army gained entry to the castle using grappling irons. They knew where we were hiding. Cara Rea must have betrayed the castle's secrets. I was too weak to stop them. Nicolaus threw down the statue of Danu and smashed the bottle of myrrh on its broken pieces, thinking he had destroyed the Luck of Rabenwald. Mother Agatha tried to stop him. The Duke crushed her throat for being a heretic and a witch.'

Count Bertram broke down and wept. I wished I had chosen my words more carefully, recalling too late that Mother Agatha must have been his grandmother. To give him space to grieve, Fadrique spoke of his own part in the rescue.

'I was in Aunsberg when the Duke's forces returned from the campaign. Count Bertram had sent me back to the city to find out how many of the clan had been taken prisoner. You were the only one.'

'He must have known Rabenwald had no money to pay ransoms after paying Maladriuzzi. He thought he could exact payment from my previous benefactors to help pay for his military forces. When their envoys arrived instead, he must have been very disappointed.'

Fadrique laughed. 'He knew they were sending envoys. They had not recognised you in his description of Knight Gendal, the rebel leader, and told him so.'

'How do you know this?'

Fadrique laughed again. 'I became acquainted with the Widow Astra, hoping for better accommodation than Nedauf. I knew from what you had told me of your exploits in Aunsberg that she would be an ally, not a foe. She took me in as her Father Confessor, or as you would call it, Anam Cara. From there, I got to hear all the court gossip, and all the Duke's news.'

He saw my doubting face and smiled to reassure me.

'Widow Astra is very skilful at walking that fine line between keeping her position at court and her loyalty to you as the person who saved her husband and brought him home. It is a role she was born to play, and she played it to perfection.'

'Including escorting me from the ball to the Chancellor's coach and certain death?'

'Yes, including that. She had won the Duke's complete trust. He told her everything: how you would appear at the ball to satisfy the envoys, how he would use the reforms you suggested to further his plot to have you killed, how he would make your death appear an unfortunate accident in a clash between your kidnappers and his soldiers.'

'Yes, I thought my kidnap from the ball might be the Duke's

work.'

'Astra told me all the details. That gave us enough time to put together our plan. Count Bertram was already in Aunsberg, posing as a wool merchant as he looked for a way to rescue you, the way you had rescued him. It was easy for him to replace the Chancellor's coachman.'

'And most convincing he was too. But to be reunited with my horse?'

'Astra had bought your horse from the Duke after he found the beast unrideable, and stabled it for us outside the city walls. She also offered to have your possessions laundered and mended as a favour to the Duke, and had them sent to the stable too, together with your swords. She just kept back the surcoat and breeches she knew the Duke wanted you to wear to make you stand out in the crowd.'

'So that's why my saddlebags were so empty. And the men waiting for us on the other side of the South Gate?'

'I called on some of my friends from Nedauf who love a good scrap at the Duke's expense, and they were there ready to stop the only coach that would pass through after the lifting of curfew.'

I shook my head, humbled by the organisation of the people who had risked their own safety to rescue me.

'How can I repay you all so great a debt?'

'The time will come, Gendal, when they shall send for you. While Count Bertram lives, the desire for a better world shall not die in the hearts of the children of Rabenwald. And powerful allies still live in Danuvia to overcome Nicolaus.'

'But why did Rabenwald fall if such allies still exist?'

'Rabenwald thought to destroy the poisonous thorn by cutting off its branches. When the first branches fell, the thorns destroyed Rabenwald again. Count Raban and you saw you had to destroy the roots for the tree to die. Raban tried in the summer when the tree was strong and failed. You tried in the autumn when the fruit fell to produce a thicket, and so almost died. But those who are left shall wait until winter weakens the tree. Like the patient farmer, they shall poison its roots and strip a girdle of bark from its trunk, and the tree shall fall.'

'Are you are throwing in your lot with Rabenwald, then?'

'That, Gendal, is in God's hands, not yours or mine.'

We slept the night in the hay barn and set off again soon after first light. Friar Fadrique returned to Aunsberg to support Widow Astra. Count Bertram and I headed towards the river border between north Danuvia and Erhart Huber's County of Aacheim. I felt as if I had been brought back from the dead, to be astride my faithful Finstar once more, with my trusty brigandine and chainmail to protect me, and my longswords to hand. I rode north west, adventuring with Bertram as I had once ridden with Rehlein.

The memory of that golden prince mouldering in a battle grave, clouded my spirits. Rehlein's ring and letter were still in my safekeeping, waiting for me to carry out his last instruction and take the news of his death to Harzland. Before I could do that, I needed to escape Danuvia.

The northern marches were flooded after the Danube had burst its banks with the unusually heavy autumn rains. Bertram and I arrived in the region two days after the midnight rescue, to find the ancient Roman road over the border impassible with flooding. The bridge that should take us out of Danuvia and into freedom, looked so close and yet was tantalisingly out of reach.

We stayed that night iat the Danbrucke Inn on the forested flood bank south east of the swollen river. The innkeeper was grateful for some custom. He had put up few travellers recently as the weather had been so poor, people had not venturing out of the safety of the cities. We sat down with him, his wife and children to a simple yet heartening rabbit stew with home baked flat bread.

'Yes, the floods have come early this year,' said the innkeeper.

'They came on so suddenly, they ripped all the boats from their moorings and washed them downriver,' said his wife.

'Yes, and the water's not covered the full flood plain yet, so things may well get even worse.'

'But there's no need to fret: you're safe enough waiting here till the floods go. The water's never come this high, in all the time our family's lived here.'

Bertram and I got up the following morning to inspect the flooding from the vantage point of the forested flood bank. The waters were still too high to risk taking the road to the bridge. The ancient arched spans rose out of the waters that surrounded them on all sides, impossible to reach. Between the swollen river and the bank where we stood, lay a swathe of undulating land which looked as if the dip had been an earlier course of the river. The rough grass gleamed wetly in the weak early November sun.

For a while, the only sound we heard was the wind blowing through the bare branches of the trees. Then the birdsong stopped. We became aware of the distant rhythmic hoofbeats of horses cantering towards us along the road from Aunsberg,

Bertram and I looked at each other in dismay.

'The Duke has caught up with us,' he said.

'Ride for your life,' I urged him. 'There is no sense in us both dying here, when Rabenwald needs you to rebuild it again.'

'Perhaps not, but there is honour. You fought my battle at Dernfels. So now I must fight yours at Danbrucke.'

Once again, I marvelled as a commoner at the strange concept of chivalrous honour which so inspired this able man to risk his life with me.

'If you must, then let us at least choose our battleground.'

'Let's take to the last ridge before the flood. Then at least our foes are all out in the open before they attack.'

We rode off down the old Roman road towards the bridge, across the wide grassy dip to the top of the ridge which stood about a man's height above the lowest point. There we turned our horses to face the Duke's cavalry with the floods behind us, our longswords drawn ready for the final confrontation.

Chapter 30
The River Decides

The November wind chafed our faces as Bertram and I waited on horseback with our backs to the flooded road, preparing to face Duke Nicolaus and his men. All too soon, the cavalry coming against us topped the brow of the road, the weak winter sun gleaming on their weapons and armour.

The standards of the Wolf and the Eight-Pointed Star fluttered above the horsemen, warning us this would not be an arrest but a fight to the death. The cavalry deployed against us, fanning out in a semicircle on the edge of the bank above the floodplain. Their formation ensured they would push us back into the flood waters if we did not stand and fight. They stood waiting before they advanced towards us across the grassy dip: a hundred horsemen and fifty lances ready to fight just two. The Duke and the Condottiero were so confident of their victory, they rode side by side at the centre of the arc of cavalry, their horses more sure-footed on the Roman road.

My heart fell, as the forces ranged against us intended. Then I heard shouts from behind us. Bertram and I turned to look back.

Eight flat-bottomed zillen boats were sailing across the water towards us from upstream. They were powered by the river current and their four-sided balanced lug sails. Their canvas bore the Boar's Head standard of the Count of Aacheim, Erhart Huber, who had ridden with the Duke against Rabenwald at the Battle of Dernfels. The boats each held eight armed men. Their weapons included pikes, halberds, flails and spiked morning star clubs.

'We are surrounded!' I cried in alarm.

'Don't worry! They're here for the scrap, not for us,' Bertram said.

'What? Has Erhart come to help us?'

'No. They're here to take advantage of our situation. If we defeat the Duke, Count Erhart will make his son Sigfrid, duke.'

The zillen came in as close to us as their shallow drafts would allow on the floodwaters. They dropped their sails and anchors. As the Danube was the border between Aacheim and Danuvia, the boats were still politically on the border where they had anchored, even though the river had burst its natural banks. However, Duke Nicolaus took their position southeast of the normal river bank as an invasion. He ordered his men to advance.

The Danuvian cavalry charged. As they cantered forward down the slope, an uncanny roar augmented the thud of their horses' hooves on the road and the turf. Movement to my right made me look aside. A wall of angry water was flooding down the dip from the west, dragging debris along the old watercourse they were crossing. Before the horses could cross the gully, the flash flood was upon them. The powerful waters swept the legs from under most of the horses and dragged them downstream with their riders. Only Nicolaus and Maladriuzzi could outrun the torrent, as their horses fled towards us along the solid Roman road.

Our ridge had become an island. Behind us, the zillen boats had raised their anchors again to run with the flood, leaving Bertram and me to face Nicolaus and Maladriuzzi alone. We rode our horses to the brink to meet them, our longswords drawn.

Maladriuzzi's bay horse was the first to scramble out of the water onto the grassy bank. The bay stumbled as he struggled up the slope, throwing his rider to the ground. Before Bertram had thought to use the advantage of his height on horseback to attack, Maladriuzzi sprang to his feet and hit Bertram's horse hard across the nose and face. The horse backed off and reared, throwing the Count. He landed with a thud at Finstar's feet, making him shy to the side. I kept my seat and used my sword to keep Maladriuzzi back, while Bertram recovered.

The Count rolled over and onto his feet in a smooth, skilled movement, well used to handling falls. He brandished his longsword and fell on the Condottiero. At last he could avenge all the wrongs Maladriuzzi had committed against his family and clan. The Italian repulsed his wild swinging with calculated calm. He blocked and dodged his wild longsword swings with relatively little effort. He was letting Bertram tire himself out.

I turned Finstar towards Nicolaus as his horse scrambled out onto the grassy bank. The Duke's lance bucked wildly, exaggerating the stumbling gait of his horse up the slope. I struck across the bucking lance with my longsword, using its momentum to help me knock it out of the Duke's grip. He drew his sword from its saddle scabbard and rode straight at me, intending to injure my horse. I turned Finstar's head aside to avoid the attack, but yanked his reins so harshly, he reared and plunged back down with his hooves across the withers of the Duke's steed. This knocked Nicolaus out of his saddle as I fell out of mine.

We stood and faced each other on the narrowing bank, our sword blades almost touching. His fine Italian blade crossed my heavier Spanish longsword. As we circled each other, we could hear Bertram still slashing at Maladriuzzi. The Italian jeered each time the Count's swing failed to make contact.

Nicolaus lunged. I stepped back and aside to dodge the stab, then swung my blade to knock his blade aside. He used the movement to swing his sword in a circle and come under my guard. I stepped back again and realised he was trying to force me off the bank into the raging water. I corrected my footing and forced him to turn so that we faced each other along the length of the bank rather than its width. He tried the thrust again. This time I turned my body and swung my sword with a double handed grip. My blade crossed under his swing as his sword passed my side without making contact. My blade cut a tear in his surcoat.

'I should have had you killed the day we met!' Nicolaus snarled.

'The way you murdered the Countess of Rabenwald?' I replied.

'I executed a heretic. And I shall do the same here too, kidnapper!'

He lunged and swept his blade across my legs. I had to leap above the sword to dodge the blow. As I landed, I swept my blade down and caught him where his shoulder met his neck. Though saved from the mortal blow by his chain mail, he staggered under its force and drew back to recover, panting. I rested briefly too, feeling my own relative weakness after weeks of idleness through fever and imprisonment, despite my measures to counter it.

Maladriuzzi was fighting Bertram back now, taking control of their duel. The Count was tiring and struggled to stay engaged.

'Don't forget Raban, Count!' I cried to him: 'Don't forget Hans and Anna and the Iyver! Don't forget the betrayal and the gold!'

A fresh fury came over Bertram. He stabbed and jabbed and swung in such a frenzy, the bulky Condottiero could not move quickly enough to retaliate. Blow after blow crashed through the Italian's defences. He fell to the ground, helpless to defend himself. Bertram dispatched him with a blow of such force across the throat, it broke through his chain mail and severed the jugular artery. Still maddened, Bertram rolled his dying body into the raging river. The powerful current dragged it away.

Nicolaus saw his ally fall and turned to face me once more. For the first time, I saw a look of fear on his long, arrogant face. I slashed my sword across the front of him, forcing him to step backwards with each swing. He parried and thrust in response, but with an uncharacteristic wavering of co-ordination. His feet were now planted in rising water, and the water had seeped through his chain mail overshoes. My own feet were also standing in water, kept dry by the leather riding boots I was wearing.

I slashed my sword across his body one last time. He staggered back and felt the bank crumbling beneath his feet. Desperate to avoid being dragged away by the waters, he dropped his sword and reached out to grasp my leg.

'Help me! Save me from the river!'

'The mercy you showed is the mercy I give. You threw down Danu from her shrine. Her river, Danube takes revenge.'

'I smashed the Baal!' he protested, fighting against the torrent dragging him down towards the river. 'I destroyed the heretic!'

His head went under, weighed down by his armour and mail. As he drowned, the river torrent dragged his body away.

Chapter 31
The Boar's Head

A cold rain was falling as I turned back from the water's edge. The water droplets hit my face like tiny needles with the strength of the wind blowing up the river. Bertram stood at the far end of our rapidly shrinking bank, trying to reassure the four horses. He looked worried. The flood waters were rising rapidly, and he did not want us to suffer the same fate as our foes.

'Should we make a run for it?' he asked.

'It's the best we can do,' I said.

We sheathed our swords in our saddle holsters and were about to mount up again when we heard more shouts coming from near the marooned bridge. Four of the zillen boats had come back for us, pushed back upstream by the strength of the wind. The boatmen dropped anchors and furled their sails. Then they shouted instructions to us.

'Throw your saddlebags on board. Give us the reins. Then climb aboard. The horses will swim if we keep their heads above water.'

We struggled to wade the short distance through the floodwater to the anchored zillen. The warriors reached out to help us while the boatmen strove to keep their boats steady against the current. We passed over the horses' reins, giving one horse to each boat, and threw their saddles into the boats so that the horses could swim unencumbered. I helped Bertram heave himself into the boat towing his horse. Then I heaved myself into the boat towing Finstar, just as the river obliterated the last small traces of ground from beneath my feet.

The boatmen raised their anchors and let the current take the zillen, leaving their sails still furled. Bertram and I joined others in encouraging our frightened horses as they swam behind us. The current dragged us downstream while the wind strove to push us back. The journey seemed endless.

Eventually, the boatmen steered the four zillen into the calmer waters of the main river and crossed to the far riverbank. They moored near the four other zillen we had seen earlier. Strong arms helped us onto the bank and unloaded our gear. Other men coaxed our terrified horses out of the water onto firm ground. We gave thanks to God and to the men of the Boar's Head for our deliverance, and flopped back on the wet grass to recover from our ordeal.

The boatmen lifted their zillen out of the water and carried them high enough up the river bank to keep them from floating away if the river rose even higher. Then we made a weary and wet two-hour trek across sodden fields to Erhart Huber's fortified manor house. This rambling half-timbered farmstead had been built on a high bank well above and overlooking the flooded river.

Count Erhart himself welcomed us as we entered the courtyard. Stable hands took the horses and servants brought in our possessions. Bertram and I dried ourselves by a roaring log fire blazing in a large stone fireplace. The Boar's Head motif decorated the dark wooden mantlepiece over the fire. While we enjoyed the Count's hospitality in the entrance hall, he spoke with his warriors elsewhere.

The outcome of those talks must have been favourable for us. That evening, Erhart set a winter feast before us all. He feted everyone who had been involved in the day's events, and celebrated the victories: ours over Duke Nicolaus and Maladriuzzi, and the boatmen's victory over the water.

THE EAGLE AND THE RAVEN

Erhart had the sort of youthful-looking face which made it hard to judge his age. He was fair skinned with grey-blond hair and a ginger beard. His blue eyes crinkled at the corners as if he saw the absurd in everything. I could see why Sigfrid, Nicolaus' son, had taken to him.

Sigfrid sat on the top table with us at the feast. He was a coltish young man, with the same long face and black hair his father had had, but without the arrogance and cruelty of expression.

'I offer you my condolences for the loss of your father, Sigfrid,' I said.

The young man blushed and made no comment. I sensed his inner conflict as he faced the dilemma between feeling glad his father had gone, and his fear of the enormous changes which the future now held for him.

'Yes, and not by your hand,' Erhart said.

'It was a close-run thing,' said Bertram.

Erhart frowned at him with crinkling eyes and stated firmly, 'Yes, not by Gendal's hand. My men saw it all. They told me how the river dragged Nicolaus away.'

I realised Erhart was emphasising this to save Sigfrid from the need to avenge his father's death, and so spare Bertram and me.

'I saw Duke Nicolaus desecrate Danu's shrine at Rabenschloss,' I said: 'He murdered Countess Agatha in front of me, when she tried to protect the statue of the river spirit from his zeal. He smashed the statue on the ground where her body lay, by the stream there, which runs into the Danube.'

'Clearly Danu's river did not forget,' said Erhart.

'What of the other horsemen who rode out against us with Duke Nicolaus and the Condottiero?' asked Bertram.

'My men have recovered some thirty bodies and a similar

number of horses. All drowned. Some others may have escaped, but most of them would have been swept away, further downstream. It was unusual for that flood bank to breach so suddenly.'

The twinkle in Erhart's eye told me that some men in zillen had assisted in the fortuitous breach.

'How did you know to send boats to aid us?' I asked; 'And how are you even here? The last time I saw you was three days ago, at Duke Nicolaus' Mischief Night Ball.'

'What a night for mischief that was, too!' Erhart laughed. 'We all saw how the Duke had singled you out, Knight Gendal. You stood out like a bright lantern on a dark night. All the guests noticed when you left. A short while later, I danced with a beautiful woman in a crimson dress. She told me, "If Gendal survives the Duke's assassination plot, go back home at once. Take Sigfrid with you. Your opportunity will unfold at Danbrucke." Then the Duke stopped the dance to announce that you had absconded. And I realised the plot she spoke of wasn't against the Duke, but against you.'

'How did she know we would go to Danbrucke?' I asked, astonished.

Bertram smiled. 'Mischief night indeed! That was where Widow Astra told me to take you if we managed to free you. She also told me to make sure we took two days to get to the inn south of the bridge. She wanted to give the Duke enough time to catch up with us, and Count Erhart enough time to get home by a more direct route, so that his warriors could be there too.'

'But why did the Duke chase after me? Why did he not just let me go?'

'Because he received a note shortly after Count Erhart had left with Sigfrid, saying you had kidnapped Sigfrid to use as your shield. Widow Astra knew that would be too much of a blow to the Duke's pride for him to ignore.'

I shook my head in horror at the nature of the plot Astra had contrived to save me. Riddled with falsehood and manipulation, it was all that I hated about court and its politics. Truly, her cunning of the court had far outwitted my cunning of the road.

'Forget your moral compass, Gendal,' said Erhart: 'Good has won through; the ends have justified the means. Duke Nicolaus is dead and Duke Sigfrid will shortly return to Aunsberg to take his place, with Count Bertram and a phalanx of my warriors to support him. A new era will dawn for Danuvia and for Rabenwald, as Sigfrid rights the excesses of his father, while Bertram and I guide him. Peace and prosperity can now prevail.'

'But not for the fallen,' I said, remembering Rehlein and Sinter, and all the other precious children of our Lord who had fallen in the rebellion and its aftermath.

'They died for a better future for those who survived,' Bertram said.

I turned to the coltish youth who would be Nicolaus' successor.

'And is that what you want, Duke Sigfrid?' I asked.

He looked at me with glistening eyes.

'Though I loved my father, I know he had many faults. He also caused a lot of damage. It is my desire to heal those wounds, repair that damage, and rebuild my land. With the help of my God and the support of Count Erhart and Count Bertram, I am confident I can. Will you join us, Knight Gendal?'

'I am honoured that you should show me such respect when your father found me so troublesome. Sadly, I have another commission to complete first. Before the battle of Dernfels, Prince Rehlein instructed me to take the news of his death to his family in Harzland, should he not survive the day. And I must tell them his cousin Sinter Schwarzenberg also fell in that same battle.'

'A mighty Prince of princes, Rehlein proved – taken too soon,' Bertram agreed, 'Though I did struggle to like his cousin.'

'Knight Gendal, of course you must go,' Sigfrid said.

We stayed with Erhart some five days until the waters of the Danube had receded enough to travel safely again. Sigfrid and Bertram crossed Danbrucke and rode south for Aunsberg, escorted by ten of Erhart's best warriors.

I turned Finstar's head north to ride for Harzland, in respectful memory of my friend and hero Prince Rehlein. The last of his three stars had burned brilliantly, only to be extinguished too soon on the altar of my quest: to seek justice for the poor, to defend the oppressed, and to set the captive free.

THE END

GENDAL'S STORY CONTINUES
in
THE EAGLE AND THE HART
due out 2022

THE EAGLE AND THE RAVEN

Characters

Agatha   Countess of Rabenwald; Raban's mother, very old
Aldwin Rabenwald General, responsible for the army
Astra   Widow, lives in Aunsberg; courtesan

Barthram   Bertram's page and cousin, child of Rabenwald
Bertram   Count of Rabenwald, son of Raban, rebel leader
Bertrand   Bertram's grandfather, father of Cara Rea and Raban
Bishop of Munster   Gendal's past benefactor

Cara Rea   Bertram's aunt; witch who joins Nicolaus' court
Cunrad   Rabenwald warrior sent to assassinate Nicolaus

Danu   Water goddess of the Danube, revered by Rabenwald
Ditwin   Count Bertram's standard bearer from Rabenwald

Ened   Count Bertram's bride; Countess of Rabenwald
Engel   Frau: keeper of the Inn and Eiswald
Eregendal   The younger idealistic Gendal
Erhart Huber   Count of Aacheim, ally of Nicolaus

Fadrique   Lapsed Black Friar, befriends Gendal and Bertram
Finstar   Gendal's horse, a black stallion

Gawin   Rabenwald warrior sent to assassinate Nicolaus
Gendal   Free Knight, Ministerialis, the one telling the story
Giacomo Maladriuzzi   Condottiero, General of a mercenary army
Gotfrid   Rabenwald warrior sent to the Wolfholz Tavern

Hans and Anna Inn Keepers at the Rabenwald Iyver hostel
HermanOstler at the Inn at Eiswald

Ilse   Daughter of Hans and Anna at the Iyver
Imperator   The Emperor of the Holy Roman Empire
Isadora   Wife of Duke Nicolaus of Danuvia

Characters (continued)

Johannes	Rabenwald warrior; Ened's father
John Silvio	John O' The Woods, brigand leader
Leander	Inn keeper at Aunsberg in Danuvia
Marie	of Burgundy; a witch who stole Cara Rea's identity
Meyer	Freeman of Aunsberg, attends Nicolas' ball
Nicolaus	Duke of Danuvia, cousin to the Imperator
Nyze	Rabenwald warrior sent to assassinate Nicolaus
Oscar	Prince of Harzland; Rehlein's younger brother
Othmar	Knight, ally of Nicolaus and Isadora's lover
Raban	Count of Rabenwald, Bertram's father
Rehlein Hirschmann	Gendal's travelling friend, prince of Harzland
Rupert	Prince; Gendal's past benefactor
Sigfrid	Nicolaus' heir; future Count of Danuvia
Sinter Schwarzenberg	Prince, Rehlein's cousin; assists Rabenwald
Thiemo	Youth who asks Gendal to tell Bertram Raban is dead
Ulrich	Rabenwald warrior sent to the Wolfholz Tavern
Walther	Rabenwald General, responsible for infrastructure
Ziegenhein	Count; Gendal's past benefactor

If you have enjoyed this book, please consider leaving a review where you bought it online, or on our website: www.eregendal.com.

About the Author

Author Maggie Shaw creates her stories from her many and varied life experiences. A teenage runaway who made good after overcoming depression caused by undiagnosed ASD, Maggie writes as one who has walked the walk in recovery and spiritual development. Her degrees in science, divinity and church music, and her career as a Mental Health Dietitian, give a solid framework to the exciting adventure stories she loves to tell. The Scottish hills and Lakeland fells where her grandparents farmed often feature as landscapes in her work.

Maggie is also a church musician, composer and song writer. Many of her songs and poems are inspired by the stories she writes.

This is the sixth book Maggie has published through micropublisher Eregendal. Her other titles are *The Vision and Beyond* (2018), *Diviner's Nemesis I: Avenger* (2019), *Diviner's Nemesis II – Retribution* (2020), *The Eagle and The Butterfly* (2020) and *The Last Thursday Ritual in Little Piddlington* (2021). She has broadcast music and short stories on Radio Carlisle, Cat Radio, and Red Shift Radio; and contributed articles to The St Raphael's Guild *Chrism,* The Chronicle, The Church of England Newspaper, and *Soul and Spirit* Magazine. Online, Maggie publishes through ArtSwarm, YouTube, Sound Cloud, Facebook and the Eregendal website www.eregendal.com .

Maggie lives in Cheshire with her husband Alan and their cat Tarby.